APOCALYPSE LAW 2

By
John Grit

Also by John Grit

Feathers on the Wings of Love and Hate:
Let the Gun Speak
(Volume 1)

And

Feathers on the Wings of Love and Hate 2:
Call Me Timucua
(Volume 2)

And

Apocalypse Law
(Volume 1)

Chapter 1

Nate Williams knew the men were killers.

Five of them, all armed. Two rode a Caterpillar bulldozer. Three more rode on a trailer pulled by the Cat, rifles at the ready, their eyes searching for prey. The Cat dozer was clearly marked with bold black letters on yellow paint as county property. They were not county employees.

Nate hid in brush in the shade of trees and observed through 10X50 Zeiss binoculars as they turned off a clay road onto the one-lane track leading to his farm.

Heat waves distorted his view through the glass. A bright summer day, relentless in its reminder that he was in Florida in August, made the shade he utilized for camouflage all the more effective. However, there was no refuge from the muggy heat. Tension made his body even hotter.

When he first saw them coming, Nate hoped they would keep going down the road. He sighed and pushed the safety off his M14 with the back of his trigger finger, shouldered the rifle, and waited for his best chance to kill them cleanly, with one shot each. That was his plan.

The forty-foot-long flatbed trailer was loaded with diesel fuel in fifty-five-gallon drums near the front. Just in front of the drums, three men rode on a crude bench seat made of scrap lumber.

A gray steel shipping container sat on the back end of the trailer. Nate had no idea what was in it but guessed it was food and other items necessary for survival. More than likely, they had killed for it.

Slipping the rifle sling on his left arm while watching the Cat inch closer, he prepared to fire from standing. He must shoot fast at moving targets. The prone position would not allow enough speed, and there was too much brush in the way to see while that low to the ground.

Aiming for the driver, Nate held his breath and started to squeeze the trigger.

A nagging doubt stopped him.

Just maybe, they're not a threat. Am I about to kill innocent men?

The longer he waited the more risk he took.

One hundred yards now.

Nate still hesitated.

They're not coming to my farm to invite us to a Sunday church meeting.

Sharpening his sight picture, he started to squeeze the trigger.

When he heard the Cat's engine slow, he stopped again. They parked eighty yards away. The driver killed the engine, got out of his seat, stepped off onto the track, and then jumped to the ground. He bent over backwards, stretching.

Another man who was riding the Cat jumped down off the far side and said something to those on the trailer. They slung their rifles across their backs and also jumped down. Two of them went to the back of the shipping container and opened the double doors. Swinging them all the way over, they backed off ten feet and motioned to someone inside.

Nate watched the scene unfold. *Someone is in that thing? It must be over a hundred degrees in there.*

A woman in her late twenties staggered out and lifted her chained arms to shield her eyes from the sudden sunlight. She wore tattered jeans and nothing more. Her bare feet were crusted with dried blood and dirt. Her body was marked with bruises, her raven hair tangled and matted. She looked around after her eyes adjusted to the brilliance. When she turned Nate's way, he saw signs of repeated beatings on her face. There was little life in her blackened eyes, only dread. It seemed to Nate that she was looking right at him.

Nate lifted his rifle and waited.

One of the men standing by stepped closer, swung an open hand and slapped her down. She landed on her face in the dry dust.

Nate's ears stung when the crack of the impact reached him.

All of them laughed as she pushed herself to her hands and knees.

His face contorted with scorn, the same man kicked her in the ribs. She fell on her side and coiled into the fetal position, breath knocked from her lungs. She held her stomach and gasped.

How much of that can she take? That may have broken her ribs.

Another man who was close to her, reached down, grabbed a fist full of hair, and dragged her away from the trailer to an open area off to the side.

All five leaned their rifles against the shipping container and gathered around her. She looked up at them from the ground, her eyes flitting from one to the other as she lay on her back, covering her face with her arms. The next blow could come from any direction.

One of the men went back to the trailer and pulled a canteen out of a backpack. He turned to watch, and laughed as the others circled her, each kicking as she squirmed in the dirt. When he brought the canteen to his lips, his head exploded.

A mad rush for their weapons was cut short by a flurry of shots from Nate's rifle. Only one was able to touch his before he died.

~~~~~~~~~~~~~~~~

A thirteen-year-old boy and a man in his forties worked in a field of vegetables. Rifle shots echoed through a stand of pines and oaks. The boy put a wheelbarrow loaded with tomatoes down, slid his lever-action rifle off his shoulder, and ran toward the driveway and the sound of the shots, rifle in hand.

Mr. Neely dropped a hoe he was using to weed between rows of tomato plants and ran for the house, his shotgun already off his shoulder. "No, Brian!" he yelled. "Get in the house."

Brian kept running as fast as he could. His father needed help.

In the kitchen, Deni and Mrs. Neely were making tomato paste and canning it in Mason jars, when the shooting started.

They both had a rifle in their hands in seconds. Now, they were looking out windows, searching for danger.

Mrs. Neely looked at the tree that she knew her daughter was under, standing guard over those working in the field.

"Cindy's okay," Deni said. "The shooting came from the road where Nate is." Nevertheless, her eyes searched the tree line on both sides of the field as much as Mrs. Neely's.

A little boy came running into the kitchen. "What's wrong?"

Mrs. Neely spun around, rushed to her son, and pushed him under the dining table. "Lie flat on the floor and don't move!"

The little boy's eyes rounded, and he did as ordered. "More bad men have come to hurt us?"

"Shut up and just lie there!"

The little boy shook as he cried.

Mrs. Neely's face softened. She turned to her son who peered up from under the table.

Mr. Neely charged through the front door and slammed it behind him, bolting it. "Brian has run after his father." He heard his son crying. "What's wrong with Tommy?"

"He's scared and I yelled at him." She dropped to her knees and motioned for her son to come to her. The boy crawled out from under the table and hugged her, still crying. "Sshh, it's okay," she said.

Deni's eyes met Mr. Neely's. "Check the back windows, Ben. Make sure they're all shuttered. Martha and I have the front covered."

Ben ran into the living room. Finding all the window shutters closed and barred, he ran down the hall to check the rest of the house.

Strained with worry, Deni's face belied her young twenty-four years. She looked through the window down the dirt drive where Brian had disappeared. "Damn it. Damn it. Damn it. What's going on over there?"

Ben came back into the dining room. "Windows and doors are all secure."

Martha spoke, still holding her little boy. "Ben, maybe you should go."

Deni snatched up two, thirty-round magazines for her AR 15 from a small table by the door and stuffed them into back pockets of her baggy jeans. "No. I owe them. You stay here and protect your family."

"We all owe them," Ben said. He looked at his wife. "Don't we, Martha?"

Deni did not wait for her to answer. She opened the front door and said, "I'm going."

~~~~~~~~~~

Nate waited ten minutes before making his way around to the back of the trailer, keeping in the woods and behind cover, trying to see into the shipping container.

The woman had not moved. She just lay there on her side and stared at the dead men, a demon-like smile on her face. Yellow clay dust was plastered to her sweaty body.

That suited Nate. She was out of the way. He could shoot without worrying about hitting her. He still did not know what was in the shipping container.

He was forced to leave the cover of trees and walk into the clay one-lane track in order to see into the open end. Carefully, he "sliced the pie" of angles, jerking his head back after quick looks, until he had edged around enough to see most of the inside.

There was a cage on the right just inside the door. Its dimensions were four feet square—a cube. A nude girl sat in it, her knees to her chest, arms wrapped around them, her head bent over uncomfortably. Nate judged her to be about fifteen.

No one else seemed to be inside the container. There were many boxes and barrels, some marked with brand names, but no other people.

Nate eased closer, keeping his offside foot in the lead and his rifle shouldered, the way he was trained in the Army.

The woman on the ground began to laugh. Her bruised body shook, and her laughter became more and more hysterical. She rolled from her side onto her back and looked over at Nate, her face full of amusement and glee, giving him a toothless smile. "Shoot the bastards again! Do it. I want to see it. Shoot them again. I don't care what you do to me after. Just let me see it again."

The look on Nate's face made her laugh more. She tried to turn her lungs inside out with her crazy cackle.

He circled around her and walked up on the men. Not wanting to be shot in the back, he pulled his .44 magnum revolver and shot them in the head, one at a time.

The woman shrieked with glee with each shot. "Oh, thank you! Do it again."

Nate kept her in the periphery of his vision and walked up to the cage.

The girl inside recoiled and pressed herself against the back bars with her bloody feet. She shivered and made a sound he had never heard come from a human being. The cage stank of raw sewage.

"Oh God." Nate put a hand to his mouth. The smell didn't bother him as much as the sight of her.

Boots pounded on the hardpan clay. Heavy breathing rushed nearer.

Nate ducked behind the shipping container, swung around, rifle shouldered, ready to shoot. He peered over his rifle sights, around the corner.

His eyes flashed fear. "No, Brian. Stay back."

Brian stopped, his shirt soaked, chest heaving, and eyes wide.

"I'm okay. It's over," Nate told his son.

When he saw his father was not hurt, he looked at the woman on the ground. She was still staring at the dead men, laughing like a crazy woman. His jaw dropped at the site of her bare breasts.

Nate rushed to him and turned him around. "It's over. Go back and get Deni. There are two girls here who need help."

"What happened to them?"

"They've been beaten up." He took a canteen from his load-bearing harness and poured some water over Brian's head while keeping an eye on the laughing woman. He handed it to him. "Take a drink."

Brian gulped it.

"Whoa. Slow down. Not too much. You're way overheated. You shouldn't have run up here. You know you should have stayed at your post to protect the farm and the others. Walk when you go back for Deni, don't run. They need help, but a few minutes are not going to make any difference."

"You were alone," Brian said.

"I'm okay."

"Yeah, but I didn't know." Brian looked up at his father. "What do you expect?"

Nate did not answer. He looked at the laughing woman. She was crawling toward the dead men. The guns were what concerned him. There was no telling what she would do. "Go on. Get Deni. Do what I say for once. You're not helping me here."

"All right. All right." Brian walked away.

Nate put himself between the guns and the laughing woman.

She stopped crawling and looked up at him, her chained arms raised above her head as she sat in the dirt, shivering in fear. Her wrists were rubbed raw and bleeding.

He opened his canteen and reached it down to her. "I won't hurt you. Have a drink."

An animal sound came from her lungs and she snatched it from his hand. She kept her eyes on him while she drank, gulping it down. When he took it back, it was empty.

Reaching her wrists up to him, she made a sound, "Ugh." Her eyes were insistent, pleading.

He saw that the chain had been tightened on her by putting bolts through two links on each wrist and turning the nuts down with wrenches or pliers. Her hands were swollen from lack of blood circulation.

"We'll take them off as soon as we get you to our home where the women can take care of you and the girl. I'll need wrenches to get the bolts off."

Her eyes told him that she did not believe him.

"Hey!"

He turned and saw Deni taking cover behind a tree seventy hundred yards away, her rifle ready.

"It's safe," he said. "Come on over. I need your help."

Deni came running up, scanning the scene as she ran.

"It's bad. There's a girl locked in a cage." He motioned toward the container. "You watch this one for a second." He walked behind the woman so she could not see and made the crazy sign by circling his ear with his right index finger and mouthing the words, *be careful with her.*

Deni nodded and stepped back.

Nate stripped T-shirts off two of the dead men and handed one to Deni. He draped the other across the woman's arms so she could hold it to her chest. "I'll watch her. You do what you can for the girl. Try to determine if it's safe to let her out before we take them home. I don't want to leave her in there, but if she's…"

Deni nodded and walked toward the back of the shipping container. Ten feet from the opening, she stopped in her tracks and gasped. Recovering, she walked closer, trying not to gag. Behind the bars, she saw an undernourished, filthy, bruised, and scarred human being looking back at her with terror-filled eyes through tangled black hair plastered to her skin with dried blood and her own sewage.

"The men who did this to you are dead. You're safe now. We will help you. Do you understand?"

The girl nodded. "Will you let me out?" She seemed immediately calmed by Deni's voice and demeanor.

"Of course we will." Deni pulled on a padlock. "Do you know which one has the key?"

She shook her head.

Deni stepped back.

"Don't leave me." The girl pressed against the cage.

"I'm getting the key. It will just be a few minutes."

She started breathing fast and shaking the bars. "Oh, please let me out."

"I'll be right back with the key."

Nate heard them talking. "Watch her. I'll find it."

The woman was still sitting in the dry dirt, laughing with glee at the sight of the dead men. She had already dropped the T-shirt Nate gave her. Deni kept watch from a safe distance.

First, he gathered all the weapons he could find and put them on the front of the trailer next to a barrel of fuel, including two handguns and five knives he found on the bodies. Then he emptied all the guns of ammunition, putting it and the knives in a toolbox on the Cat. Only one of the men had any keys in his pockets. Nate handed them to Deni.

"Be careful," he said. "She's been through hell."

Deni took the keys. "She seems okay but I'll definitely be careful."

The woman shrieked. "Don't let her out! She's crazy."

"Calm down. We're trying to help both of you," Deni said.

"I tell you, she's crazy. She killed one of them. That's why they put her in the cage."

Nate watched as the woman's eyes went from wild to tearful.

"Oh, how they beat her for hours and hours, taking turns when one got tired." She lifted her arms and tried to cover her ears, but could not because of the chains. "Her screams. Why didn't she die? It should have killed her. How could anyone live through that? Oh God, put her out of her misery. The poor girl."

Deni shivered and walked to the back of the trailer.

When the girl saw Deni, she rattled the cage. "Let me out." No longer pleading, her voice resonated with sharp command. "Let me out."

"I will. What's your name? Mine is Deni."

The girl stared at her as if she had just said the strangest thing she had ever heard.

"Name?" The girl asked.

"You don't remember your name?"

"They hit me. My ears ring in my head. I can't think." She shook the bars. "Let me out. Everything hurts. I can't move in here."

"Think about your name while I find the right key. Can you remember?" Deni pretended to try several keys.

She tilted her head, eyes staring a thousand yards. "Bitch."

Deni looked at her. "What?"

"That's my name."

"No it isn't. That's what they called you. They're dead now. You're not a bitch. You're a teenage girl. What's your name?"

She stared out of the cage into a less dark place in her mind. "My mother called me Carrie."

Deni smiled. "That's a nice name. We are going to take care of you, Carrie." The lock opened with a turn of the key and Deni swung the cage door out of the way.

Carrie recoiled in terror, pressing against the back of the cage. "Oh no! Not again."

"Think, Carrie. No one is going to hurt you. Those men are dead."

Looking bewildered, she looked out past Deni. "Where are they?"

"Over there, dead. No one will hurt you now. Come on out." The girl did not move, so Deni came closer. "Let me help you." She reached into the cage.

The girl kicked at her with both filthy feet. "Stay away. I'll get out when I'm ready."

"Both of you need a bath, medical care and food. There is no need for you to stay here." Deni stepped back. "See if you can get out and walk."

Still timorous, she stuck her head out of the cage and looked around inside the shipping container and outside at the trees. Gaining courage, she slid out of the cage onto the edge of the trailer and pulled her numb legs around with her hands, so her feet could fall to the ground. She moaned with pain as she straightened her back, and her eyes swept the area in front of her. "Where are they?"

Deni pointed. "You're safe now."

She leaned far enough to see. Her body shook with tremors. A wave of comprehension washed over her face and with it a toothless smile. Her cut lips began to bleed.

Deni handed her the T-shirt Nate had taken off one of the dead men. "Put this on. It's big enough to cover you until we get you home."

Still smiling, she slipped it over her and pulled it down to her waist. When she tried to stand so she could pull it down all the way, her legs buckled.

Deni was not quick enough to catch her. "Why don't you stretch your legs out and sit there a few minutes so your blood can circulate?"

The girl said, "I'm dizzy." She held her hands to her head.

After a few minutes, she managed to get up with Deni's help.

"It hurts."

"I know. We will soon have you all cleaned up and fed and in a soft bed. How long have you been locked in there?"

She did not answer.

They got both the woman and the girl on the front of the trailer. Nate closed the container door, while Deni watched them.

He climbed into the driver's seat, started the Cat, and had them heading for his farm, leaving the dead men where they lay.

Chapter 2

Brian heard them coming and ran out of the barn. This time he did not gape at the shirtless woman.

Martha followed him. She braced herself and walked up to the trailer. "We have a tub for each of you in the barn. Water's not too cold. Then we'll take care of those wounds."

Brian handed Nate two glasses and filled them from a canteen.

Nate handed them to the girl and woman. Both drained their glasses in seconds.

"Go in the house and get out the medical kit. Clear the kitchen table," he told Brian.

"We already did that. I told them," he motioned with his head, "about them."

"Good. Now go and keep watch out of the east windows. You never know when someone may come along looking for trouble."

Brian rolled his eyes, sighed, and walked into the house with the empty glasses.

~~~~~~~~~~~~~~

The woman cleaned herself, but Martha had to wash Carrie while Deni kept her rifle ready.

Outside the barn, Nate whispered to Ben, "Stay close. They may need your help. Both of them are about half crazy, especially the girl." He motioned for Ben to follow, and they walked to the back of the trailer.

Ben stared at the stinking cage. "Holy hell!"

"No telling how long they had her locked in there. They were beating the woman. I mean they were going to beat her to death. As soon as they walked away from their rifles, I killed them."

"I don't blame you." Ben stepped back from the stench. "Why? Why turn animal just because there's no law? What's the point of this kind of cruelty?"

Nate had no answer. "I don't trust them. Better get close to the barn, just in case."

"Right." Ben walked to the closed barn door.

The girl was whimpering. "It hurts."

Martha said, "I'm sorry, but those gashes are festering. They have to be cleaned. It'll be over soon, and you will feel a lot better."

The men looked at each other with pallid faces.

Nate grabbed the cage, all one hundred pounds of it, yanked it out of the trailer, and flung it against a pine tree.

Ben watched.

Nate headed for the water pump to wash his hands.

Brian came out and pumped the handle for him.

When Nate was finished, he stood and looked at his son.

Brian looked up at him. "What?"

Nate patted him on his left shoulder. "I'm sorry."

"For what?"

"I…I just want you to know that I'm proud of you. You're a good son, but you've got to start doing what I say. It's dangerous to disobey me like you have several times today. We can have a good life someday, but we have to be careful until it gets better."

"I don't see any sign it's going to get anything but worse. If people would just leave us alone, we would do okay. It's not so bad on this farm for us at least." He pointed up the drive and then the barn. "But others don't have it so easy."

"It'll get better. There are five fewer…"

"I guess the bad ones are being thinned out."

"Yes."

"By people like you."

Nate glanced down the driveway for a second. "Go inside now and watch the east side. Cindy is still out there. She will have to be relieved soon."

Brian looked up at his father. "Did they rape them?"

Nate did not answer.

"I guess I'm supposed to be too young to talk about it."

Nate's chest lifted high and held for some seconds. "They didn't spare them anything else."

Brian went back into the house.

~~~~~~~~~~~~

Dark of night blanketed their farm by the time they fed the woman and girl and got them settled down enough to sleep.

Martha sat at the kitchen table to rest for the first time since the girl and woman arrived. She cried and held her little boy. Talking to Cindy in the kitchen, she said. "We had to cut all their hair off so the gashes and cuts could be cleaned." Holding Tommy to her, covering an ear with her hand, she said, "It's going to be hard feeding them since they can't chew."

Cindy stopped doing dishes and left Nate at the sink, who had just brought in more water from the pump outside. She held her mother and brother for a while and then went back to work.

"It seems they finally comprehend their ordeal is over," Martha said.

From the sink, Cindy said, "Things will never be the same for any of us. The plague was just the beginning." She shook her head in amazement. "Why did so many people go crazy as soon as there was no police? All that rioting and killing! And I had no idea it was possible for our country to run out of food so fast."

Nate joined the conversation. "None of it surprised me. I've seen riots reported on the news where local police were overwhelmed by just a few hundred yahoos. Imagine tens of millions all over the country going nuts from fear. I've read many times that America had only about four days' worth of food in the pipeline at any time. Without trucks and people to load and drive them, nothing moves. And without fuel, they don't move anyway. During the Depression, most Americans knew how to produce at least some of their own food." It was not common for Nate to give a speech, and the others listened intently. "When the sickness came, only one percent had any idea where food comes from. As far as they were concerned, it came from a grocery store. No, none of it is really that surprising. You just have not been on this earth long enough, Cindy. And the cruelty, while sickening, is not surprising to me. I've seen it before in other countries. In some societies, women are just slaves. Without the force of law, all of the old demons are unchained. The only thing between us and animals like them," he pointed toward the driveway, "is a gun. But a gun is useless if you let your guard down. We have no choice but to maintain twenty-four seven security."

~~~~~~~~~~~~

Carrie slept in Brian's bed, the woman on the floor in the same room. Her swollen hands caused her much pain, and she moaned for hours before falling asleep. She seemed to be trying to be as quiet as possible, but the pain was too much now that blood flowed to them and reawakened nerve endings.

Brian slept on the floor in the living room.

Nate stayed up all night, keeping watch for danger outside and from Brian's bedroom.

Ben slept five hours, then ate a quick meal, grabbed his rifle, and walked out into the dark night to man the observation post on the field's east side. From midnight to false dawn are the hours when most raids come.

Deni slept on a couch in the living room. She woke four hours before dawn.

Nate cooked breakfast for both of them. They talked quietly as they ate.

"I'm afraid they both may die, despite all we can do," Deni said.

"That's possible. They need a doctor and hospital. Both have broken ribs, probably internal injuries."

Deni's eyes filled. "Why?"

"They were just sadistic assholes. I don't know any more than you."

She looked at him from across the table. "Yes you do. You're a man."

Nate's chair scraped on the floor. He stood up, his face hard, and left the dining room.

"Oh, I didn't mean...I'm sorry." She started to reach out as he passed but stopped short.

He was silent as he kept walking. He went into the living room and lay down on the bare wood floor by Brian, his rifle beside him.

Just after sunrise, screaming came from Brian's bedroom.

First through the door, his revolver in hand, Nate stood there watching the girl scream. The woman had stumbled and fallen against Brian's dresser, causing a gash to bleed again.

The girl sat up in bed, staring off into space at some invisible horror, turning her lungs inside out. She looked at Nate and recoiled in fright. Her screaming grew more intense.

Nate gently took the woman by her shoulders and pushed her past Deni and Martha, who stood at the foot of the bed looking aghast at the girl.

They continued down the hall to the dining room. "Sit here, Caroline. It will be okay, stay calm."

She shrugged. "Too far gone. Nothing you can do. Been through too much pain and terror. Should be dead. Death is the best kindness she's got waiting for her." She smiled up at Nate, careful not to show toothless gums. "That was the first time a man called me by my name since they killed my husband and baby three weeks ago."

Both could hear Deni and Martha trying to console Carrie.

Brian walked in from the living room, eyes full of sleep, and his face showing concern. "What is it, Dad? She having a nightmare?"

Nate's voice rose. "Where is your shotgun? Never walk away from your weapons."

"It's right there on the floor where I was sleeping. We're in the house."

"It doesn't matter. Your pistol and rifle are locked in the safe for a reason, and your shotgun should be in your hands or slung on your shoulder at all times."

With his voice also rising in anger, Brian said, "Even when I sleep?"

"Yes! Goddamn it, yes."

"Shit. I just woke up 'cause of her screaming. And you're pissed already."

Caroline sat at the table looking at Brian. "You're a cute little boy. You should do what your father tells you." She looked at Nate. "Maybe he doesn't understand that Carrie's dangerous." Turning back to Brian, she said, "She's crazy.

Been through too much. She's not tough like me. I lost my Carl and Jacob, but—"

"We don't need to hear that now," Nate said.

"First, they made Carl watch as they used me. Then they made me watch as they killed Carl slow. He screamed for hours. Burned and cut him. After that, they cut Jacob's throat. Got tired of hearing him cry for me. That's what they said, but I think they would've done it no matter how quiet he was. They didn't have any use for a baby, but enjoyed the hurting." She shook her head, eyes cold. "But I'm not crying about it. You see me crying? No way. They did things. But I'm not crying."

Cindy stood in the dark hallway, listening, her cheeks wet. She went to her mother and Martha saw. She left Deni alone with the girl and took Cindy to the bathroom where they talked in private until Tommy woke and cried out for his mother. Martha and Cindy both went to him.

Nate walked over and put his hand on Brian's shoulder. "Get your shotgun. Deni and I have already eaten, but I'll cook breakfast. Everyone is awake now anyway."

Brian came back with his shotgun slung over his shoulder and Nate's rifle in his hands.

Nate looked up from scrambling eggs on the wood stove.

"You left your rifle," Brian said.

"You were there."

"Yeah, never admit you made a mistake."

"I make plenty of mistakes." Nate smiled. "And don't be a smartass."

Brian looked away, a smirk on his face.

Caroline shrieked with laughter. "You don't know about mistakes, but you'll learn."

Nate stopped stirring the eggs. Brian and he both stared at her.

~~~~~~~~~~~~

The sun inched up over the eastern tree line. Nate and Brian worked in the field.

"Dad, you shouldn't be out here. You've been up all night." Brian leaned on his hoe. Sweat ran down his face.

"I pulled security yesterday while Ben and you worked. Now it's my turn," Nate said.

"You have to sleep sometime."

"I will. While you and Deni pull security tonight."

"Shit. You wouldn't let me go without sleep."

"That's true. But I'm your father, so you don't have any choice. If you feel sorry for me, milk the cow and put her in the pasture for today."

Brian looked up at his father from under his boonie hat brim. The sun's heat would soon beat down with no mercy, and his T-shirt already clung to him. "What about the girl and woman?"

"What about them?" Nate knew but asked anyway.

"You know. You're scared they're going to grab one of our guns and kill us."

Nate stopped hoeing. "We have to watch them."

"You left your rifle this morning."

"I had my forty-four, and I knew they were in your room."

Brian had a half-smile on his face. "Yeah, right. One of them could've snuck out while we were asleep."

"Deni was up."

"Uh huh."

"Not to change the subject, but what you did yesterday was stupid. Stupid, because it was dangerous."

Brian looked hurt.

"I don't mean *you* are stupid, what you did was."

"So I was supposed to leave you up there alone?" Brian kicked at a clump of dirt. "Bullshit."

"You are supposed to stay with standard operating procedure. There's a reason why we all went over how to handle emergencies, and it's not so you can just ignore SOP when you're worried about me. I know why you did it. But—"

"You would've come running faster than me. I've seen it before. No way would you have stayed in the house while I was being shot at."

"I have a responsibility. I'm your father."

"I'm your son. And you made me…So don't give me anymore shit about running to help and not staying in the house."

"I know I'm asking a lot. The world is what it is. I'm sorry. I told you yesterday you're a good son. I meant it. But you still should have stayed in the house."

"Bullshit."

"And if you're going to come running, for God's sake, don't come running right up in the open. If I had been dead or wounded and down, they would have just killed you too. What's the point of that? Stay behind cover—always. Deni did it right. She came in careful, Army style."

Brian looked away. "I guess you didn't train me to not give a damn about my father. And I was never in the Army. I want to be a fighter pilot anyway."

"I have the feeling you will be someday, but if you want to be in the military you must learn to obey orders."

"I'm not in the Air Force yet."

"You won't be if you don't start using your head more. We can't depend on luck. Sooner or later, our luck is going to run out. We were lucky yesterday."

Brian looked up at his father. "You killing them before I got there was not luck. You're as tough as they come."

"Not when it comes to you." Nate looked his son in the eye. "You need to control your emotions—and your mouth. Lately, you've become enamored with the word shit. I've been lenient because of all that you've been through with the loss of your mother and little sister. But I can't keep letting you talk back to me like you've been. If I let my emotions go and my mouth run like you do to me, you would be a sad boy from all the cussing and put-downs. In the military, you are expected to remain calm under stress. That means you keep a level head when scared, worried, or angry. You can't think straight when you let your emotions run your head for you. To be the pilot you want to be, you have to be an officer, and an officer must have a level head under stress. You will be evaluated on that very thing. Spouting off is immature, and in the military it's unprofessional. Control your emotions."

"So I'm not supposed to care about you anymore?" Brian looked toward the house.

"I didn't say that and you know it. You're my son and I'm your father; that will never change."

Brian's face reverted back to his usual boyish self as he turned his head and then looked up at his father. "So I can forget everything you just said?"

"Uh, no. Smartass." Nate knocked Brian's hat off. "This conversation is going in circles. Get back to work."

Brian picked his hat up. "But what about them? We can't watch them all the time. And how can we feed them?"

"They can work in the house and field after they're well." Nate kept his doubts the two could do much heavy labor after the injuries they suffered to himself.

"We didn't plan on two more mouths to feed." Brian reached down to pull a weed growing close to a tomato plant. "It's too late to plant more this year."

"All I know is we can't just turn them away. We'll make-do. We'll plant a larger winter crop."

Brian pulled a bug-eaten tomato off the vine and chopped it into the soil for fertilizer. "Not if it's as cold this winter as last year and the one before. You said it yourself: The climate has changed. It gets colder in the winter now."

"So much for global warming, huh? In my lifetime, it's snowed in Orlando a few times, even south of Orlando, and it snows about every year in North Florida. In 1882 or so, it snowed in Florida in July. But that was because of a big volcano eruption blocking the sun around the world. Krakatau, I think it was. I've never seen it like it's been the past few years or heard of it being like it has lately though." He looked toward the backyard where his wife and daughter lay in the ground. "Some diseases spread faster in colder weather, like the Black Plague. It got colder and wetter just before the plague spread over Europe. Something about the disease living in the gut of fleas on rats." His face washed over with sadness for a second, but he recovered quickly before his son noticed. "Maybe that's what's happened with this sickness."

"I remember seeing something about that on TV," Brian said. "I don't think this disease is spread by rat fleas though."

"No," Nate said. "But colder weather means people stay indoors more and that means they're coughing and sneezing in the same room as others. The government never was sure of much of anything. They told us one thing one day and then the opposite the next. The sickness spread so fast they did not have much time to determine exactly how it was spread. It wasn't long before so many had died there wasn't much government left."

Nate stopped talking. He turned away and hoed with more force than necessary, attacking the weeds with a vengeance.

Brian went back to work. After a few minutes he stopped. "I miss them."

"I know." Nate's voice sounded distant. "So do I." He stopped hoeing, waiting for Brian to say what was on his mind.

"You started to say something to Mom once when the disease was first on the news," Brian mopped sweat from his forehead, "but you stopped talking when Beth and me came in. You were saying something about the disease spreading too fast not to be weaponized. I never heard that word before. What did you mean?"

Nate straightened and his chest rose, he turned to look his son squarely in the face. "I have my suspicions. I don't know any more than anyone else does, but it seems to me the disease spread way too fast and it was way too deadly to be a product of nature. And why did it start in America and then our allies like England and Israel? The sickness spread around the world after that, but it started with America and our allies. That is suspicious as hell. It may have been designed by some government or terrorist group."

Brian blinked. His mouth was open. "Our government?"

"Doubt it," Nate said. "It's possible that our government designed the disease and it was accidentally released or some terrorist got his hands on it some way. More than likely it was an enemy—another government or just a terrorist group." He seemed disgusted. "Whatever happened, we're left to live with the results."

Brian's face turned red. "If our government killed my mother and sister, they can forget about me being in the military. Even if it was an accident. What good is a weapon that kills good and bad people the same? What's the point?"

"All weapons kill good and bad people the same, Brian." Nate put his left hand on his son's shoulder. "But you're right. Now calm down and don't let it eat you up. We have to get this done. There are more mouths to feed now."

They went back to work.

After a few minutes, Brian spoke. "Now that Carrie and Caroline are with us, do you think the food will last until the next harvest?"

"There's fish in the river and hogs and deer. And there's food in that shipping container. It's more theirs than ours. So they brought food with them."

Brian looked toward the house. "I can't tell which one is worse. Both make me worry."

"We can't trust either of them," Nate said, "that's for sure. Don't leave guns or knives lying around."

"I know. You told me that." The tone of Brian's voice was not as belligerent as usual, but he added, "I hear you."

"And don't go near them alone, only when someone besides Cindy and Tommy is around. Better yet, stay away from them for now except at the dinner table."

"Okay. I will."

Chapter 3

A rifle shot shattered the peaceful night. It came from downriver and snaked along bottomland, reverberating through hammocks and then uphill to the farm.

Nate stood watch at the observation post. He estimated it to be half a mile away and gripped his rifle tighter. It is hard to judge how far a shot is in thick trees and fog; it could be much closer.

False dawn came an hour later. Nate stood still, listening, watching. He had not moved since the shot. Dew falling from tree limbs above fell on underbrush, bombarding palmetto fronds, sounding like rain. Mosquitoes buzzed around his head.

Brian, stay in the house this time, please.

Sunrise came, but he could see only his side of their field; cornstalks grow high. Most of their tomato plants had stopped producing, but the beans, okra, and peppers continued in plentitude, likewise the second planting of cucumbers. The potatoes had been harvested and put away. They would have to eat them before they spoiled or started to grow eyes. Green onions were just growing large enough to pull.

Dry leaves crunched behind him, further back in the trees. Nate eased around, his movement flowing. Though he wanted to swing around fast to see, he knew better. Movement catches an enemy's eye. It can nullify all efforts of camouflage.

More noise in the brush revealed someone's route. Nate waited, his rifle shouldered.

"Nate, it's me." Ben's voice came from out of the wall of green.

He lowered his rifle but kept it shouldered. "Come on in."

Ben appeared from out of the brush. "Time for me to relieve you."

Nate put a finger to his lips and motioned for him to come closer.

Neely looked around, his shotgun ready. He walked up as quietly as possible.

"I take it you didn't hear that rifle shot a couple hours ago," Nate said.

"No. No one did. Otherwise Brian would've come running." Ben smiled.

Nate nodded. "Well, maybe not. He's learning."

"He's a good kid. You've done a great job. Anything other than the one shot?" Ben asked.

"No. I think it was in the swamp. Downriver a ways. Maybe a half mile. Hard to tell. But nothing since."

"Hunter probably," Ben said.

"I hope he was hunting animals for food."

"And goes back where he came from," Ben added.

"Keep your eyes and ears working. I'll go to the house and warn the others, grab a bite, then patrol downriver, see what's up."

Ben turned to watch the field. "Be careful out there. Tell my wife and daughter to work in the house. The crops can wait one day."

"All right, but I'm not their boss. I can't even control my son."

Ben smiled. "Well, just tell them I would like for them to stay inside today."

"Will do." Nate walked away, watching where he stepped, not making a sound.

~~~~~~~~~~~~~~~

Martha looked out the living room window. "That corn's got to be shucked, scraped off the cob, and canned. We can't stop work around here over one shot in the woods."

"Ben would feel better if you three stay in the house. So would I. I want Brian to stay in too, and I don't want him alone in here," Nate said.

Brian sat on the wood floor, cleaning his shotgun on a coffee table in the living room, old newspapers spread over the table to soak up dripped cleaning fluids. He looked in their direction but said nothing.

Caroline had a washtub on the kitchen floor, washing clothes, rinsing in one sink, wringing them out in the one beside it. "I'll go and cut corn, if you trust me with a sharp edge. I promise I won't slit my wrists or stab anyone. I'm feeling better nowadays."

Cindy was helping her mother shuck corn at the table. She looked at her mother and Nate. "It wouldn't be right."

"What?" Martha asked.

"Sending her out like we don't care what happens to her. She's with us now, and we should treat her the same as anyone else. That goes for Carrie too."

Caroline said, "Nobody is sending me, Cindy. I want to go. I really don't think anything is going to happen. I'll stay on this end of the corn. Some of the beans can be picked too. They're right in view of the house. You can keep watch. And Ben is out there."

Nate's chest rose and held. "Okay. If you want to."

"I want to help."

"And Cindy is right," Nate said. "You're not expendable. You and Carrie are part of our family now." Nate saw her eyes fill. "Oh come on. Let's not start a crying session. Go out and pick some butter beans."

She wiped her face and went out the front door.

Avoiding the other's gaze, Nate walked over to Brian and took his shotgun from him.

Brian looked up from the table. "It's not loaded, Dad. You taught me better than that."

"Teaching you doesn't always stick. But you've been careful with guns as near as I can tell." He handed it back. "Looks clean to me. Wipe the bore almost dry and load it. I have to go back out there and patrol the downriver side of things. Check out that gunshot."

Brian affected his best western hillbilly accent. "I guess I'm s'posed to protect de women folks whilst you're gone."

"Hey. Smarty." Deni smiled. "I am...was a soldier."

"Just kidding."

"Well, I've got to eat and run." Nate went into the kitchen.

Deni followed him. "Carrie's still in bed. She doesn't seem to be coming out of it. I don't know if it's depression or what, but she sleeps way too much."

Nate made himself a wild hog sausage sandwich by putting it between a sliced biscuit. "I don't know either. She was injured more than Caroline." He pointed to his head. "And up here too." He looked out the window over the sink, watching Caroline pick butter beans, throwing them in a two-gallon pail. "And don't ask me why those bastards enjoyed hurting. I don't know why."

"I wasn't going to ask." Their eyes locked. "How could you? You're no more like them than Brian is."

Nate stopped chewing.

She touched his hand lightly and let hers fall away. "We all appreciate your generosity and kindness."

Carrie limped slowly into the living room, sleepy. "I'm hungry."

Deni heard, but her eyes were still locked with Nate's.

Cindy jumped out of her seat. "Come on and sit down. I'll fix you something." She pulled a chair out.

Nate took a glass down and filled it with water from a pitcher.

"I'll take it to her," Deni said. "Be careful out there. You're the one who makes this place work. We can't make it without you." She turned and walked away.

Nate filled two one-quart canteens and put them in carriers on his load-bearing harness.

When Deni turned back to him, he was already out the door.

"I expect to be back by dark," he said over his shoulder at anyone interested and was gone. He entered the woods as Deni watched.

Brian stood in the open door, shotgun in hand. "He didn't even say good-bye."

"Yes he did." Deni slung her arm across his shoulders. "What do you think he was doing, admiring your shotgun?"

"I thought he was picking on me about gun safety."

"Picking on you?" She whispered in his ear. "I doubt he has ever picked on you since the day you were born, kiddo."

"He doesn't boss you like he does me."

She laughed. "He's your father. You want to know something?"

"What?"

"I'm jealous."

"Whaaat!"

She bent down to his ear again. "I wish someone loved me like he does you. I had someone once, but I'm sure he's dead by now."

"Maybe not."

"True. But there's no way I can get to him and no way he can even know where I am if he was trying to find me."

Brian didn't seem to know what to say.

She ran her fingers through his hair and left him needing a comb. "You have a kind heart, like your father."

He rolled his eyes and closed the door. "If Dad saw us standing in the open like this, he would be pissed."

~~~~~~~~~~~

It took Nate over three hours to find his trail. Another hour of tracking brought him to the kill site. No animal had found the doe guts yet, but flies were blowing. All the heat and humidity of early morning had intensified with the sun's skyward climb and turned Nate's private wild world under the swamp's heavy canopy into a sauna. Sunlight filtered in nearly straight down now. Clothes clinging, his boots filling with sweat, he stalked closer to danger. The smell of his own body often overpowered the smell of the swamp. He had eaten a lot of tomatoes lately, and he could smell tomatoes in his sweat.

Nate was able to learn a lot about the man he was hunting by reading his trail. The route he chose was calculated more for hunting deer and wild hogs than travel through hostile territory. Trails, worn down from use, fanned out from a center, a hub, like a wagon wheel. All were marked every thirty yards with gashes in tree trunks. *A machete probably. Maybe a big knife.* Obviously, the man worried more about finding his camp again after a day of hunting than keeping a low profile. *Perhaps he has no compass. And he must believe he is far enough in this swamp not to run into danger: people.* He expected to find the man's camp in the center of that wheel. *Raised a country boy for sure. Not military trained though.*

In the middle of Marion's Bay, a ten-mile-wide swamp that drained into the river by way of a small creek, Nate found more sign the man had been living in the area for weeks. Several times, he found catfish heads that had been buried shallow and then dug up by coons or fox, or maybe a bear. They were picked clean by ants. Old campfires had been set farther up creek. Next to them, fish and squirrel bones were scattered by animals.

Trailing him was easy, he had a heavy load across his shoulders, and the tracks he left were deep. Nate had no idea if the man would shoot first or wait and talk, but he felt there was a good chance the two could come to an understanding and avoid violence. Still, he felt that familiar weight on his chest, a rise in his heartbeat and breathing, lacking only the strong fierce pull of blood, like when he killed those who shot his son so many months back. He did not hate this man, nor did he despise him, like the sadists who tortured Carrie and Caroline. Nate hoped they would not kill each other. If they could live with peace between them, everyone's chances of survival would be improved. Whatever happened, he resolved if someone had to die, it would be the stranger.

Nate stopped, froze. The coffee smell of hickory smoke drifted to his nose from upwind.

A man around thirty years old cut a strip of meat from a skinned and gutted doe and hung it on a rack made of branches. He had a makeshift smoker, fabricated from what he could gather from the swamp, and a slow, cold fire underneath. Thin green branches, woven into a tight mat, held smoke from the cold fire in. His venison would be preserved through drying and smoking. In the meantime, smoke was keeping most of the flies away.

Nate appreciated his ingenuity and equally appreciated the fact he did not have to eat it.

He watched the man work. In tattered and dirty jeans and green T-shirt, dark hair down to his shoulders, tall and thin, Nate outweighed him by a hundred pounds. Holes in his shirt revealed protruding ribs and a hollow stomach. There was little loose skin hanging from his waist, telling Nate the man was already thin before he lost weight from near-starvation.

Moving closer, he inched along a well-worn trail. There was something about a thin young cypress off to the left of the trail that stopped him in his tracks. It was bent over into a half-circle, the top tied down to something. Brush would not allow him to see what. An attempt had been made to hide the bowed tree, but Nate's trained eye caught it. He had dealt with booby traps in two wars and lost friends to them.

There was no wind, so the swamp's silence allowed the man to hear Nate click the safety off his M14 with the back of his trigger finger.

The man froze, and then whirled around in a blur of motion.

Nate yelled out, "I mean you no harm."

He froze again, standing there, eyes hard, his useless knife in his hand.

"Just be still and we'll talk." Nate held his rifle ready.

The man's lever-action rifle stood against a tree beside his lean-to of cut pine saplings covered with brown palmetto fronds, overlapped like shingles to shed rain. It was twenty feet from him; too far.

His eyes appraised Nate in a second, lingering on the M14's muzzle. "What's the rifle for then?"

"Self-defense. You have nothing I want." Nate lowered the rifle's barrel a little more.

"What *do* you want?"

"Heard your shot this morning," Nate said. "I'm just checking out the area. With things as they are, I can't be too careful."

"Kind of nosey, aren't you?" The man seemed to be more defiant than scared.

"Just being careful. I've had trouble." Nate found himself liking the man. He certainly had spunk.

"Not from me." The man's eyes were locked on Nate's.

"That's why I don't want to shoot you. So don't make me."

"This is public land. I'm just weathering the storm." The man sighed. "I was hoping no one could hear the shot this far into a swamp. I was trying to stay clear of trouble."

"I heard it," Nate said. "You're right. This is public land, or at least it was. Either way it's not mine and you have every right to be here. I just had to check to see if you're a threat to me."

"I'm no threat. And I can prove it."

"How's that?"

"I've seen your farm, seen you, and your entire clan. Don't know who's related to whom, but you got quite a bunch living in that little house."

"So?" Nate pulled his rifle tighter against his shoulder.

"So I've been close enough to do damage but didn't. I admit all that produce in your field and those yard chickens running around were a real temptation. Been living on fish mostly. But I knew you would kill me or I would kill some of you if I went stealing. So here I am." The man gave Nate a hard look. "And unfortunately there you are."

"No harm done by me being here." Nate moved closer, down the trail.

The man's eyes changed, but he said nothing.

Nate took two more steps and was about to stop when the man spoke.

"There's a trap just in front of you."

"Oh?" Nate feigned mild surprise.

"Won't kill you. But you'll be upside down with a snare around your leg if you keep walking."

"Nice of you to warn me."

"Yes. Wasn't it?" The man smiled for the first time.

Nate relaxed. "Next time you set one, hide your spring tree better. I saw the bent cypress before coming on in."

The man laughed. "You were testing me. What would you have done if it looked like I was going to let you walk into it?"

"Nothing. I would have backed away and left you here. With instructions to stay away from my farm. And I never would have trusted you again."

"Well, if you're not going to shoot me, I need to get back to work." The man pointed at the doe carcass with his knife.

"Go ahead. Just stay away from that rifle."

He cut another strip of venison and hung it on the rack. "What now?"

"Haven't decided," Nate said. "Either I walk away and leave you to your caveman life or invite you to dinner."

"You mean that?" The man stopped cutting a strip off the deer.

"Sure. I would like to know a little about you first."

"Not much to know. I owned Sam's Garage. Inherited it from my father. I'm sure you heard of it."

"Been there," Nate said. "Or my wife has. She had a breakdown once, and called you. She said you came out with a wrecker and brought her and the truck to your garage. Treated her honestly. Even let her keep the groceries she had just bought in your frig while you worked on the truck."

"My father taught me that you'll make more in the long run if you value your reputation and treat people right." The man put his knife on a log. "Grew up on the other side of the county. When the plague hit, everyone was dead in three months. I mean everyone in my house and my wife's family too. Then I got sick and it nearly killed me, but for some reason I pulled through. This old woman saved me. She lived down the road. And God or luck I guess. Now I'm glad we never had kids. Would've been one more hurt to go through." He scratched at his thick black beard. "Emily and I talked about it. Business was doing good. We had a little put away so she could stop work at the Greasy Spoon. That's what we called the Country Cooking Restaurant she worked at." He looked away. "That's all over now."

Nate could not look at the man for a few seconds. "Can't say as I trust you completely after our little talk, but if you want to come in for food to take with you or a meal, we can spare some. Just don't steal it or sneak around. We're a bit jumpy about that."

"Don't blame you. I stayed back from your farm for that reason." The man looked down at the mud in front of him. "It's been getting worse. I was thinking people would be working together by now. But it's even worse than the initial panic. Travel is suicide."

Nate's jaw set. "People will reorganize. Don't know how long, but it will happen."

The man shrugged his shoulders. "Got to deal with today first. I don't even think about tomorrow."

Nate got the feeling he was saying he did not care anymore. "Come in with your rifle over your head in daylight and in the open. No one will shoot. You will be welcome."

"Thanks. My name is Sam Boonbeck."

"Nate Williams. You really should come over sometime soon."

"Maybe in a few days."

"Good." Nate backed away and headed home.

Chapter 4

Nate pumped fuel from a fifty-five gallon drum into the Cat dozer's tank.

Brian looked up, squinting in the sunlight. "I don't see why I can't go. You need someone to ride shotgun."

"Deni will do that. I need you here, protecting the farm. There's still produce to be harvested too."

Brian sulked away without a word.

When he had the tank full, Nate jumped down and continued to check the Cat over.

Deni met Brian at the door. She smiled, but he brushed by her.

She joined Nate and watched him tighten the fuel drum's lid with a spanner. "You two have a fight?"

He threw the spanner in a toolbox and slammed the lid shut, snapping its two latches down. "No. He wants to go. I guess it's a boy thing."

They started for the barn, he carrying the toolbox and fuel pump.

"More likely it's a father and son thing," She said.

"Could be a lot of things. Maybe he just wants to get away from the farm, spend time with me, or get out of working the fields. He's a boy. Boys don't always think like adults."

She waited until he set the toolbox on a workbench and hung the pump on a wall next to other tools. "He's a good boy being raised by a good man."

Nate was bent down to pick up a coil of heavy cable. He stopped short and stood, looking at her.

"He needs to know you can trust him in an emergency," Deni said. "Taking me with you—a woman— in his eyes makes it look like you don't. He's at the age that he's trying to be a man."

"I don't want him to be a man yet. I just want him to do what I say. And he does not need to prove anything. I want him to live long enough to get to be a man. Proving what kind of man he is could get him killed."

Deni's face revealed she meant what she was saying. "He will be with you. And that's the safest place he can possibly be."

"You have military training. The fact you're a woman has nothing to do with it. He's a thirteen-year-old boy. I need you out there and him here. It's as simple as that."

"It's not that simple and you know it. You didn't get this far with him not knowing things like that."

"It could be dangerous."

"You're only going to the bridge, but he's your son. I'm just saying his heart is important too."

She walked out of the barn.

He carried the coil of cable out to the Cat and draped it over the engine cowling. Deni headed for the observation post to relieve Cindy, rifle in hand.

Starting for the barn, he turned on his heels and then went looking for Brian.

Nate found him at the dining table, helping Caroline with butter beans. Martha was there also.

"Brian, where did I put the logging chains?" Nate asked.

"It's in the wood box where all the chain is. I didn't touch it." Brian dropped beans in a bowl.

"I need your help." Nate motioned for Brian to follow. "We'll need the chain too. Cable's not long enough."

Brian got up, a puzzled look on his face. He slung his shotgun on a shoulder and followed his father out the door.

When in the barn, Nate stopped and turned to Brian. "This is what we in the Army called an all-or-nothing mission."

He looked up at his father. "What?"

"If we don't come across anyone who wants to hurt us, it will be an easy ride to the bridge and back. But if there is anyone on the road between here and there, we'll be sitting ducks on that dozer. I don't want you sitting behind me."

"If it's that dangerous, why go at all?"

Nate checked a can of hydraulic fluid, finding it nearly empty. He put it back on the shelf. "Destroying the bridge means less trouble coming down the road. Any gas left is getting old now, but diesel will be good for some time. More trouble could drive right up to the farm any day."

Brian looked down with his shoulders slumped. "I don't want you to go."

"Why?"

"Because."

Nate cleared his throat. "Now you know why I don't want you to go. It's that simple. There's nothing more to it. And since I'm your father I get to tell you to stay while I go."

Brian looked up from the ground to his father. "Shit! That's real nice."

"The decision is all on my shoulders—and the consequences—that's what's real nice. So stop bitching and help me with the chains."

Brian did not move. "It's all a matter of luck then. And you always said to never trust your life to luck."

"If you have any ideas on lowering risks, speak up. But for now, we have to get those heavy chains to the dozer."

"When are you leaving?"

"Tomorrow morning." Nate reached for the chains.

"Sorry I said shit. I forgot you don't want me to cuss anymore." Brian looked up at his father. "That's two times."

~~~~~~~~~

Nate woke with a feeling something was wrong. He turned his head to look where Brian slept on the living room floor a few feet from him. In the dark of 2AM, someone stood over Brian. The form moved away and into the dining room where dim starlight streamed in from a window.

It was Caroline.

She got a glass of water and quietly slipped past him and down the hall. Brian's bedroom door closed. He could hear whispering between Caroline and Carrie. Their voices rose for a short time and became insistent. Then the room fell silent.

Nate did not sleep. An hour before he planned to wake, he got up, stood over Brian, and struck a match. Flame flared up. For a few seconds, Nate saw his son sleeping peacefully, his chest rising in slow rhythm.

Brian's eyes opened partway. His father's face glowed in the flame's light, eyes warm and soft. Such a rugged face did not often reveal tender emotions. All sleep fled from Brian, but he did not stir, mesmerized by what he saw. The flame in Nate's hand died, but the image lived on.

~~~~~~~~~~~~~

"Someone's out there in the beans," Cindy yelled. "He's got a rifle, but he's holding it over his head like he's surrendering or something."

Nate grabbed his rifle. "Don't shoot without good reason."

Everyone in the house scrambled to look out a window toward the field. Everyone but Ben. He did what SOP dictated and went to the east window to stand watch.

Deni was pulling security at the observation post, her second shift in fourteen hours. Still early, the sun not yet over the tallest treetops, fog obscured much of the lower field, but Nate was certain she had her rifle on him.

Caroline's hands were wet from doing dishes. She glanced at Carrie who was leaning against Martha, shivering, eyes wide.

Carrie grew more upset. "Don't let him. Please, kill him now before he hurts me."

"You're safe here," Martha said, "No one is going to hurt you ever again." She held Carrie with one arm, holding a rifle with the other.

Tommy came running down the hall. "Mommy! Daddy said to stay with you." Now Martha had two frightened children to console. Her arms were full. She could not shoot if she had too.

Brian stood beside his father just long enough to appraise the scene, and then ran to a back window, his shotgun ready.

Nate turned from watching the man approach. "Brian, get your lever-action."

"Okay." Brian ran into Nate's bedroom and opened the safe. Slinging his shotgun across his back and grabbing a box of cartridges and the rifle, he swung the safe's heavy door closed and spun the lock's dial. Boots pounding on the wood floor, he ran down the hall into the living room.

"Catch your breath," Nate said. "It's the man I met in the swamp. I don't expect trouble, but be ready to shoot if necessary. Deni's out there too, remember."

Brian nodded and jacked a round into the chamber.

Nate brought a chair over so Brian could sit back from the window. Then he brought another chair over and set it with the back toward Brian so he could use it to steady his aim. "Keep yourself calm so you can think and shoot straight."

"He probably just wants a handout," Brian said.

"More than likely. I told him he could visit." Nate walked out into the front yard and pushed his M14's safety off.

The man stood, his rifle held over his head. He had to yell to cross the distance. "I decided to take you up on your offer. Hunger drove me to it."

"Most of us already ate, but you're in time for breakfast anyway. Put your rifle down and leave it, then come on in the house, Mr. Sam Boonbeck."

He did as directed and walked up to Nate. "I cleaned myself up as best I could, but I'm still not fit for socializing."

"Don't worry about that," Nate said, "we all are just surviving nowadays. There's a bar of soap by the pump. I'll work the handle so you can wash your hands."

After he washed, Nate opened the door and the man followed.

"Here." Nate gave him a towel from the kitchen counter to dry his hands on.

Carrie became more upset.

"Come with me," Martha said. "You too, Tommy." She led Carrie and her son to Brian's bedroom and closed the door.

Sam seemed uncomfortable. He stood there as Brian held his rifle, pointed safely at the ceiling. There could be no mistake about Brian's and everyone else's distrust of him.

"This is Sam Boonbeck, everyone," Nate said. He introduced all in the room. Brian merely nodded, but the others were friendly enough.

Caroline blushed when Sam's eyes lingered on her face, despite her scars. She lowered her eyes and gave a slight smile, running her hand over her short hair self-consciously. He smiled back with confidence.

Nate and Sam talked while Nate scrambled eggs. Caroline left and joined Martha in Brian's bedroom. Brian slung his rifle, kept his shotgun in his hands, and stayed back, watching.

They had leftover pork already cooked, so Nate heated it and sliced and buttered bread for him.

Sam wolfed down the food. "You guys have it made here."

"I guess we have it better than many," Nate said.

His mouth full, Sam nodded. "I'd say. Damn, this is good." He took a drink. "Pork's wild, isn't it?"

Nate sat in a chair across from him. "We've been eating a lot of wild pork lately."

"You got some chicks I saw, so you'll be enjoying a chicken dinner or two soon."

"Come winter, we'll slaughter a few of the older hens. Their egg production will be dropping off soon. We're not exactly overburdened with supplies though. There are a lot of things we could use more of."

He wiped his plate with a slice of bread. "But at least you're not going hungry and you have a roof over your head."

"That's true."

Sam scratched his face and pulled at his beard. It reached down to his chest. "That was the best food I've had in months. Food hell, it's the only *real* food I've had in months." He looked Nate in the eye. "I thank you for it. And I thank you for not shooting me out there in the swamp."

"I don't shoot unless I have to, and we help people when we can. So far, you've given me no reason to consider you a threat."

"I'm not, but me just saying it will never be enough. I wish there was some way to convince you. I think maybe I could be of use to your clan...and improve my living conditions considerably."

Nate's face was unreadable. His eyes fixed on Sam. "Seems you've been doing some thinking."

He smiled. "Yep, and I'm hoping you wanted me to. I'm hoping that's mostly what that visit you paid me was about. That and checking to see if I needed killing."

Cindy broke in. "He's the best friend you could ever have—and the worst enemy. Everyone here but Tommy can shoot. We won't be easy. If anyone comes to raid us, they'll pay a high price."

"I don't doubt it," Sam said. "It's obvious you're proud of your father."

Brian nearly shouted, "He's not her father, he's mine. Her father's in the back room watching with a rifle in case you got people out there waiting."

Sam smiled. "Sorry for the mix-up. Thanks for setting me straight. I don't know the familial situation around here."

Nate leaned closer and put his massive arms on the table. "Just so you know: This is not a clan, as you call us. My son and I took in the Neelys and they've been a great help. Recently, Carrie and Caroline kind of fell into our lives when they were captured by two-legged animals. They put those scars on them. Those two are less trusting than the rest of us. So keep that in mind."

"Oh, God. That's why the girl was upset when I came in? Caroline seemed to be...well, some women are kind of shy even at her age. I didn't think she was overwhelmed by my masculine charm." He laughed. "My aroma maybe. But...I thought maybe there was something about me that bothered her."

Nate leaned back in his chair. "Just be mindful of what they've been through if you want to impress me."

"I will."

"There's another woman living here too," Nate said. "Don't be worrying about scaring her. She'll cut your head off and hand it to you if you try anything. She's Army, and she knows her way around guns and combat. Right now, she's pulling security and over watching from a distance."

"Damn. She probably had me in her sights the whole time I was in the field."

"No doubt," Nate said. "I warned everyone you might show up. That may have saved you."

Sam's eyes lit up. "So, she's kind of a he-man woman?" His mouth turned to a smirk surrounded by beard.

"Actually, Deni is beautiful and every bit a woman," Nate said, wanting to change the subject as soon as possible.

Sam broke out into a laugh. "Oh? So you have quite a setup here for yourself."

Nate stood. "There is only one married couple here. The rest of us have a totally platonic relationship."

Sam swallowed. "I apologize if I misspoke. I meant no disrespect."

"None taken—this time."

"I guess I'm a little rough around the edges after living like an animal in the woods for so long. Sorry."

"Do you want to clean up?" Nate asked, hoping the conversation was over. "We have soap. Be sparing with it though. We'll run out soon enough as it is."

"Sure. You have scissors?" Sam pulled on his beard. "I'd like to cut this fuzz ball back."

"Got a razor too."

"I don't know about shaving. My face is kinda raw after going so long without cleaning. Cutting it back to an eighth of an inch will help. That and soap."

"Well, come out to the barn and you'll have privacy for a bath." When they were outside, Nate pointed at the pump. "Grab that bucket and fill it. There's a washtub in the barn."

While Sam took several trips to the pump bringing water to the tub, Nate got the scissors.

"I'll try to find some clothes for you," Nate said. "We're running low on that also, but there should be pants and a shirt you can use." He looked down at Sam's boots. "I've got a very old pair of boots that might fit. They're in bad shape, but they're better than what you're wearing."

Brian watched the barn from a living room window while Nate searched for clothes.

Nate walked by him, heading for the front door, a shirt and pants in his hands. "Where are those old boots I don't wear anymore?"

"Mr. Neely's wearing them." Brian did not divert his eyes from the window. "Dad, why are you giving this guy so much? We will run out of soap and clothes someday, and you're always giving stuff to people."

"I'm being selfish."

Cindy was listening. Both she and Brian said, "What?"

"You two should use your heads," Nate said. "Brian, do you think the Neelys have been an asset for us? Have they helped us survive? Is having them here worth the food and other things they use up?"

"They're our friends."

Nate liked Brian's answer. "They were strangers like Sam when we took them in. Look at it cold. Forget the fact they're friends. Forget the fact they are people. Is having them here helping you and me survive or not?"

"Yes," Brian said. "But they *are* people and our friends."

Cindy blushed.

"What is he? An animal?" Nate asked. "And he is a potential friend. So far, I believe he could be an asset to our group. We just have to go slow until we can trust him."

Brian stopped looking through the window and turned to his father. "Maybe he's a hard worker and a good shot, but we're still going to run out of stuff that much sooner if we take him in. And this house is getting crowded."

"For now, he can stay in the barn," Nate said. "It's a lot better than camping in that swamp. It'll be safer for us that way too, at least until we can trust him."

"What do you think?" Brian asked Cindy.

Cindy raised her eyebrows and shrugged. "Don't ask me. I'm just a guest here, and a kid."

"If I said that," Brian said, "Dad would yell at me."

"Said what?" Cindy asked.

"He means you're not just a guest here," Nate said.

"Well," Cindy said, "ask my father or mother, not me."

Ben yelled from the back bedroom, "I trust Nate's instincts and judge of character. Give the guy a chance if he wants to join us."

The three of them looked at one another and broke out laughing.

Nate said, "I guess that's one advantage of a small house: You can hear a conversation from any room."

~~~~~~~~~~~~

Nate stoked the fire. It reached five feet high. He was forced to step back from the heat.

Closer to the barn, they had a large kettle with ten gallons of hog lard waiting.

Sam threw more oak logs in the flames. "It'll be a while before we have enough ashes, but we need to shovel some out now so it can cool before dumping it in that old hog trough." He swung the ax and split another log.

Deni stood back and watched. "Lye water from ashes? You sure that soap of yours won't take our skin off?"

"It's not that bad. Just use less of it than normal," Sam said. "Also, make sure you rinse it off completely."

Deni gave him a doubtful look.

Sam wiped his sweating forehead. "Hey, when you guys run out of soap you'll be glad to have it. I know what it's like to go months with only a river and no soap for washing my stinking butt." He rubbed his whiskered face, the beard now trimmed close. "That bath I took in the barn was worth the trip over here alone."

Deni smiled. "And now you're thanking us by talking us into using lye soap."

"You don't have to use it," Nate said.

Sam split another oak log. "She will when the other soap runs out."

"What about washing clothes?" Deni asked.

"We'll make it a little stronger for that and for the dishes." Sam's eyes lit up. "Just don't get the bars mixed up."

Deni rolled her eyes. "Wonderful."

Caroline watched from a living room window.

Martha handed her a pail. "Why don't you get us some water and we'll finish the dishes?"

"I…" Caroline touched a deep scar on her left cheek. "He makes me nervous."

"Who? Mr. Boonbeck? He seems okay. Besides, Nate and Deni both are out there. And I'll be in here watching from the kitchen sink."

She took a timorous step and stopped, swallowed, and walked out the door.

Nate saw her and took three long steps to the pump. "We'll need the pail when you're through with it." He pumped the handle until it was full. "I'll take it in. Why don't you take a rest in that chair?" He pointed to a cheap patio chair made of plastic.

Caroline's eyes were fixated on Sam. Her left hand shook as she tried to cover her worst facial scar.

"Where's that brave woman I saw the day we met?" Nate asked.

"Brave?" Caroline turned her head to glare at Nate. Her eyes turned to slits.

Nate could not tell if the sun bothered her or if she was angry. "Yes. That's what I said. And there's no need to hide those scars."

She spun around, facing him.

They stood looking at each other.

"All I've ever done is try to help," Nate said. "And all I ask is you do me and those I care about no harm. What do you think I am doing now? My words were not meant to hurt."

Caroline walked into the house without a word.

Nate brought the pail of water in, set it down by Martha, and then went looking for another pail or bucket.

Chapter 5

Sam yawned and walked out of the barn where he spent the night. His worn out boots were still untied, and his T-shirt only half pulled down. He scratched at healing sores on his face and pulled at his shirt.

Nate got up on the Cat and cranked it.

"Hey," Sam yelled above the Cat's engine as he ran, "you're not going to destroy the bridge alone, are you?"

"Tomorrow maybe," Nate said. "I'm going to clear more land for planting and give us more shooting distance, so we can keep raiders off the house."

"Need any help?"

"Nah. Go on in and get some breakfast. The women will put you to work, I'm sure." Nate put the Cat in gear and drove toward the nearest tree line.

Deni met Sam at the door.

He stepped aside. "Where you going?"

"To relieve Brian at the OP." She kept her AR15 pointed skyward. The carbine had been taken off a man she killed in self-defense many months back.

Sam's eyebrows knitted. "OP?"

"Observation post," Deni said.

He nodded. "Oh. Military talk."

"Yeah. Sorry. I'm used to Nate knowing what I'm talking about since he was in the Army too. Everyone else around here knows what an OP is by now, since most have stood watch many times."

"Didn't know he was in the Army."

"Not surprising, since you haven't been here long." Deni looked across the field toward the tree under which Brian was standing watch. "I could tell though, even if he had never told me. Soldiers carry themselves differently." She smiled to herself. "They walk faster and stand more erect. They also treat others with respect and expect the same back."

"Did he see any combat?" Sam asked.

"Two wars. He was a Ranger. I rib him about Rangers being overrated, but, to tell the truth, I have always been in awe of super soldiers, as some call them. Not just Rangers, but all the elite military and all branches, not just Army. Ranger school is a real ass kicker, they say." She looked toward Nate. He was pushing a big pine tree down with the Cat. "You can also pick a Special Forces warrior out of a crowd—even a crowd of military members—because you can see it in their eyes.

"What?" Sam asked.

"They don't quit—ever." Deni's eyes grew distant. "And they are confident. There is no swagger or posturing. They have nothing to prove. You don't wear an Army Ranger Tab, or a Navy SEAL Trident—they call it a Budweiser—or a green beret without earning it."

"I can tell that you respect them," Sam said, "but you were a soldier too."

Deni flinched, and her eyes changed. Returning to the present, she said, "My father was a Ranger. I was thinking of him too."

"Was?"

"He's gone now," Deni said. "My mother died years ago."

"Sorry." Sam looked straight at her. "I guess I shouldn't have asked."

"No problem." Deni smiled. "I don't mind thinking about my father, or…the military. They are a special family."

"I wouldn't know," Sam said. "Just a hick car mechanic. Be careful out there. Way things are now; you never know when trouble can come hunting."

"You bet." Deni walked away, heading for the tree line and woods.

Sam found Martha folding clothes. Towels and shirts were folded and stacked on the dining table.

"Breakfast is waiting for you," she said.

"Thanks. I know you're busy enough around here without cooking for me." Sam took a plate of eggs and ham off the wood stove where it was being kept warm and set it on the table between piles of clothes.

"It was no trouble to put extra in the pan." She smiled. "Besides, Nate cooked it."

"Where's your husband?" Sam filled a glass with milk and then sat down to eat. "I was thinking of using the tractor's power takeoff to pump water from the river and irrigate. It hasn't rained since I've been here, and Nate agrees the crops need watering."

"Ben's manning the road OP." Martha started on another basket of laundry.

"Oh. That's where trouble is most likely to come from, isn't it? They can just drive right up here."

She nodded. "But some have come by river. Brian was shot in the leg by two men who showed up in a canoe. That happened before Nate took us in. Deni helped them stop a gang of cutthroat prison escapees early on after the plague killed nearly everyone. I don't know the whole story. He found us starving not long after and gave us food." Martha looked out the window, watching Nate bull trees down with the Cat. "He saved all of us. Certainly Tommy would not have lasted much longer." She seemed to shutter and went back to work, her chest deflating as she sighed. "Then Carrie and Caroline showed up needing help."

"Now me." Sam held a fork loaded with egg halfway to his mouth. "I'm trying to pull my weight around here. I want to go with Nate when he destroys the bridge. He is hesitant to allow it."

Martha finished folding another towel. Then she sat at the table to drink water from a glass and rest her back. "He says he's better off with Deni." She looked across the table at Sam. "I'm worried. They will be easy targets on that bulldozer."

"I get the impression he would rather go alone because it's so dangerous."

"Yes." Martha's hands clasped against her stomach. "I wish they wouldn't go. And I certainly don't want Ben to go either."

"Seems to me I'm the one who should do it." Sam washed eggs down with a mouthful of milk. "I'm the most expendable person here, being the newest member of this outfit, and I have not yet repaid you guys for taking me in."

"We don't feel that way." Martha gave him an anxious look.

"Let's put it like this: Nate is the least expendable person here. You're obviously worried. I know for certain that Brian is. He told me in not so many words."

"Those two would die for each other in a second."

"Yeah," Sam said, "I got that feeling too." He took another bite. "Maybe I still have a chance to talk him into letting me do the job for you guys. More than likely, there won't be a soul between here and the bridge, but I feel like I owe you all. If something does happen, what have I lost? Really? Everyone in my family is dead. Might was well die trying to help people as grow old alone."

She started to speak but stopped short of uttering a word.

~~~~~~~~~~

"Whoa! Give me a chance to catch my breath." Sam staggered back from his end of a two-man crosscut saw.

Nate pulled a rag out of his left back pocket and wiped his face.

They had a log chained to the tractor's front-end loader and lifted to a convenient height for cutting.

Brian laughed. "Dad is working you to death and he's older." He stacked another oak log on a pile.

"Brian." Nate gave him a stern look. "He's still recovering from overdosing on venison."

"Oh, he's just being a boy," Sam said. "A smart aleck one."

"I should feel sorry for anyone who has been forced to live on venison. It's not your fault you're so weak." Brian's eyes were full of mischief.

Sam waved him off. "You're a good kid. A smartass, but a good kid."

Nate pulled the saw across, starting a new cut eighteen inches back from its end. Saw wood poured out onto the ground next to where a foot-tall pile had collected. "We've got a lot of trees to cut for firewood with winter coming. Let's get busy."

"Winter will come and go before we get half the trees you pushed over cut and split." Sam took his end of the saw and pulled.

Nate pulled the saw back his way. "Winters are bad now for some reason. We need seasoned firewood to stay warm. Might as well cut all we can now. The splitting should wait until the wood's dry though."

Brian interjected. "You guys need to stop talking and start sawing. It'll take forever at the rate you're going."

You know, I think Sam is right," Nate said, "you are a smartass."

"A chip off the old block," Brian said, smiling.

A shadow landed on Nate's face. He opened his eyes. In the dark of 4AM, someone was standing over Brian, who slept on the floor next to him. He looked around, right hand tightening on his revolver. A form moved away and moonlight lit Caroline's lower half, her bare feet stepping around and past Nate's boots where he put them before going to sleep. He watched as she went down the hall and into Brian's bedroom. He heard whispers between Caroline and Carrie, then silence.

There was no sleep for Nate the rest of the night.

Brian, Deni, Sam, and Nate ate breakfast just after sunrise.

Caroline and Carrie were still in what used to be Brian's room. There was no sound coming from down the hall, and Nate assumed they were asleep.

"Why don't you let me take the dozer and destroy that old wood bridge?" Sam's voice was persistent. "I've seen it and know exactly what supports need to be taken out to do the job."

"Been thinking on it. That's why I haven't done it myself yet." Nate pushed a plate of sliced bread over to Brian. "With first one thing and then the other, I've been sidetracked. But I have been thinking on it."

A fork of eggs halfway to his mouth, Brian said, "As long as you know you're not going alone."

"Sometimes you forget who the father is." Nate's voice rose just enough to let Brian know he should be careful.

The fork fell to Brian's plate. He got up and walked out the door.

Nate spoke before he had gone too far. "Take your shotgun with you and don't go farther than the barn."

Brian swiveled on a heel and went back for his shotgun, then ran outside.

Sam pointed at the door. "There's a damn good reason why I should go and not you."

Deni's face showed concern. "Nate…," she started.

"I'll explain to him that I'm not going alone." Nate got up from his chair. "If I can talk him into coming back and finishing his breakfast, I'll tell all of you what I have planned."

Sam and Deni looked at each other.

"Okay," Deni said, "we'll wait."

Four minutes later, the two walked in.

Brian put his shotgun in a near corner and sat down to finish eating.

Nate stood by the table. "We can make it a little safer by having two people walk down the road just back in the woods on each side to scout ahead and make sure no one is waiting in ambush. They will have to be ahead a ways, since the dozer can move faster than a person walking can, so it's possible someone could set up an ambush after the scouts go through. It'll be a slow process, but safer than just driving down the road."

"You and I will be the scouts, I presume," Sam said.

"No, Deni and I will. You will drive."

Sam's eyes flashed to Deni. "Why her? I'm a good woodsman and hunter."

Nate folded his arms and leaned back against a wall. "Yes, I noticed that the day we met. There were signs of it anyone could pick up while tracking you but you're not military trained. Deni is. Being a hunter is a good start, but military training goes way beyond that when it comes to surviving a fight with the deadliest killer on earth."

"You have a lot of respect for her, don't you?" Sam asked.

Brian broke in. "She saved my ass that time when some convicts were breaking in. Put .22 bullets in them with that rifle she got off the man who shot me in the leg."

"Anyway," Nate said, "I figure you should give us a two-hour head start. When you catch up, I'll step out into the road so you can see me. You pull off into the woods to give us another head start. Then we do it all over again. We'll keep doing it that way till we get there."

"We'll have to do the same thing returning," Deni said.

Nate nodded. "It's a pain but it's worth it. We're talking about two days there and two days back."

"What if someone drives up on me from behind?" Sam asked.

"We will come running, but if they hit when Deni and I are a mile or two down the road, you're in trouble. Head into the woods and parallel the road heading for us. That thing can push down and go over all but the largest trees. This isn't going to be one hundred percent safe no matter how we do it." Nate looked at the others. Any questions?"

Brian said, "Yeah. What if you don't come back by nightfall the second day? How long are we supposed to wait before looking for you?"

Nate shook his head. "You don't. All of you stay here and keep this place guarded."

"Bullshit!" Brian nearly yelled. "You're always doing that. You expect me to do something you would never do."

Nate ignored him. "I have to get with Ben and work out a security plan that compensates for the reduced manpower here at the farm while the three of us are gone."

"They won't be getting much work done in the field," Deni said.

Nate nodded. "Security will be enough to keep them busy. I don't think anyone should be in the field at all." He looked across the table at Brian. "I'm sure you will do your part."

Brian looked up at his father. "The cow and chickens will still have to be fed and let out every day."

"And that will still be your job," Nate said. "The cow can stay in the barn though."

"That just means more crap to shovel out of the stall." Brian got up and headed for the sink with his plate.

"Tough, ain't it?" Nate did not smile. Neither did Brian.

Nate looked at Deni and Sam. "You two pack enough for five days in case something does go wrong. Bring plenty of water." He grabbed his rifle and started out the door.

"Where are you going?" Brian asked.

"To get Ben. There's no need to man the OP since no one will be working in the field today or tomorrow."

Thirty minutes later, Nate and Ben went into the barn. Brian saw them and grabbed his shotgun.

Deni put a full canteen in her backpack. "Stay in the house until your father gets back."

"They just went into the barn," Brian yelled over his shoulder as he rushed out the door.

Brian found them having a serious conversation. They stopped when he came through the wide doorway.

Nate waved him closer. "We need to have a talk about how to handle security while the three of us are gone."

"You want us all to stay in the house as much as possible," Brian said. "I got that."

"Yes. When you take care of the cow and chickens, Ben will be watching. Never leave the house until you have Ben at the window over watching."

Brian rolled his eyes. "Right."

"While I'm gone, Ben is in charge."

Brian started to make a face but caught himself.

"There is something else." Nate glanced at the open door. I do not trust either Carrie or Caroline. I want you to sleep only when Ben is on watch. And then you must sleep where he can watch you while he pulls security."

Brian's forehead wrinkled and eyes narrowed. "What?"

"Twice now, Caroline has stood over you in the middle of the night while you slept. I don't know what that's about but it could mean trouble. Both of those girls have been through hell, and there's no telling what their mental condition is. So stay away from them."

"Uh, okay," Brian said. "But if one of them is crazy, what are we going to do?"

"That problem is for later. While we're gone, you just be on the watch from danger—both inside the house and out."

"Nice." Brian sighed. "More lost sleep."

Ben spoke up. "And don't worry about me bossing you around. If you do what your father just told you, I won't need to say a thing. He's covered the situation well enough."

"Yeah, he's always thorough when it comes to bossing me," Brian said. "He doesn't need any help from you."

"Hey," Nate warned.

"He doesn't mean any disrespect," Ben said, chuckling.

"That's right, Mr. Neely; my wrath was directed at him." Brian smiled at his father. "I will do what you said. But if you don't come back, I will be pissed."

"I'll be back," Nate said. "I might be late, but we will all be back here in a few days."

The expression on Brian's face changed. "I wish we didn't have Caroline and Carrie to deal with on top of everything else. We already had enough problems without two crazies in the house."

Nate's eyebrows knitted. "So I should have just told them to hit the road? Is that what you think?"

Brian lowered his head. "No. But we should lock them in my bedroom at night."

Nate's voice rose. "I'm ashamed you would say that."

"Only when we're asleep." Brian's voice exuded apology. "It won't hurt them to be locked in my room nights. They could be dangerous. You said that yourself."

Nate's chest deflated with disappointment. "I was hoping you were not serious, that you were just joking like you always are."

Brian turned red. "I don't see where that's mean. People lock their kids in their room all the time."

"You were never locked up," Nate said. "And if you saw Carrie in that little cage with no room to move at all, you would not be talking like this. The last thing we need to be doing is adding to their pain."

Brian looked insulted. "I didn't say a thing about hurting them. I would never do that."

"I know that you do not realize it," Nate said, "but it would hurt them. They have not done anything yet to cause us to go that far. Just be careful and do what I said. I really don't think they will be a problem. Just be careful."

"Yeah, careful. Anything else?" Brian looked away. "I didn't say anything about hurting them."

"I know that." Nate laid his heavy hand on Brian's shoulder. "But locking them up would destroy their trust of us and may push them into doing exactly what we're afraid of."

"Your father's right, Brian," Ben said. "We must show them they can trust us, even if we're leery of them. They can't be given any reason to feel like prisoners here."

Brian nodded. "Okay. It was just a suggestion. I didn't mean any harm."

"No one is judging you," Nate said. "I just don't think you thought it through. Let's leave that behind and move on to preparing for the trip."

"What?" Brian asked.

"While we're getting ready to leave, bring in plenty of water for drinking, washing, and flushing the toilet. The safest place for everyone is in the house, so fill every bucket and water container now before we leave."

He rolled his eyes and picked up two pails. "You guys are the ones who should be careful." He headed for the pump.

Ben looked like he had something on his mind.

"What is it?" Nate asked.

"He has a point. I mean maybe we could ask them to stay in the bedroom at night for safety reasons."

Nate shrugged his shoulders. "You could ask. That does not mean they will. And what are you going to do if they don't?"

Ben blew out a lung full of air. "I'll tell my wife and daughter what's going on and remind them to keep an eye on those two."

~~~~~~~~~~~~

Nate tied a five-gallon fuel can to the Caterpillar.

Deni walked up, her backpack on and AR15 in hand. "There's plenty of diesel in the tank. Those things don't get much mileage, but you don't need the extra fuel for this trip."

"You go heavy on ammo?" Nate asked. He glanced up at her while working.

"Six extra mags."

"Get another six or eight," Nate said, "and put them in my duffle by the door. I'll throw it behind the seat. That way we won't have to carry it."

Deni gave him a quizzical look. "Okay."

Nate answered the unspoken question. "No. I don't know anything you don't."

"Just in case, huh?"

"That's it." Nate finished. They walked into the house.

The shortwave radio was on. A woman talked about problems with hungry people showing up and demanding food she could not spare. She was alone and afraid. Everyone but her son died in the plague. Then her son was killed in a gunfight a week ago. She lost her voice in a fit of crying. The signal faded.

Brian came down the hall and into the living room with four boxes of 30/30 rounds. He handed them to Sam for his lever-action carbine. Before Sam could thank him, Brian said, "That sounded like Mrs. Benton."

"Yes, it did," Nate said. "You turn the radio on?"

"I...thought we should try to learn what's going on before you guys left," Brian answered.

"Good idea. I should have thought of that." Nate glanced at Deni as she walked by.

Deni opened Nate's duffle bag on the floor by the front door. She hesitated. Inside were a dozen magazines for his M14. After putting hers in, she zipped the bag closed and stood.

Nate put his backpack on. "We're already running late. Get your packs and let's go."

Sam and Deni were following him out the door when a man's voice came in over the radio.

"Anyone hearing my voice, take notice: A gang of killers just burned a wide swath through the little town of Cold Springs. They are now heading north. These bastards are ruthless, and there are hundreds of them. To stand against them is suicide. All you can do is stay out of their path. Whatever you have in your home is not worth dying for. Run and hide."

Another ham operator broke in. "Who the hell are you to tell us to leave our homes?" The man seemed as scared as he was angry. "We'll starve if we lose everything. I went into town early on in this crisis and found all the stores looted and warehouses of food taken over by gangs who would shoot you if you got too close. I worked for a grocery store chain and thought I could go to the warehouse and get supplies. My manager said he would let us take what we needed if the plague reached our town and it came to that. Well, it was under armed guard. A gang of thugs had taken over the warehouse. My manager and four employees had been shot dead and were hanging from light poles as a warning the same would happen to anyone who went against them. One of those bastards offered to trade a bag of rice for my fifteen-year-old daughter. I got the hell out of there and never went back into town. The point is we are close to starving as it is. We can't afford to just leave everything to looters."

The first voice came back. "My name is Frank Pogue. I was a captain with the Levee County Sheriff's Department before the plague. This is not an order. I am simply warning everyone that they cannot fight these people. There are too many, and they are well organized. If you fight them, you will die. It's that simple."

The second voice answered. "If I let them take what little I have my family will starve."

The deputy's voice faded and sounded like someone talking with a lung full of helium but was still clear enough to understand. "I'm sorry, but they will rape and murder your family if they come to your home. Flee into the woods and hide until they have passed through your area."

"Can you tell us where they are now?" The second voice came in much clearer, telling Nate he was probably much closer than the deputy was. "I'm hoping we have time to bury what food we have back in the woods."

"They left Cold Springs yesterday morning," the deputy said, "mostly in pickups and on motorcycles. How fast they travel would depend on how often they stop to rob, rape, and murder. There is nothing between you and them. No law enforcement agency survived the plague. You are on your own, and you cannot stand against them. Get out of their way and hide."

Nate clicked the radio off. "A change of plans. Brian, let the cow out in the pasture and fill the water tank. Put feed and water in the chicken coop. Ben, have your family pack what they can carry long distance. Get ready to lock the place up and leave."

Ben stood there looking confused. "What?"

"He's in his bossy mode, Mr. Neely, I wouldn't argue," Brian said. He looked up at his father. "You want me to take them to Mel's bunker, don't you?"

Nate nodded. "The keys are in the safe." He looked around the room at the others. "Take what you can, but don't load yourselves down so much you can't move fast. We have thirty minutes to haul stuff into the woods and hide it. I'll take care of my reloading supplies and the ammo. Brian, get the extra guns. We'll haul some of our canned goods into the woods too. Make sure you get the wheat we have in five-gallon buckets."

"Why only thirty minutes?" Ben asked.

"It's not arbitrary." Nate was already stacking Mason jars of canned vegetables from kitchen shelves in a cardboard box Martha got out of a closet. "We will never get everything, even if we worked at it for days, and we don't have days. But thirty minutes will give us time to save some of what's most important." He headed out the door with a box of canned food. Martha was right behind him with a box full of Mason jars. Deni followed with another box.

Sam had been in the barn. He came out carrying two five-gallon cans of diesel. When he saw the others heading into the woods, he followed.

By the time they came back, some with empty boxes, Brian had the extra guns and some of the ammo they had in the house piled on the porch. Most of their ammunition was buried in PVC pipe a quarter mile from the house and near the river valley, just before the land dropped off into wetlands. What ammunition they had in the house was only a small fraction of their total ammunition supplies, but they did not want to leave it to be used against them. There were also boxes of food ready to be packed into the woods setting by several five-gallon buckets of wheat.

Sam grabbed two buckets and headed into the woods again.

"That's about all we're going to be able to save," Nate said. "Brian, get the tarp out of the barn." The others were already leaving with boxes of food they picked up off the porch. Nate yelled at them. "Take a different route this time, and don't walk single file. Try not to leave a beaten path in the woods they can follow."

They spread out. Deni lead them into the woods.

Nate went into his bedroom and loaded a box with gunpowder and primers. He did not get all the powder or any of the bullets and cases. There just was not time to save it all. He also had to leave the loading press and other ammunition loading tools.

After carrying his overloaded box to the porch, Nate went into the kitchen and grabbed the grain mill so they would have something to grind wheat into flour.

Brian dragged the heavy canvas tarp out of the barn and up to the porch.

"I'll carry that," Nate said. "It's too heavy for you."

Brian stood there catching his breath. "It's heavy all right."

Nate noticed Brian did not have his shotgun. "Get your shotgun. Sling it on your back out of the way, if you have to, but never leave it. Always have it with you."

Brian started past him to go into the house.

Nate reached out and stopped him. "If there's anything you really do not want to leave behind to be stolen or destroyed, you better get it now and put it in your pack. Then take care of the livestock."

Inside, Brian grabbed two photos off the fireplace mantel. One was a photo of the entire family, including three of his grandparents, taken when he was five. The other was a photo of Nate and him holding up a thirty-five pound catfish Brian had caught when he was seven. He wrapped them in a spare T-shirt and put them in his backpack.

When Brian set his pack on the porch so he could get it later, Nate spoke. "We still have each other, Brian."

"It will never be the same." Brian's eyes were dry.

"I'm glad you chose the photos." Nate held him. "You will make memories with your own family someday." He let him go and stepped back. "Now I need your help. Get everyone to Mel's bunker."

Brian's jaw set, and he suddenly appeared more mature. "I'll get them there. *You* be careful. If they come up on you on that road, Sam's going to be in trouble."

"That's our worries," Nate said. "Yours is to get these people to that bunker."

"I will." Movement caught Brian's attention.

Caroline and Carrie stood silently just inside the door, their faces white.

Caroline said, "Don't let them take us again. Finish us first."

Nate turned to her. "Both of you just do what Ben and Brian say and you'll be safe. Once you're in that bunker, they can't touch you. They will never find that place anyway."

"There's a couple military surplus backpacks in my room," Brian said. "I'll get them so you two can load up with items you want to take with you." Brian ran past them into the house and down the hall.

Nate checked how they were dressed. "Get into the best walking shoes you have. Wear thick socks to help prevent blisters. The trip's going to be hard on you two with all your injuries, but you have to walk the whole way. Don't load your packs too heavy."

Caroline took both the packs from Brian when he came back. "I'll help Carrie get ready," she said. "We can make it. We just won't be breaking any speed records."

"Good," Nate said. "Once you're a ways into the woods, there will be no big hurry. Brian will get everyone to the bunker."

Twenty minutes later, everything on the porch had been taken into the woods. Nate and Ben spread the tarpaulin over the cache and sprinkled it with leaves and sticks for camouflage. Despite their efforts, anyone who happened to walk up on the cache could not help but see it.

Everyone stood on the porch with their packs on, ready to go. Only Tommy, Carrie, and Caroline were not armed. The house still needed to be locked up, but everyone knew that would only slow the raiders down.

Nate headed for the Cat, stopping just long enough to put his left hand on Brian's shoulder. "There's no time for goodbyes. Keep your head straight and thinking, help Ben take care of everyone, and we'll all be back together in a couple days."

Brian swallowed. "I will."

Chapter 6

Sam hung his pack on the back of the Cat and stepped up into the driver's seat. Deni and Nate held on to catch a ride.

When they got to the road, Nate yelled, "Stop here." He checked if anyone was coming and jumped down.

Deni did the same on the left side.

Nate looked up at Sam. "You two keep watch while I operate this thing."

Sam jumped down and got behind a tree, keeping his rifle trained down the road.

"What are you going to do?" Deni asked, raising her voice above the engine.

"Block the driveway." Nate turned the Cat around, lowered its blade, and pushed dirt up, digging into the driveway at the same time. He backed up and started over again, repeating five times until he had a six-foot deep trench on his side and a six-foot high mound of dirt across the driveway. Large pine trees lined the road and denied passage on both sides of the mound. A motorcycle might get between the trees, but no four-wheeled vehicles could pass. If anyone wanted down the drive, they would have to walk.

"Hop on," Nate yelled. "I'm driving. Keep your eyes open."

Deni climbed up. "Another change of plans?"

Nate waited until Sam was on. "We may not have time to screw around. We're heading for the bridge as fast as this thing will go."

She blanched, but said nothing.

Sam nodded and smiled. "Hell yes! We've got to get there before they do, or we're in trouble."

Deni added, "It's worth the gamble. Floor this thing."

Nate raised the blade until he could just see over it, wanting it in front to stop bullets. He had the Cat topped out, heading south, in less than thirty seconds.

~~~~~~~~~~~~

Brian checked the last shutter, making sure they were all bolted. "You guys wear the best walking shoes you have. It's rough country at Mel's place." He yelled loud enough everyone could hear out on the porch.

Cindy laughed. "You must think we have a choice of shoes. All I have is one worn out pair of sneakers."

Ben looked down the driveway as if he expected trouble to arrive at any moment. "Let's hit the road, Brian."

Brian checked the back door locks and slid a steel bar across it through two brackets. "Mr. Neely, get them into the woods, we're going now." He had his .22 pistol strapped on and lever-action rifle slung on the left side of his backpack, his shotgun in his right hand.

"That's a lot of iron you're carrying, and call me Ben."

Brian smiled as he locked the front door. "Better not. Dad won't like it."

"He's not here. What about this bunker, and who's Mel?"

"A neighbor and a friend," Brian said. "We haven't seen him in nearly a year. Probably the sickness got him, or bullets. He was a survivalist nut, but a good friend. He had a lot of food and stuff stored in a cave. It's not far from his bunker. Anyway, we can stay in there a long time. The bunker's got a well and hand pump and a toilet and freeze-dried food, so we don't even have to go outside. We can get more out of the cave if we need it, but Dad and the others should be back before then."

"Why didn't you and your father tell us about all this before?" Ben kept checking the driveway for trouble.

Brian hesitated, thinking. "Well, at first we wanted to wait until we were sure we could trust you. Then the subject never came up. Mel said we could use whatever we needed, but Dad felt that we should do our best to provide for ourselves in case Mel showed up. It wouldn't be right if he fought his way back here, thinking if he just made it home he would be okay, only to find out we had used all of his supplies."

Ben nodded. "That sounds like something your father would say."

"Also," Brian added, "he wanted to leave Mel's stuff in reserve for when we really need it, like if our crops fail. He always told me we should raise or own food on the farm because Mel's stuff will only last so long anyway."

"Won't it get old?" Ben asked.

"Nah. That freeze-dried stuff will last decades."

Ben seemed surprised. "No kidding?"

Martha interrupted. "We're ready. Let's go."

Brian took a last look around outside the house and barn. Their cow munched peacefully on grass in the pasture. He pulled a compass out from under his shirt where it hung on a string from his neck and headed into the woods. Ben stayed back ten yards to guard their rear.

~~~~~~~~~~~~

Nate had the Caterpillar bulldozer in high gear, and its engine roaring. Still, their progress seemed agonizingly slow. They found the ride smoother than expected, considering the poor condition of the clay road. Summer rains had washed deep gullies across it, and two creeks overflowed two months back during a tropical storm that dumped torrents into north Florida, cutting ravines deep enough Nate was forced to slow when traversing them. The Cat climbed out of them with little trouble. Water levels in every creek in the area were still high. There had been some argument over whether it was a full-fledged hurricane or just a tropical storm at the time. The Neelys were from the North and had never been through a real hurricane like Nate and Brian had. Normally, the Weather Service would have settled the argument before it started, but there was no government left as near as they could tell. Certainly, their radio gave no hint of one. Nate insisted there was a government still in Washington, even if you could not prove it from their farm.

Nate stopped after crossing a washed out ravine and had the others jump off while he cut the gully deeper and pushed dirt into a long berm all the way across the road just behind the ravine, leaving it impassable. "It will slow them down at least," he said.

They took off again and were soon going at top speed.

Sam's face revealed little concern. He looked down the road up ahead and occasionally turned to look behind them, but he did not watch the tree line on his side as carefully as Nate thought he should. Nate wondered if he understood just how easily he could be shot off that dozer by anyone hiding in the woods.

Deni's eyes were hawkish, constantly searching the woods on her side of the road. Nervous tension kept her face taut. Nate knew the look well: He had seen it on many soldiers' faces, but never on a woman's. Women did not fight with his Ranger teams. It made her look ten years older. He nodded to himself. *She knows the danger. Either Sam does not give a damn anymore, or he does not realize our situation.* He had an idea Sam did not give a damn about his own life, but did feel obligated to do his part.

They passed a bend in the road that Nate recognized, and he knew they were making good time. What would have taken all day had taken little more than an hour, not counting time spent on the roadblocks. So far, it appeared their gamble paid off. "We got about a mile to the bridge," he yelled above the engine's roar.

Another turn, sharper this time, and they were heading down slope into wetter land. Deni yelled, "People down there!"

Nate eased the throttle back and slowed to a stop. He saw half a dozen motorbikes parked on the bridge. As many young men stood watching.

"Get on the tracks and squat down so the blade will protect you," Nate said. He estimated the range before getting out of the seat: six hundred yards.

Bullets pinged off the dozer's blade.

"We got to get closer," Sam yelled.

Nate jumped down and lay beside the right track so he could shoot from prone under the blade. "You two are safe. Just stay where you are."

Sam was incredulous. "They're shooting at us, goddamnit!"

Deni fired two deliberate rounds over the top of the blade. "Stay calm, Sam."

By now, Nate was in a tight shooting sling and in his natural point of aim. He had already adjusted his back sight for range and wind. His first shot took a man's heart out. He aimed at another man who fired at the Cat and missed completely. He too fell to Nate's shot.

Deni managed to hit a motorcycle, and then put a man down.

Nate fired again, and another man fell.

Fewer bullets hit the blade and Sam began to fire back also, but his rifle, with its open sights and short-range caliber, was not up to the job. By aiming more feet high than he could hazard a guess to put a number on, he managed to hit a rail on the right side of the bridge, causing a man nearby to stand and give Nate an easier target.

Nate took advantage of the opportunity and killed him.

A last man ran to a bike and got it cranked before Nate put a bullet through his chest.

The woods continued to echo with gunfire for a few seconds, then silence but for Sam's heavy breathing. "They just started shooting for no reason," Sam said. He gulped air.

Nate still lay on the yellow dirt road. "Scouts for their main raiding party. They were supposed to secure the bridge until the others got there."

"They failed," Deni said.

"I didn't think anyone could hit anything that far off." Sam's eyes were focused on the bridge. "Must be a quarter mile."

"No," Nate said, "quarter mile is four hundred fifty yards. It's six hundred."

"How do you know just by looking?" Sam asked.

"Long practice. If my range estimate were off fifty yards, I would have shot over or under them at that distance. My rifle sights don't lie. Those on the bridge are dead."

Deni clicked the safety on her rifle. "The main bunch will be coming anytime. We better move."

"Sam, you drive," Nate said.

"Okay but…," he sat in the seat, "how do we know there's not more in the woods?"

Deni answered, "Six motorbikes, six men."

Sam put the Cat in gear. "They could have ridden double." He raced the engine and let the clutch out. The dozer lurched and headed for the bridge.

Deni smiled, but said nothing.

Nate kept his eyes working the tree line on both sides of the road. "When we get there, you stay in the Cat. Deni will keep watch while I hook the cable and chain up."

When they were close, Sam slowed to a stop off to the right side a little so Nate could stretch the cable to the nearest pillar.

The old wood bridge had seen its better days, and Nate hoped taking a pillar out on each side would bring down a twenty-foot section. He slung the cable end with its hook around a two-foot support pole and caught it as it swung back to him. He hooked a loop and pulled it tight.

As Nate expected, the cable was not long enough, so he got the heavy chain and hooked the cable to it. Pulling it tight, he had just enough length to wrap it around a brace behind the dozer's blade. He looked up at Sam. "Keep as low as you can in the seat in case the cable breaks. It will whiplash back and cut you in two."

Sam nodded and waited for Nate to run back into a stand of trees for protection. Deni was already in cover on the far side, watching the other end of the bridge.

Backing up slowly stretched the chain and cable tight. The loop end around the pillar began to cut into wood, and their end of the bridge groaned. The Cat's tracks slipped a slight amount in the clay and limestone of the road until the pole came loose from heavy beams it was bolted to. Before Sam could react, he had pulled the pole several feet from the bridge. The cable slipped off the top end and came whistling back, harmlessly lashing off to the side of the Cat and throwing dust ten feet into the air.

Nate came running. "Great! Might as well keep working on this side. We'll take out the last long pillar. That should collapse the section on our side and leave them with only a footbridge. If we have time, we'll take out the left side and leave them with nothing." He snatched up the cable end and ran back onto the bridge.

A low rumble warned Nate that Harley's would be bringing trouble across the bridge in minutes. He scrambled to drag the heavy chain and cable, and then lay on his stomach to reach around and swing the cable end with its hook so he could loop it around the next support post. He was not able to catch the hook on his first try. He gave it more slack and slung the cable end around with more force, catching it as it whipped around and slammed into his hand.

Shots echoed in the river valley.

A group of men rode up on motorbikes, stopping on the other end of the bridge. A few fired before they got off the bikes. Four-wheeled vehicles followed close behind. Men shot at them from the back of flatbed trucks, shooting over the top of the cab. More jumped out of pickups, shooting as soon as their feet hit the ground.

Deni cut loose with her AR15, emptying what was left of her thirty round magazine.

Nate pushed up from the bridge planks and ran for the tree line on his side. "Rip it out," he yelled over his shoulder.

Sam backed the Cat, leaning over to keep low. This time he hurried it. The chain and cable snapped tight. The pole jerked loose and moved several feet from the beams it supported, leaning at a fifteen-degree angle. The cable set the wood to smoking as it pulled tighter and slid up the pole at the same time. Finally, it slipped off the end, flew back, and slapped the roof over Sam, its end whipping around the back end and just missing him.

"Son of a bitch!" Sam stared at the two inch deep, eight inch long bend in thick steel just above where his head would have been if he had not leaned down and to the left as much as possible.

Nate and Deni fired into a gathering crowd of vehicles and men on foot. Gunfire from both ends of the bridge roared, making it impossible for Sam to hear Nate yelling for him to back down the road. Nate was too busy aiming and firing to worry about it at the moment.

Instead of backing away, Sam put the Cat in neutral and fired into the gang with his 30/30. He left the blade down, exposing him to gunfire.

One look at the bridge told Nate they were in trouble. It sagged on their side but had not collapsed and fallen into the river. More support posts needed to be taken out. He ran for the cable.

Sam saw and brought the Cat closer to give Nate enough slack to work with. He stretched to look over the top of the blade, exposing more of himself as bullets hit all around. Sparks flew off steel when a bullet ricocheted off a roof post near Sam's face, leaving him temporarily blind. He rubbed his right eye.

Deni continued to provide suppressive fire.

Crimson mist sprayed the Cat's roof, and Sam's head whipped back, then forward. His body went limp and left foot slid off the clutch pedal. The Cat lurched, the engine nearly died, then caught itself, and the dozer started to creep forward.

When the Cat reached the bridge, Nate felt vibration coming from the wooden planks he lay on. Turning to look, his eyes grew wide and he rolled off the edge of the bridge just as the Cat's right track was about to crush his feet. Landing in brush, he continued to roll down the slope and stopped at the river's edge. He jumped up and ran for the cover of a stand of cypress trees as bullets whistled by. Behind him, he heard timber splintering and snapping. By the time he was able to look, the bridge had collapsed and the Cat was lying on its side, half submerged in the river. He could not see Sam. Perhaps he was under the Cat.

Nate's blood boiled. *Okay, you bastards, you want to cross? How high of a price are you willing to pay?* Nate wished he had the duffle of extra magazines, now lying in the river with Sam and the Cat. He wanted to put that ammo to good use.

Deni kept up a steady rate of fire, taking a deadly toll.

Nate crawled upslope through trees and brush until he could turn back to the road in safety. A lull in the shooting allowed him to hear Deni yelling, asking about Sam. He had no time to answer. After slamming a fresh magazine home, he killed two more that were careless in their choice of cover.

The shooting stopped. Someone yelled, "Who the fuck are you, and what do you want?"

You shot first, you son of a bitch. Nate searched for the one yelling.

"Why don't you assholes just leave while you're still alive?" The man stood. "You're outnumbered."

Deni stopped firing.

Nate saw the man who was talking when he stood from behind a bush. He took careful aim and put a bullet through the man's chest. *I haven't left yet because I'm not through killing, and this is a damn good place for it.*

Deni found more targets and began to fire at her steady pace.

Nate knew they both were going to run out of ammo at the rate they were firing. They had to make their ammo last until nightfall so he could sneak down to the Cat and retrieve that duffle bag. By then some of them would already be across on their side. He knew, at that moment, men were running both up and down river so they could swim across out of Deni's and his sight. It was only a matter of time before the tables would turn and they would be in serious trouble. *However, there is no better place between here and the farm to slow them down.* He killed another one and relocated farther back.

Another man yelled, "Why don't you want to talk? What did we ever do to you?"

Nate detected a hint of desperation, or perhaps exasperation, in his voice. *They're in a hurry for some reason.*

Deni took Nate's cue and emptied the man's head. She was answered with a sustained rain of bullets that sent her ducking behind a log.

Men ran from cover to a pickup, one got in the driver's seat, four in the back. The driver sped down the bridge until Nate put a bullet through the windshield and killed him. Deni started in on those in the back. Nate joined her, and they soon had all of them dead or lying wounded in the bed of the pickup.

Reaching into a pants pocket, Nate pulled out four tracer rounds. He removed the magazine from his rifle and loaded them. The truck had come to a stop at an angle, leaving the gas tank exposed to rifle fire. It took three rounds to set the truck ablaze. Nate hoped the bridge would burn too. If not, the truck would be one more obstacle the killers would have to overcome if they wanted to rebuild the bridge well enough to get their vehicles across. *Why don't they turn around, unless they plan to repair the bridge? They must need to get across bad.*

He moved closer to the road, looking for Deni. He needed to talk to her. But how could he cross without being shot?

Water had washed a gully across the road two hundred yards back from his position. It was only a foot deep in places, a little more in others. He thought about trying to cross there, but his pack would be visible above the shallow gully, and he did not want it shot up. It was not enough protection anyway. A quarter mile down the road there was a hill. He could get there safely by staying in the trees, then crossing on the reverse slope. *I hate leaving Deni unsupported for so long, but it's the only way.*

By running as fast as he could, weaving through trees and brush, he made it to the hill in five minutes. Firing intensified while he crossed the road on the reverse slope. He fell to his stomach and crawled to the top of the hill. They were rushing the bridge, and Deni was struggling to drive them back.

Nate adjusted his back sight for range and a five mile an hour wind coming out of his right, then slipped his left arm into the shooting sling. His withering fire halted them by the time they got to the break in the bridge. Before they were able to get back behind their vehicles for cover, Deni and he had killed ten more.

Nate accessed the situation. *They won't try that again. The deputy said these guys are organized. I see no evidence of that yet.* He crawled across the road and headed for Deni, using the cover of trees.

Deni did not hear him coming up behind her, so Nate stepped behind a tree and called out. "Time to relocate, Deni. We have to go."

She turned her head around. Relief on her face, she ran toward him. They left the river valley behind, stopping after one thousand yards.

They sat on a log to talk.

"What about Sam?" Deni asked.

Her eyes told him she knew the answer, but he dreaded telling it anyway. "I think he was shot and his foot slipped off the clutch. That's why the Cat wound up on the bridge, collapsing it and falling in the river. I could not see him after. I guess he ended up under the Cat. I'm sure he's dead."

She looked away. "I hate it."

"So do I. But we're not out of this yet, so we've got to keep our heads working fulltime."

"I don't get why they didn't leave already," Deni said. "They can't get their vehicles across now."

"I've been wondering about that too. They must think they can repair the bridge. They're in a hurry and don't want to turn around and go another way, I know that. But I don't know why."

Her eyes lit up. "They're being pursued. But by whom?"

"Bingo. Either way, we have to hold them here as long as possible. The more time they lose here, the less time they'll have to stop and raid our farm. They may keep driving by, especially since our drive is blocked."

"If we get lucky, whoever is chasing them will catch them on that side."

He nodded. "We can't bet our lives on luck though."

She checked her magazine pouches. "I've got a mag. and a half left."

"I'm running low too. We need that duffle full of ammo."

She stood. "There's no way. Don't even think about it."

"Oh, I've thought about it, but you're right; there is no way. At least not now."

Deni's eyes showed worry. "They've sent men up and down river to swim across out of our sight."

"Yep. They're hunting for us as we sit here."
"If you don't want to run, what?" Deni asked.
"Come on, I'll show you."

Chapter 7

Deni looked downhill at the men milling about on the bridge. "One thousand yards?"

"That's what I estimate," Nate said. "And I better not be off or I'll miss every time." He raised the back sight on his M14 to shoot high at one thousand yards so he could aim low and the front sight would not obscure his targets. At that range, the front sight would appear larger than a man's chest. "Wind's in our face—zero value."

"I knew a couple snipers out of Benning, you sound like them."

"I wasn't a sniper, but Rangers are trained to reach out past normal carbine range. I have fifty rounds for my revolver. You may see some long-range revolver shooting before this is over." He glanced at her, a slight sign of mischief on his face. "And I damn sure did not learn that in the Army."

"Yeah. I got to shoot one magazine of pistol ammo a year. Army doesn't think much of pistols in combat."

Nate handed her his Zeiss binoculars. "You're my spotter. Try to see where the bullets hit so I can adjust my range."

"Okay." She glassed the bridge. "Who are you going to kill first?"

"The one standing on the hood of that two-ton flatbed truck. He has binocs and is trying to find us up here."

He sharpened his sight picture and held his breath when the front sight was low on the man's chest, then started to squeeze the trigger.

The M14 barked. The man doubled over and fell headfirst off the truck.

"A foot low," Deni said.

"Yep." He could see men on the bridge running for cover. One man looked over the hood of a pickup. Nate shot and missed.

"I didn't know which one you were aiming for, so I didn't see where it hit."

"I missed," Nate said. "The target was too small for long range—his face."

He aimed for a man in the open and took out his heart.

"You got that one in the chest," Deni said.

The M14 barked again and a man fell behind a pickup.

"Not sure where it hit," Deni said.

"That's okay, he's good. One more and we have to relocate."

He fired, wounding a man in his right arm.

Firing from below roared.

Deni handed him his binoculars.

"They're shooting blind again," Nate said. "But we must move. Others are coming at us through the woods right now. Bet on it."

"Close quarters stuff from now on, huh?"

"I hope to avoid that by backing off," Nate said.

Deni seemed relieved. "How far do you think they'll come before turning back to the river?"

"Don't know, but we won't be there. We'll swing around downriver and come at them from the side tonight."

Deni's eyes grew wide. "Oh. Shit."

"You don't have to come."

"I didn't say that."

Nate stopped walking and turned to her. "I know you didn't; I did, and I meant it. I want you to stay back while I raid them tonight." When she said nothing, he started walking again.

She followed him as he worked his way through thick brush. "No time to argue about it now."

He nodded and kept moving.

They walked three miles downriver and stopped to eat for the first time in sixteen hours. Neither was really hungry, but they needed to keep their stamina up.

Mosquitoes feasted on their blood. They were both soaked with sweat and exhausted. Night sounds of the swamp forest chirped, buzzed, and hooted around them. Water moccasins were coming up out of the water onto land to hunt.

"I don't think you should go alone," she said, resting on a log. "I can keep your escape route clear at least."

Nate kept his ears on the woods in case someone tried to sneak up on them "You will, by staying here."

"This is way too far back to do you any good."

"It will be morning by the time I'm through, and I'll need you awake while I sleep tomorrow."

"You're not in the Army anymore," Her voice was somehow different. "How long has it been since you were a Ranger? You're not twenty, you're pushing forty. You have to be young and in your prime for combat. Now you'll be using your knife in the dark. It's all crazy bullshit."

"You mean you have to be young and stupid enough to think you're bulletproof and it will happen to the next guy but not you."

"Well, you're not a twenty-year-old kid with a body full of testosterone. And—"

"Piss and vinegar," he interrupted.

"Whatever," she said, "there's no need for you to push it."

"Deni," his voice rose above the whisper he had been talking in, "those bastards are heading for my son and friends. I'm not going to let them by without doing everything I can to stop them. And this is the place to do it. Once they get that bridge repaired and they're over the river, we can do nothing but kill one or two as they drive by."

"And you think they're being pursued, so you want to hold them here as long as possible."

"Why else are they so damned determined to cross here? There's another bridge twenty miles north. Why didn't they turn around when Sam and the Cat collapsed the bridge? Why have they been willing to take such losses? They know there will be more if they try to cross."

"Yeah, they know we're not playing." Deni sighed with fatigue. "But they think they can hunt us down out here. We're in deep shit and you know it."

"Yes we are," Nate said. "We have to be careful. One screw up and we're dead. But them not turning around and crossing somewhere else means more risk. Why? Why do they need to cross the river at this one spot?"

Deni stood and came closer. "I understand all that. Just keep in mind I can't stop them alone. So be careful and come back. And remember…you have Brian waiting for you."

Nate stood. "Always. Well, I have to go if I'm going to have time to travel quiet there and back."

"You damn sure snuck up on me in daylight," she said. "I guess you can sneak up on a bunch of yahoos in dark."

"Why don't you get on that big cypress log we passed twenty yards back and lie down and rest?" He took his pack off and handed it to her.

"Damn, this thing is heavy," she said.

"It's got .44 mag. ammo in it. Don't lose it; we'll need all the ammo we have before this is over."

"You have a lot of killing in mind, don't you?" Deni's voice revealed worry.

"Deni," Nate said, "If we don't stop them here, we don't stop them. We will lose the farm. More than likely, they will burn the house and barn to the ground. This year's harvest will be lost, and we will all go hungry." There was silence between them for some seconds. "You should take this time to rest. Just keep your ears working so you can hear someone coming up on you."

He left her standing there in the dark, listening to an owl.

"Yes, who will die tonight," she said to no one, "that is the question."

~~~~~~~~~~

Nate swam across the river. He kept his M14 out of the water, and that required him to use only one hand. Then he made his way upstream, praying he did not step on a cottonmouth in the dark.

He heard chainsaws long before he got close. They were back from the river bottom, up on drier land, where pine trees grow. *No. You're not going to repair that bridge tonight, assholes.*

A pickup's starter groaned. It did not start and the battery was nearly dead. A door slammed in the dark. "Sonofbitch," a man said.

"Gas is getting old," another man offered. "That stabilizer works only for a while with ethanol gas. If it was the old shit with no ethanol, it would still be good."

"There's still some of that spray stuff to put in the carburetor to help it start," the first man said.

"Where is it?"

"In the glove box, idiot. Bring it here so we can get this load of logs to the bridge. They'll be shooting at us again, come daylight."

One of the men scrounged around in the glove box, feeling in the dark. "I got it. Ain't much left."

"The filter's off the carb. Get your flashlight on it and be ready to spray once I start cranking. Soon as it fires up, stop spraying. We can't afford to waste it."

"Right. Batteries are almost dead, but it should light up long enough for this." A dim light came on, shinning on the engine. "Ready when you are."

The starter groaned.

The man in the pickup noticed the flashlight went out, but kept the starter going. He could not see much with the hood up. It didn't start and the battery was nearly dead. "Shit." He got out. "What happened, asshole?"

A massive hand clamped over his mouth and nose and pulled his head back. A sharp pain cut across his neck, deep. He gurgled as the hand released its hold and he fell to the hard-packed clay of the county road next to the other man.

Nate's right hand and wrist were wet and sticky. A copper smell Nate knew was blood permeated the air for some seconds, and then a drifting breeze blew it away. He slid his Ka-Bar into its sheath and checked their weapons. One carried an AR15. He took the ammo for Deni. There were only eighteen rounds. The other carbine was a semiautomatic AK47 clone in 7.62x39mm caliber. He threw both carbines in the back of the pickup on top of logs that were so long they hung out past the tailgate eight feet.

Grabbing the flashlight, Nate searched for the chainsaw and put it in the back. There was a one-gallon can of gas and oil mix for the chainsaw near the cab on top of the logs.

He went around to the front, dragged both men out of the way, and picked up the can of starter fluid. Then he ran around the open door and jumped in the driver's seat. There, he released the parking brake and made sure it was in neutral and the ignition on. He got out and pushed until he had the truck moving. The road sloped down toward a valley between hills one hundred yards ahead. He planned to push the truck until he had it going down that slope.

After only fifty yards, he had to stop and rest. Two more tries and he had it near enough for one last push. He got out and sprayed the contents of the can into the carburetor, then pushed until the truck was rolling downhill, his legs and back screaming protests. He jumped in and let the truck gain momentum for a few seconds, then pushed the clutch in and put it in gear, letting the clutch out. The engine sputtered and the truck nearly stopped rolling. He pushed the clutch pedal to the floor and the truck gained momentum again. When he let the clutch out the engine sputtered and caught.

It ran rough, but it ran, and that was good enough for Nate. He reversed back up the hill and found a place wide enough to turn around. After three miles, he saw what he was looking for. There was a side road, little more than a jeep trail. He turned off, found a place to park, and back up in the wet mud. There, he unloaded the logs and hid the guns behind a windfall. Someday, he might come back for them.

A tall thin pine tree grew nearby. He soon had the chainsaw working and the pine tree down and limbed. It was forty feet long, so he found some rope in the cab and lashed it to the right side of the truck. He hid the saw and can of gas next to the guns.

Nate jumped in and raced the engine a little because it was idling so roughly that he thought it might quit. Tires spinning, he headed for the road.

Two miles from the bridge, Nate got out and lashed the tree crossways behind the cab, taking great care to lash it tight with rope and chain so it would be sturdy. It was about chest high on a shorter man but waist high on him. The tree reached nearly all the way across the road. He drove slowly at first, using the headlights for the first time, and keeping in the middle so as not to hit an overhanging roadside tree limb.

Several fires in the road and people standing around drinking beer alerted Nate it was time to speed up. When he was doing forty, he let up on the gas and then kept going at a steady speed. He took a hasty count and thought there might be thirty men standing around those fires eating and drinking. There were as many more lying in the road resting or asleep.

He hoped to kill some of them too.

A man with a shotgun stepped out from behind a tree, waving his free arm. "Slow down, fuckers!"

Another man appeared on the right, yelling something Nate could not understand, but he had a good guess. With the high beams on, neither could see the danger as Nate drove between them. The pine tree caved their chests in and killed them where they stood, throwing them both into the ditch on their side of the dirt road. He tightened the seat belt and hit the gas.

Men flew on impact and died in their tracks; some lived only long enough to wonder what hit them. Others were crushed under tires as Nate ran them over, some died in their sleep. More would die after hours of agony.

Nate slammed on the brakes and skidded twenty yards, crashing into the rear of a Ford F150. He grabbed his rifle, rolled out, and kept rolling until he was out of the road and in six inches of swamp water.

Firing from the bridge killed many in the road and firing from the road killed a few on the bridge. All they knew was they were under attack. They shot at any and every muzzle flash in the dark.

Nate low-crawled farther into the swamp. The firing made it unnecessary to worry about keeping quiet, so he got up and ran.

It was tempting. Nate wanted that duffle of loaded magazines bad. However, he called it a night and circled around, crossed the road several miles back from the bridge, and made his way through the swamp to the river again, which he swam.

Deni was losing her battle with fatigue, just able to keep her eyes open, when her ears caught squelching boots in mud. Someone was working his careful way upslope from the river. She sat up and pushed the safety off on her AR15. Since she expected Nate to be coming from the same direction, she knew to wait until he was close.

Her heart rate doubled when she heard another set of boots sucking in mud as its owner lifted it to take another step. All she could do now was to wait for a shot.

They came close enough she could hear one of them breathing. Still, she could see nothing. Then a freckle of starlight that had managed to filter through the swamp canopy landed on a man's upper body. His face glistened with sweat. She took aim as best she could, not really seeing him or the carbine's sights. Just before she finished the trigger squeeze, another shadow seemed to float in behind the man. She heard a thunk, and another, then something heavy fell in the mud. Deni eased pressure off the trigger and waited. Nate was hunting.

The other man must have heard. He stopped in his tracks. He had not chosen a good place. Starlight's cool dappling painted his right hand. He pulled it away from the rifle's trigger long enough to swish mosquitoes away from his face and ears. Deni saw the movement. She aimed and waited.

The man took a timid step and entered a darker shadow. He did not come out. There was another thunk and another. Deni thought she saw a flash but could not be sure.

Ten silent minutes went by.

"Deni." A whisper came out of the dark, so close it startled her, though she knew it was Nate.

"I'm still on the log," she answered, in a low, hoarse whisper.

Nate's voice came from out of the dark again. "Coming in from the river side, don't shoot."

"Okay."

Nate emerged, appeared as a shadow in a sea of shadows where light was only light in comparison to areas of more dark. He reached for a canteen in his pack setting on the log next to her. "Got back sooner than expected." He took a long drink.

"Are you hurt?" Deni got down from the log and stood.

"No. Not a scratch," Nate said. "A bunch of them are dead or hurting though."

"Yeah, you just cured two of all their worldly worries, as well as aches and pains."

"Damn. You saw it?

"No, not exactly. Too dark."

"Near as I can tell, they were the only ones around here," Nate said. "We should keep it low anyway, just in case."

"Why don't you get some sleep if you can?" Deni said. "False dawn will be showing soon."

Nate got up on the log and lay down, his rifle across him, right hand clamped on the trigger area, trigger finger straight and against the receiver.

She leaned against the log, not three feet from him, keeping watch, mosquitoes filling her ears with their incessant buzzing.

Within minutes, Nate's breathing slowed, and he was asleep.

~~~~~~~~~~~~

Trees dripping with morning dew woke Nate. The sound of drops landing on underbrush seemed loud in the still of the swamp forest. A squirrel caught his movement when he sat up and scolded him for many minutes before barking one last time and jumping to another tree and then another, disappearing in a tall hickory.

Deni had walked away from the log not long after he fell asleep and now stood in the shade of a twelve-foot-wide cypress, long dead, but still standing. The sun was not up yet, but its light revealed fog that hung low and collected in the dips and holes and hog wallows as thick as cotton candy. It felt almost cool, but humidity clung to them as wet and uncomfortable as their sweaty, dirty clothes.

They walked over to check the dead men for ammunition. One had an AR15 with eleven rounds. Nate added to that number when he gave her the rounds he took off one of the men on the road.

She loaded them into one of her empty magazines. "I'll use these for up close, because I don't know where they'll hit at long range."

Nate nodded.

The other man had a Marlin lever-action in 45/70. They put the guns in the hollow of the cypress log along with what ammunition there was for the Marlin and covered them with leaves. Maybe they would come back for them someday.

To keep their energy up, they decided to eat.

"Any trouble last night?" she asked.

"Not really. I got a few and slowed down their bridge-building plans some."

"I was afraid you'd go after the duffle."

"I wanted to, but they were shooting everything that moved when I left. Probably killed a dozen of their own."

"What the hell did you do?" She smiled for the first time since Sam died.

He told her his short version with no frills or adjectives.

"Damn," she said. "I never would have thought of that."

"The chainsaw was there. I guess that's what gave me the idea. They couldn't see the log coming at them with the truck's brights in their eyes and thought they were safe as long as the truck didn't hit them." He searched across his field of vision for danger. "I ran over a few also."

"You sure took a chance, driving right in among them. Their confusion is what saved you. Thought you were one of them at first." She looked at him, her eyes lingering. "It's not like you to be so reckless. You usually play it safe."

Nate shrugged. "I intend to stop them from crossing. Besides, it worked." He grabbed his pack and rummaged in the main compartment. "Let's eat and make tracks. We've got a long day of killing ahead of us."

"Oh?" Deni looked inquisitively at him. "More tricks?"

"I can only guarantee you more killing."

Deni searched her side of the woods. "What fun."

Out of habit, Nate buried their food packages after eating, covering the fresh soil with leaves. "Let's make a three-mile sweep around to the road so we can get a look at what they're up to."

She slipped her backpack on. "Yeah, let's."

~~~~~~~~~~~~

Nate hid in brush by the road and glassed the bridge with his binoculars. "They're not working on the bridge. Most of them are gone. Must be hunting us." He handed the binoculars to Deni.

"I think some of the trucks are gone." She scanned the bridge and road behind it again. "Yep, I'm sure some of them are gone."

Nate motioned for her to back away from the ditch and into the woods. They crawled a few yards before standing to walk. He got close enough to whisper in her ear. "We need to back off a couple miles and wait a few hours."

She looked puzzled, but said nothing.

They walked through the forest for more than an hour. "Let's stop here and talk," he said. They sat on a limestone rock.

"What?" Deni looked hard at him. "I haven't been able to figure out what you're going to do next or what you're thinking since Sam was killed. So please tell me."

"Nothing mysterious really. They can't get much done on the bridge in an hour or so, and it's obvious they have most men out looking for us. It's just as obvious that they will patrol out at least as far as we can see and shoot. That means we didn't want to be within a half mile of the bridge. Might as well wait a while and rest."

"Okay," Deni said. "That makes sense. I wonder if you know how mysterious you've been acting since we got into this fight. You're a different man."

"Not really. I'm just falling back on my training. I'm in my killing mode. It frightened Brian the first time he saw me like this. I'm sorry if you don't like it, but I intend to stop them from crossing, and I damn sure intend for us both to go home when it's over."

Deni shook her head. "I have no complaints. Sam's death was no one's fault but those men at the bridge and neither of us have a scratch. So, just keep doing what you've been doing. I would like a little warning before game time though."

"Okay. In a few hours, after they've swept both sides of the road as far as a mile from the bridge—if they're even *that* energetic—we're going to sneak back over there and do some one thousand yard shooting."

"Sounds like a plan." Deni took her pack off and used it for a pillow, lying on the ground. Wake me when you're ready."

Nate laughed.

Chapter 8

Deni could barely see a group of several dozen men working on the bridge. "I don't know...this seems like a lot farther than before. Are you sure this is one thousand yards?"

"Fifteen hundred—I hope," Nate said. "It's hard to estimate distances this far and any small amount I'm off in my estimate will mean a miss as this range. The bullets will be dropping fast. If I hit someone it will be luck."

"Let's get closer then." She squinted and looked down the road. "No point in wasting ammo. We're running short as it is."

"Too dangerous. They know from experience we can reach out one thousand yards. So we're back here this time. We can't stay long either. Two, three shots and we're gone. This is just a harassing measure to slow them down until tonight."

"Another night raid?"

Nate kept his eyes down the road. "Not exactly."

"What then?"

"I'll tell you later." He settled down for a shot.

Deni sighed and shook her head, then glassed the bridge. "What are you aiming for?"

"Those four men carrying the log. They're in line and that gives me more leeway as far as elevation is concerned."

He squeezed off a shot.

Deni started to say, "I think you—" But before she could finish, the second man from the near end of the log collapsed and the man next to him could no longer hold his end. He dropped the log and staggered to his left. Nate fired again.

"You took out the back window of that big truck," Deni said.

He fired into a moving mass of men as they ran for cover. One fell, but crawled behind a pickup.

"Time to relocate," Nate said. They crawled into the woods, then got up and ran fifty yards before slowing to a quiet walk.

When they stopped a mile away, Deni asked, "Now what?"

"Follow me. We need a better place for an ambush."

She searched the woods around her, seeing only the wall of green. "You think they're going to get serious about hunting us down?" She kept her voice low.

Nate moved through the woods with the fluid confidence of a lion on the hunt. "You bet. And we better be ready for them."

"Or run," Deni said.

Nate waited for her to come closer. "We have to stop them at the river. But if you want to go back and help the others get ready in case they get the bridge repaired, go now."

Deni coughed. "Bullshit. I didn't say that. I do not intend to leave you. I was just saying we could retreat for now and come back tonight."

"That would be safer, but we need to slow their bridge repairing as much as possible. There may be someone, maybe the military, chasing them. We don't know how far behind they are, but if we can keep them on that side of the river long enough…"

"I understand all that," Deni said. "The question is: are you willing to die to get it done."

"If need be. This can't be done without risk."

She looked him in the eye. "As long as this isn't about revenge for Sam."

"I'm a little pissed about that, but I barely knew him. This is about stopping them before they cross, because we can't stop them once they're on this side. Sure, they *might* go on by the farm. But they may shovel that pile of dirt we left in the drive into the trench I cut and drive right up to the farm and take everything we have, leaving us with only what's at Mel's place. I can't take that chance."

"Okay." She looked behind her, toward the dirt road. "We should get closer if we want to pick a fight today. I doubt they will come this far."

"Maybe not," Nate said. "But I think a small number of them will keep coming. They've had enough of us and realize now we're not packing up and leaving—so they'll come. They know there's not many of us. They just have to kill us and then get that bridge repaired well enough to get those trucks and motorcycles across." He stopped talking when he heard a hog grunt and take off at a trot when it got a whiff of them. It crashed into palmettos.

Deni swung her carbine around and shouldered it as she turned and aimed in the direction of the sound.

"Hog," Nate said. "Nice to know you're alert though." He waited for her to turn to face him again. "We don't want to take on the whole bunch at once. I'm hoping only three or four will come this far."

"All right," she said, "what about that rise over there? We can see better and there's plenty of bullet-stopping cover."

Nate smiled. "Great minds think alike. That's where we're heading."

Deni motioned with her head. "Let's go."

~~~~~~~~~~~~

The sun was inching lower, and shadows stretched out long from tall trees. Nate thought they may not come, and it would be dark soon. He could not see Deni hiding in thick brush, but he knew where she was. It had been several minutes since his eyes caught a flicker of movement in a dappling of sunlight seventy yards back in a stand of pines where shade darkened the emerald forest. It could have been a doe flicking flies with her tail or a squirrel jumping from tree to tree or a bird. It could have been a lot of things.

Nate pushed the safety off his rifle with the back of his trigger finger. *There you are, you son of a bitch. Now, where are the others?*

Two quick shots from Nate's left told him Deni had found one of them. He saw movement on his end of the rise and aimed, waiting for a clear shot, not sure, if it was man or animal. The first man had hit the dirt at Deni's shots and disappeared, so Nate concentrated on the third man.

When shooting from behind a log alerted Nate of a fourth killer, he aimed for what he could see: the top three inches of his head. Punk wood fragmented and powdered, creating a brown puff of smoke above the log. The cloud drifted away in a light breeze, revealing brush painted red.

Deni continued to fire. Another man fell.

Not wanting to waste rifle ammunition on recon by fire, Nate pulled his revolver and fired into heavy brush where he was sure he had seen a muzzle flash, thumbing the hammer back, and firing single action. After four rounds, he could hear screaming between Deni's shots. He holstered his revolver, crawled to another position in case someone saw his muzzle flash in the darkening shade of the forest, and waited for another target.

All shooting stopped, but the man Nate wounded still screamed.

A bullet shrieked by Nate's head. He dropped behind a stump, then low-crawled to a big pine tree for cover.

Deni fired twice more.

They waited, eyes searching for danger.

The woods became silent in the dying afternoon. Except for the moaning from the man Nate wounded, the scene would seem tranquil. Nate found the contrast between the peaceful woods and the tension storming within him surreal. The realization that Brian would never feel the same about a relaxing walk in the woods came over him in a flash. Brian had been hunted, and in the back of his mind, the woods would always be a battleground where a bullet can come from behind any bush and take his life. Never again would he enjoy the wonders of nature the way only a child can. He knew this because he had been through it himself, but at a much older age.

After fifteen minutes, Nate low-crawled to Deni. "Time to go."

She hesitated. "Leave him?"

The man was still moaning.

"Yes," Nate said. "We've done what we needed to. There might be more coming. Let's go." He started crawling.

Deni followed. After fifty yards, they stood and walked, taking their time, standing, listening, and looking more than walking. They made their way farther from the road, deeper into the forest.

Nate raised his right hand, singling to stop, then came back to her. She had been keeping ten yards behind for proper spacing, so they would not both be killed in an ambush.

"We'll rest here and wait for dark," he said.

Her face was rigid with tension. "That won't be long, sun has gone down."

He searched the woods while he talked. "There was nothing we could do for him but finish it. You know that. Then we would have had to live with that. Either way, it's not a pretty picture."

"I was just thinking you might want to put him out of it." She turned and looked away. "Oh hell, it doesn't matter. Don't make a big deal out of it."

"Could have been putting on an act to lure us in. It wasn't worth the—" He saw blood on her left arm. "Sit down. You're bleeding."

She glanced at her arm and then looked up at him. "Don't make a big deal out of that either. I'm okay."

Peeling his pack off and with a worried look on his face, he said, "Sit down."

"Jeez." She took her pack off, then her long-sleeved shirt. "Don't cry about it." There was no log or rock to sit on, so she sat on the ground.

Nate examined it. "This is bad."

"Bullshit. It's only a half-inch deep. There are no blood vessels or nerves or bone involved."

He sighed. "We're not even close to the end of this fight. I was planning to swim the river just before daylight after I attack again. That's out now. You have to keep this clean."

"Get real." Deni laughed. "I don't believe you. "Get your head on straight for God's sake."

"My head is thinking just fine." His voice rose. "We don't have a thing to stop infection. I used what was left when Brian was shot." He cleaned around the wound with an antiseptic-soaked two-inch square of gauze, dropped it, and soaked another to clean the wound itself.

Wincing, she turned her head away. "That's enough. You'll just make it bleed more."

Nate rubbed harder. "Bleeding a little won't hurt you. It'll help clean it in fact."

"And I thought you were afraid I was in pain."

He wrapped the wound with gauze and taped the ends. "It'll get soaked with sweat. Nothing we can do about that. Keep it clean otherwise or you'll be wishing you had." He put his medical supplies back in his pack.

"I hope you're through acting crazy." She turned her back to him and put her shirt on. "You didn't even look."

"I've seen those things before."

"Not mine."

"I don't allow myself to think that way anymore. Not since Susan died."

"You're not *that* old."

"Too old to be looking at you that way. I've got guns older than you."

"Whatever." She turned to face him, buttoning her shirt. "Why don't you rest while I pull security? Unless you think I'm too disabled."

He did not say anything, just sat against a tree, and reloaded his revolver. Then he put his pack between two bushy scrub oaks and lay down, using the pack for a pillow. "I'm running low on rifle ammo."

Deni stopped scanning the woods and looked over at him. "How much?"

"Five rounds."

She stiffened. "How good are you with that revolver?"

"In broad daylight, if he sits still long enough, two hundred yards."

"Damn, that's hard to believe. I thought you were joking when you said that before." She kept her eyes on the woods. "Why don't you take my 1911? I have three eight-round mags. It's got to be faster than the .44 in close quarters."

"It is." He pulled his boonie hat down over his eyes. "But you keep it. For now anyway."

"Why wait?"

Nate smashed a mosquito on his face. "I should have taken that AK that one of them I killed was carrying, but I didn't want to carry the extra weight. Had to move fast when I rolled out of the truck. Thought I'd come back for it later."

"Why don't you take the .45? I've got about thirty-seven rounds left for the AR."

"No," Nate said.

"You know," she sighed, "I've noticed that sometimes you're obstinate."

"I guess."

"You're afraid I'll need it."

"Yep. Shoot me." He turned his back to her and lay on his side.

"No thanks. There are enough people trying to do that already. I've also noticed it's not healthy: You tend to shoot back."

He snored.

She looked closer, not sure, if he was pretending to be asleep or really snoring. Smiling, she muttered under her breath, "Smartass."

~~~~~~~~~~~

There was no time to wake Nate. Deni did not even know herself there was anyone near until he saw her at the same time she saw him. She had heard something in the brush earlier but decided it was a small animal. They stared at each other's white face for an eternity, which in reality lasted all of a tenth of a second. She was faster, but his shot took her hat off and some of her hair. She panicked and dropped to the ground, holding the top of her head with her left hand.

Nate bolted upright, shouldered his rifle, and looked over the sights while searching the moonlit woods. It was just a sliver of moon, but enough he could see Deni on the ground holding her head.

He crawled to her. "Are you hurt?" He kept his voice low.

"No," she said, catching her breath. "Scared the hell out of me though."

"Where is he?"

"I got him. Over there." She pointed in the general direction.

"Get your pack on and crawl to the end of this log, and get under the shade of that magnolia. The moon's out. Light is death. Stay in shade." Nate put his pack on and followed her.

They squatted on their knees under the magnolia, back to back, watching.

Thirty minutes passed.

Nate whispered, "There's another one out there."

She said nothing, just kept searching the moonlight-bathed woods, trying to penetrate the shadows. After five minutes, she said, "I didn't hear or see anything."

"He's there. To my left about fifty yards out, coming in slow."

Ten minutes passed, and Deni still had heard nothing. Then she did.

Nate saw movement. He held his fire, waiting. There was no way to know what it was, but something tall enough to be human was coming closer. When the gray ghost of motion came into moonlight and its cool dappling fell on a man's face, Nate spotted him and took a quick shot.

Deni dropped and moved fifteen feet to the other side of the magnolia, but still in shade.

Nate dropped to the ground and crawled to her. *Good. Reposition. If anyone's out there, he saw my muzzle flash and located us.*

They couldn't hear anything but the man's screaming, and Nate couldn't see where he fell in heavy brush.

Nerves strung taut, Nate whispered in Deni's ear. "Keep watch on your side of things. I'm going over to him."

She squeezed his arm, her breath rapid on his face.

"Don't shoot on my side," he whispered.

She squeezed his arm again.

Making his way to the man, while staying in the shadows and being as quiet as possible, took time.

Too weak to scream now, the man moaned. Nate moved close enough he could hear a sucking sound and knew the man was shot through a lung. He would not be able to talk and therefore was no use to Nate as a source of information. He had only a few moments before death. Nate stopped and searched the woods for more danger.

Gunshots from behind him prompted Nate to drop from his knees to his belly. He tried to see if Deni was okay but saw nothing from his position. He knew it was not her carbine by the sound.

Another shot rang out and then Deni fired three rapid shots.

Nate saw her carbine's muzzle flash but not the other gun's, despite his searching the dark woods to locate the shooter. He flinched and jerked his head around when someone shot over him at Deni. From his stomach, he shot until his rifle clicked on an empty chamber. He released the rifle, letting it fall, and pulled his revolver. Fast crawling, he moved to another shadow and lay still, listening, searching for danger, his eyes straining to probe the dark. No target presented itself. All he could do was wait.

Concern for Deni made Nate's heart race. But he did not dare call out or go to her with the other man out there in the dark. And he didn't know how many more waited for him or Deni to make a fatal mistake.

Night sounds returned while Nate lay on the ground waiting. Crickets started in, and fireflies flashed in brush and trees, some flying in a midair dance.

Movement near where the wounded man lay caught Nate's eye. He tried to aim, but the revolver's sights were useless in the dark. He had to get closer. *Safer to wait for him to come to me.*

Five minutes of silence and nothing. Nate strained his eyes, searching the dark woods.

Someone brushed against a palmetto frond, warning Nate that Deni was in danger, but he could do nothing, until he killed the man he had seen earlier.

Nate heard another, making it two, coming in for Deni. *Stay alert girl. They're coming for you.*

Out of the dark came barely discernable movement. Nate watched until he could make out the upper form of a man sneaking in for the kill, coming closer from an angle. *He must not know exactly where I am.* He raised his .44 but could not see the sights to aim. All he could do was to wait, until the man got so close, he could point shoot by looking down the barrel without using the sights.

A string of shots that Nate recognized as coming from Deni's carbine, told him she had seen the men. They must have been close for her to see them in the dark. She continued to fire so much Nate worried she may have panicked. *Maybe there's more than two.*

The one Nate had been trying to keep track of in the dark rushed to the shooting. Nate waited until he was so close he could not miss, and then shot him twice.

For cover, Nate jumped into the brush. He also needed to relocate as fast as possible, just in case someone had seen his muzzle flash. He landed on a stump, hammering the breath from his lungs. While catching his breath, someone ran by him only twenty yards away. He did not have time to shoot.

Nate heard a struggle going on. He got up and ran.

The sound of a fist hitting flesh and Deni gasping gave Nate direction in the dark.

Then a man yelled, "Son of a bitch!"

Just before Deni was knocked down, she had swung at him in the dark, but her aim was off and the light carbine glanced off his head, only stunning him. She grabbed for her pistol.

Hot blood sprayed her face.

"Don't shoot. I got him," Nate warned.

"Reloading," Deni said, falling back on her training. She felt around on the ground until she found her carbine. In four seconds, she had a fresh magazine in.

The dead man lay beside her, his throat cut and both lungs punctured by Nate's knife.

"Are you hurt?" Nate whispered.

"No. But I think we should get out of here."

Where the hell did I leave my rifle? Nate tried to get his bearings. "Are you ready?"

"Yes."

Nate felt around until he found the man whose throat he cut and searched for a handgun, finding a pistol he thought might be a Browning 9mm, but was not sure because he had not touched one in years. *Why couldn't it have been a Colt 1911?* He searched pockets and found one extra magazine. The pistol, he stuck under his belt on the left side for a cross draw and the magazine in his left front pants pocket. Feeling along the ground, he grabbed a carbine of some kind that he could not recognize by feel in the dark. "Stay close on my six."

"Right," Deni said. "There are more out there. We need to get out of here."

It took some time for Nate to find his rifle, but he was not going to leave it. He had plenty more ammunition and magazines for it at home. In the heat of the fight, he had dumped it because it was empty. He knew it was a mistake when he did it, but he had to move fast. While feeling around on the ground, they both kept their ears on high alert, knowing more killers were lurking.

Finally, Nate's left hand grasped the barrel. He slung the M14 on his left shoulder. "We have to take our time, and we're not going to get far before daylight. We'll be going about a step a minute, so be patient and stay glued to me. I don't want to lose you."

Chapter 9

It began to rain, not enough to ease the mosquito curse Nate and Deni were forced to endure, but just enough to render their ears useless in the woods. They could not hear anyone trying to sneak up on them. Nate knew this worked both ways and began to walk a little faster. But he had to rely more on his eyes to detect danger from father away now that leaves on the ground were soggy. Deni stayed close behind.

The dawning sun was not yet blocked by clouds coming in from the west and rays streamed in at a low angle, filtering through towering pines and wide oaks.

"Exactly where are we going?" Deni asked in a whisper. "We seem to be heading back to the river now."

"We are," Nate said. "I hope we have swung around them and they've gone back to the bridge. We should come to the start of the river valley soon."

"What then? How long can we do this and survive? We were lucky back there." Deni continuously scanned the wall of green around them.

Nate stopped and turned to her. "I think you should go back to the bunker and warn the others. I was hoping the two of us could hold them here long enough for whatever gang they're running from to catch them at the bridge, but now I'm thinking it may not be possible. They really want to cross here for some reason, and it looks like the group they're running from is not so interested in catching up. Maybe they stopped chasing them. Whatever. The fact is it looks like they're going to get the bridge repaired." He looked at her, his face showing determination. "I'm going to kill as many of them as I can and hold them at the bridge as long as possible. You go back."

Deni's eyes narrowed. "That's not what I was saying. I do not intend to leave you here alone. I was just thinking we have to come up with something better than what we've been doing. Some kind of force multiplier through speed and violence of action."

Nate smiled. "You're taking sound military principles and turning it into gobbledygook. We don't have any force multipliers, and we've used about as much violence of action as the two of us are capable of."

He saw the shiner on her face for the first time. The smile vanished.

She saw it in his eyes. "It can't look that bad."

Nate shook his head, sighed, and looked away. "How much ammo do you have left for the AR?"

"Less than a mag. full. I haven't had time to count."

He pointed. "Let's rest on that rock and you check. We need to assess our problem and come up with a plan for tonight. We're both too tired to do any fighting this morning. And we've got to eat."

Deni sat down and removed the magazine from her carbine. "Can't we burn the damn thing with Molotov cocktails or something? They have gas for their trucks. You snuck in among them that time and we could do it again."

"I drove in with one of their trucks. It won't be so easy to do that again."

"They do seem to be more organized than before." Deni stripped rounds from her magazine, counting. She looked at Nate. "Fourteen rounds."

Nate lifted the carbine he took off the dead man in the dark and showed it to her. "This is no better than my revolver. A cheap nine-millimeter with a ten round mag. and crappy sights." He took the magazine out and counted the rounds. It was full. Then he pulled the bolt back enough to see if there was a round in the chamber. "Cocked and locked," he said, "but chambered for a round that's notorious as too weak for the job without using several rounds per man."

Deni reloaded her carbine, talking as she pushed rounds into the magazine. "If those rounds were hollow points it wouldn't be so bad."

"Just full metal jacket," Nate said.

"Figures. Well, what are we going to do?"

"Eat and get some shuteye." Nate yawned. "I guess you should stand first watch."

"That's not what I mean."

"I know. We need more time to think on it." He took his pack off and reached in for some food.

~~~~~~~~~~~

Nate heard them coming. One of them walked through the mud of a slough Deni and he had just gone around. It did not take him long to realize they were military trained. They came in a wedge formation, spaced perfectly to prevent more than one from being mowed down with the same gun. They were quiet in the woods, but not so much as he could not hear them coming.

Deni heard too. She found cover and waited.

Nate's eyes desperately searched the swamp around them. They were in a bad place to execute a hasty ambush. There was not enough concealment, though tree trunks, windfalls, and rotted-out cypress stumps offered cover. What they needed was enough concealment they could retreat without being seen. The swamp floor was thinly covered with brush because the canopy of treetops did not allow enough sunlight to get through.

Deni had found a stump solid enough to stop bullets. The problem was a lack of concealment for retreat once the men located them—and they would, the instant they fired a shot. Once the fight started, it would be to the finish, or at least until Deni and he managed to kill enough they could retreat without being shot in the back.

Nate rushed to her and pointed to a hollow cypress log barely large enough for her to fit into. "Crawl in as far as you can." He kept his voice low.

Deni blanched. "No way! If they find me I'll be helpless."

"They won't find you if they're looking for me elsewhere. I'll lead them away."

She shook her head. "No. We can fight them."

Nate grabbed her pack strap and yanked her to him, her face inches from his. "They're not a mob of yahoos, they're *military*. And this is not the place for an ambush. Now get in there, so we'll have half a chance to get away from them."

Her eyes widened. "Why would soldiers be out here? Why would they be hunting us?"

"Who knows?" Nate practically dragged her to the log. "Hurry."

Deni took her pack off and shoved it in front of her as she crawled in, disappearing into darkness.

Taking off on a run, Nate headed upslope, hoping to make it out of the river bottomland and into heavy brush where he might have a chance of shaking them off his trail.

One of the men heard Nate's headlong crashing through the woods. He caught a glimpse of him, a blur between trees, and fired with an automatic weapon.

Nate feinted to his right, but then turned left and kept running. Bark flew off a cypress as he ran past, with wood fragments blinding him. Now desperate and running recklessly, he could not stop in time to prevent his fall into a muddy creek, landing on his stomach with a splash. He pushed up with both hands, coughing. He pulled the carbine out and hoped its barrel had not been plugged with mud.

The squad size group of men maneuvered toward him, still in formation. They rushed, but were cautious.

Nate crawled out of the mud and peered over a root, looking for his pursuers. A man in his early twenties saw him and veered to his left, taking cover behind a tree.

Shit! I'm in trouble now. Nate could not run without being shot in the back, and he could not shoot, unless the man came out from behind that tree. In seconds, more men would be surrounding him.

Doing the only thing he could, he jumped up and rushed the man, firing the carbine. When he got within ten feet, he stopped firing and veered to his right, the carbine shouldered and ready.

The man heard him and leaned out to see and shoot.

Nate shot first, putting two bullets in his face. He dropped the carbine, snatched up the dead man's M4, and sprayed another man across his chest just as he ran around a wide cypress trunk. Another man rushed toward him, raising his carbine to shoot. Nate fired a burst into him, noticing for the first time they wore body armor and helmets. He had been too busy for his mind to register such details. He took careful aim and shot the last two again, before they could recover from the bullets' blows, in the face this time. Then Nate grabbed two magazines out of the nearest dead man's load-bearing vest and took off on the run.

Bullets ripped into trees. He kept as much wood between him and his pursuers as possible until the shooting faded. He was able to leave the soldiers behind in ten minutes.

Farther upslope, it got dryer and the brush grew thick. Now Nate turned and began to circle back and come in from the side. While waiting, he removed the magazine from the M4 and put it in his back pants pocket, then inserted a fresh one. Sweat dripped from his face and mosquitoes droned around his head. Dead tired, he waited to see if they were still hunting him. His chest heaved. *I'm too old for this shit.*

Nate hoped they would keep hunting him and moving away from Deni so he could circle back later and rejoin her. Then, together, they could lose the soldiers for good.

More than an hour later, Nate listened to them come, following his trail. He crouched low in heavy brush, keeping behind bullet-stopping cover, and watched one of them slink by. The others were too far into the brush for him to see, but he could hear their progress. He waited several minutes, and then crept away, heading back to Deni.

The bodies of the men Nate shot had been stripped clean of weapons and ammunition. The armor had been taken, but he suspected they hid it nearby, as it would be too heavy for them to carry on top of everything else.

"Deni," Nate spoke before approaching the log's opening.

"Get me out of here. I'm stuck." Her calm voice did not mesh with her predicament.

Nate put his arm in, but he couldn't reach her boots. He took his pack off. His shoulders were too wide, and he still could not reach her. "Hold on, I'll get a pole to reach in so you can grab it."

Deni yelled out, "That won't work." The sharpness of her now higher pitched voice was dulled only a little by the hollow space that kept her pinned in. "You need a rope."

"Calm down. I have a rope in my pack. I'll tie it to the pole so you can hold it while I pull you out."

His Ka-Bar sliced into a young tree three inches thick near the bottom. Bending it over made cutting into the wood easier, and he had it down and limbed in less than five minutes. He left a stub of a limb two inches long near the end to hook his rope. After tying a loop on the end, he hooked it on the pole and carefully pushed it in. "Watch for the pole with the rope on the end. It's coming in above you."

"I got it." Her voice seemed calmer.

He pulled the pole out two feet. "Tie the rope around your waist with a bowline knot." He knew she had to know what a bowline is because of her Army training.

She huffed inside the tight space. "Damn it. There's not much room to move my arms and work the rope around under me." After several minutes she said, "I got it."

"Okay, grab hold of the pole with both hands. We'll use both the rope and pole to get you out."

Holding the pole above her, he pushed it back in so she could reach it. He had to work blind because it was dark inside the log.

"I have a good hold on it," she said.

He reached in, wrapped the rope around his left hand, and grabbed the pole with his other. "Kind of squirm a little while I pull."

When her boots appeared, he let go of the rope, took the pole out, and pulled her out by grabbing her legs.

Deni sat on the ground, soaked with sweat and obviously in distress. Her eyes told him she barely had control of herself. She looked around, blinking in the sunlight. "It stopped raining," she said.

"Yeah, an hour ago." He kept his eyes on her.

She swallowed. "Go ahead and laugh at me. You can see I was scared you weren't coming back."

He saw her eyes were wet.

"I heard the shooting," she said. "For all I knew you were dead."

"I'm sorry," Nate said. "I thought that log was plenty big enough." He reached over and touched her face lightly, then let it fall. "Nobody's laughing. Maybe in a year or two we'll both think it's funny, but not right now."

Her chest began to convulse with restrained laughter. She shook her head. "You bastard. The log gets smaller farther in."

Nate clenched his jaw and looked down at the mud. "Why don't you get a drink from my canteen, while I get your pack?"

Working blind, he used the pole to hook a strap by twisting until the short branch he left on the end tangled in the cloth and got it out in less than a minute.

Deni looked around as she drank. "What happened?"

"Three are dead," Nate said. "About eight more are still hunting me. We need to get downriver a ways and swim across."

She stood and slipped her pack on. "Let's go. I need a dip to cool off anyway."

Nate slid into his pack and grabbed the M4. "Okay." After handing her one of the full magazines he took off the soldier, he said, "You're tough." He pointed at his head. "Here."

She rolled her eyes, but could not hold back a tight-lipped smile.

"I'm a little claustrophobic myself," Nate said. He led the way, downriver.

Forty minutes later, Nate found a firm sandbar that made it possible to walk across with his head above water. Being shorter, Deni had to swim part of the way. Nate made two trips. First, he helped her keep her wounded arm out of the muddy water as she crossed, then he went back for her pack. She over watched for security during his second trip, her carbine shouldered and ready.

Later in the day, Deni looked up at the sun. "The road is north. You're taking us southwest."

"Yep."

"Why? We can't fight them from miles away."

He kept walking.

She gave him a dirty look he did not see. "What's going on?"

Nate stopped and turned. "I'm afraid the ones we've been fighting until now were just a scouting party. The real threat has arrived. We met some of them this morning." He sighed. "We can't take on a platoon or company of veterans. Dumbass cutthroats, yeah, but not military-trained cutthroats."

"So why didn't we just head home?"

"I'm still thinking on what we can do to slow them down a little more," Nate said, "that's why."

"The answer to that is get ourselves killed." She shook her head. "You're not able to make a decision on this for some reason."

Nate smashed two mosquitoes on his right cheek while looking off into space. "Those trucks and motorcycles—we could shoot them up. If I had ammo for my M14, I could shoot up the engines, but that's out." He looked her in the eye. "These little carbines can take out their tires. I doubt they have many spares."

Her face told him she was not impressed. "It's just as dangerous to get close enough to shoot at their tires as it is to shoot at them."

"True enough. I'm just thinking out loud."

Deni came closer and spoke in a tone he had never heard her use before. "You're desperate, grasping at straws. And that's more dangerous than anything we've done so far."

Nate stifled a laugh. "We've been desperate since the shooting started." He rasped on his dirty face with his knuckles. "I'll go in from their rear and kill a few of them tonight. Tomorrow morning we'll cross the river and head home. In the meantime, you come with me and take that chainsaw and can of fuel I stashed back to the sandbar where we crossed before and wait."

"What's the chainsaw for?"

He looked away. "On the way home, we'll cut trees across the road several places until we run out of gas."

She tilted her head and gave him a look he could not read.

"I'm not giving up until I've done everything I can," he said.

"You mean we, not just you. And cutting trees across the road is hardly worth the bother. It won't slow them down much."

Nate looked her in the eye. "As long as you know I don't expect you to stay. You can go anytime."

Her jaw set. "That's a hell of a thing for you to say. Don't you know me better than that by now?"

Nate suddenly found the ground between them interesting. "I just didn't want you to think…" He looked up, his eyes locking with hers. "I trust you with my life, and there is no one I'd rather be here in this mess with." He looked up at the sky. "So leave it at that." He walked by her. "Come on, it's getting late in the day. We might as well get closer to the road before we rest up for tonight."

~~~~~~~~~~~

Nate shook Deni awake.

She stirred, opened her eyes.

"Time to go," Nate said. "I plan to have you heading for the river with the chainsaw and fuel can by two hours before sunset. It'll give you time to just about get to the sandbar before it's too dark to see."

Deni stood and put her pack on. "Ready when you are." She checked her carbine. "We're not exactly overloaded with ammo."

"No." Nate handed her his last spare magazine. "And you're not going to have fun toting that saw and gas can so far. And if you get shot at, it might catch one and soak you with gas if you carry it in your pack. I think you should carry the saw in your pack and the can in a hand. The saw might even stop a bullet."

"Well," Deni said, "there's plenty of room for it since I'm also nearly out of food and water."

Nate stood there for a few seconds looking at her, not moving or saying anything.

"What?" Deni asked.

"I think my idea is not so bright. Forget the chainsaw. Let's go home."

She threw her hands up. "Oh hell. I wasn't bitching. I was just saying there's plenty of room in my pack."

"That's not it."

"What then?"

"I changed my mind." Nate's Adam's apple moved up his throat. "I'll stop them on the road some way."

Deni leaned her carbine against a tree and stared at him. "One thing I've never seen you be—until lately that is—is indecisive."

"Maybe I'm getting too old for this. Let's go." He walked away.

"That's all bullshit, but I guess you're not going to tell me what's really going on in your head." She snatched up her carbine and followed.

~~~~~~~~~~

They came to the place where rain had washed a deep gully across the road. The bulldozer had little trouble traversing it on their way to the bridge, but the raiders' trucks could not get across without a lot of shovel work.

"This is where I'll make my first stand," Nate said.

"I don't get it," Deni said. "If you were going to continue to try to stop them, why didn't we just stay at the bridge and fight them there?"

Nate took his pack off and untied his empty M14. "Give this to Brian."

"Okay," she said. "But you might as well keep it and give it to him yourself."

Nate's face hardened. "You go on back to the farm, feed and water the chickens and cow, eat and rest up, and fill your pack with food and water. There's plenty of ammo for your AR under the couch in the living room. Then you go back to your camp where you hid before you joined us. Get away from the farm before these bastards arrive. I'm not going to get them all."

Deni stood silently, staring at him for so long Nate started to speak. "Go on," he said, "I've got to get—"

"No. Hell no," Deni said.

Nate sighed. "I need some of your ammo."

Deni's voice rose. "You're not listening. I said I'm not leaving you."

"This is not a survivable scenario. There's no need for both of us to die."

"No!" Deni's voice echoed in the woods. "Brian will be okay even if we don't stop them. They will never find that bunker. But he won't make it without you."

"And how long will he survive after they raid the farm?" Nate's voice was flat and hard. "He, you, and the others will starve when Mel's supplies run out." He looked her in the eye, showing no emotion. "You don't know where the bunker is, so—"

She yelled, "Shut up and listen."

"So you will have to wait until it's over and Brian or one of the others shows up at the farm. In the meantime, stay hidden in the woods."

Anger contorted her face. She stood there and said nothing.

"You can be pissed if you want, but there's no reason for you to stay," he said. "You're not standing between them and your son. Those people back there are your friends, but you don't love any of them."

"Oh?" She stared him down. "Don't tell me what I feel. And Brian won't make it without you. None of us will."

"I know you will take care of him."

"Okay," she said, "then *you* go—and give me your ammo. You take care of him. It's not like I can't fight."

Nate stepped back, turning his eyes away. "I can't." He recovered and looked at her, his face unreadable again. "That would be more cowardly than both of us leaving. The fact is I am standing between those killers and Brian. I'm the one who has to stay."

Deni tilted her head, staring at him, her face a question mark. A gradual realization washed over her, changing her eyes.

Nate pretended he did not notice. He took all his .44 magnum rounds out of his pack and put them in pants pockets, filling all four.

She watched, not saying a word.

He looked up from his pack just before standing and slipping the straps on his shoulders. "You need to leave now, while you can."

Deni stood there for half a minute. Finally, she said, "I won't go. Now what?"

"You owe me that."

"Yeah, I owe you." She held her chin up defiantly. "But maybe you're asking too much. Maybe there's another way."

Nate pointed down the road toward the bridge. "They're coming, my son is back there," he pointed toward the farm, "and I'm here. That means I'm staking claim to the ground between them and Brian, and I will keep it until they kill me."

"I think you're letting your feelings cloud your judgment."

"No kidding."

"Not just Brian. Ever since I got this shiner, you've been different. One thing I liked about you and Brian is you treated me as a friend from the start—one of the guys. Well, I am a friend, just like Sam was."

Nate scanned the woods for danger. "We barely knew him."

"His life was no less important than mine. Now stop worrying about me, just because I'm prettier than Sam was, and act like the father I know you are. Concentrate on Brian. He is your responsibility, not me. If Brian is your main concern, you should accept my offer to help save him. If you're willing to sacrifice your life for him, you should be at least willing to let me stay and help."

"You know what will happen if they catch you alive?" Nate stared her down. "Even if you're only a little alive, they will make you wish you weren't."

She swallowed. "Stop talking as if I don't know all that already."

Nate blew out a lung full of air and waved her off.

"And stop thinking of me as a woman, I'm a soldier."

"Yeah, right." He blinked, looked down the road, and turned back to her. "I've asked you to go, and you say you won't. Well, I can't make you, but if you stay, just understand fully that this is not a survivable battle. We can't win. All we can do is slow them. Maybe there is someone chasing them, but we can't be sure of that, and we have no way of knowing how far behind they are. All I do know is they are not going to get to my son and my farm and my friends without killing me first."

Deni gave a half-smile. "I saw wheels spinning in your head a second ago, just before you looked down the road. Tell me what you have planned."

Chapter 10

Night sounds, frogs along the riverbank and a whippoorwill on a tree branch, drowned out the sound of Nate's knife slicing into the man's kidney. His cry was muffled under Nate's hand. He was the second one to die by Nate's knife.

Nate had ammunition now, seven full magazines for the M4.

The killers had already repaired the bridge enough to get several motorcycles across, now parked less than fifty yards down the clay road. He planned to take one, the rest he rendered useless by slashing the tires.

Son of a bitch. Nate kicked to start the old Harley three times and it had not even stuttered. He heard men coming down the road, as he made sure the gas valve was on.

Someone yelled at him, "Where the hell are you going?"

The motor roared to life. Nate turned on the seat and sent a flurry of shots toward the bridge, killing two.

From two hundred yards down the road, Deni fired into a rushing mob.

Nate immediately rode the Harley into a ditch and opened the throttle, fishtailing, throwing mud, leaning low over the handlebars. The ditch deepened and he was behind cover, safe from a now growing hail of bullets.

Despite all of Deni's efforts to provide covering fire, the men on the bridge increased their fire.

He rounded a curve and slid to a stop. Deni came running out of the thick gloom of night-darkened woods, huffing. "I'm out…of ammo."

"Hop on," Nate said.

Deni sat behind him and held on with her left hand, the other held her carbine.

They rode several miles, headlight bouncing, revealing dangerous washouts just in time for Nate to brake and swerve around.

Stopping at the deep ravine Nate had dug deeper with the dozer, he said nothing, as he reached over his right shoulder to hand her fresh magazines for her carbine.

Deni got off and jumped into the deep chasm, then dug her boots in, climbing up the other side onto the mound of dirt piled high by the Caterpillar.

He revved the bike's engine and headed for the ditch again, going around the worst of the washout, but still nearly going over backwards when he climbed the other side.

She was waiting for him, her carbine already loaded with a fresh magazine.

He got off and held the Harley up until she was seated. "Ride safe. You have plenty of time. I doubt they will be coming after us until tomorrow morning."

Deni slung her carbine from her neck across her chest so she could use it in a hurry. "Don't lie. They'll send a hunting party out on each side of the road through the woods tonight. But I won't push it, don't worry about that. Just take care of yourself."

Nate watched her take off, shifting smoothly, throwing dirt behind her, looking small on the big bike. *She wasn't lying. She has ridden a Harley before.* The sky was partly overcast, and the moon would not rise until late, and then only a sliver. A little less moon than the night before would light the night. He dimmed the Aimpoint's red dot on the M4 so it wouldn't overpower the image of his targets when he aimed. *The killing woods will be dark tonight.*

~~~~~~~~~~

A summer of heavy storms had made the road unsafe to travel faster than thirty miles an hour. Deni was reminded of this for the fourth time when she came to a rain-washed gully deep enough to send her over the handlebars if she had not skidded to ten miles an hour just as she dropped into it.

Deni bounced along at a speed that would get her to the farm in less than an hour. She sped up when it seemed safe and slowed when the road forced her to.

It took some time for her to find a pathway through thick-growing trees to get around the mound of dirt Nate pushed up in the driveway. When she emerged from the woods, Deni twisted the throttle. The big tire broke loose and the bike fishtailed. In seconds, she was roaring down the driveway.

Deni skidded to a stop at Nate's front door.

First, she hastily watered and fed the chickens and cow.

Running to an old oak behind the house with a small flashlight in hand, she found a limestone rock ten feet from the oak's trunk and rolled it over. Then she got down on her knees and began to dig with her sheath knife until a nylon rope was exposed. Wrapping it around her hand, she pulled and yanked until something gave and the rope came up along with a PVC pipe tied to it. It was heavy, but she managed to drag it out.

At the barn, she pounded on the lock with a two-foot long length of heavy steel pipe she found exactly where Nate said it would be. On the eighth blow, it gave way. She came out of the barn with an ax. Three swings and she had the glued-on plastic cap on the PVC pipe cracked open. The contents, she dumped into her pack. Rushing to the pump, she filled Nate's and her canteens.

Back in the barn, Deni unfolded a stepladder and searched until she found a can of freeze-dried soup wedged up in the rafters and another of something else. She didn't bother to read the label, just stashed them in her overflowing pack.

Outside, she swung the barn door shut and piled firewood against it to keep it shut and wild animals out. Shaking with nervous tension, she said to no one, "Move it. There's no telling what he'll try while I'm gone. The poor guy can't handle women in combat." She laughed. "One little shiner and he feels sorry for me. The big lug."

She ran to the front door and unlocked it with Nate's key. In the living room, she turned a couch over and found the ammunition she needed for her carbine and put it in her pack. After putting the couch back upright, she rushed outside and locked the door.

In seconds, she had the Harley flying down the drive.

~~~~~~~~~~

Nate walked out onto the hard clay and into the motorcycle's headlight beam.

Deni slowed and stopped beside him. "Any trouble?"

"I'm not bleeding, and they haven't moved one step closer to the farm," Nate said. "That's all that matters."

"This is a long ways from the bridge. You've backed off miles."

"That's temporary. I didn't want you driving into an ambush." Nate turned toward the woods. "Follow me. Let's get that bullet magnet off the road and in the brush." He stepped across a shallow ditch.

Deni revved the engine and followed.

After they hid the motorbike, Deni held her small flashlight while Nate loaded his magazines with black-tipped armor-piercing military rounds for his M14, all seven magazines. He stuffed more rounds, most of them special target loads for high accuracy, in his pack, wrapping them tight with a spare shirt to keep them from rattling.

Nate held the flashlight while she loaded all the magazines she had for her carbine and then the military magazines he had taken off dead men.

"I've got plenty of ammo now," she said.

"I suggest you take this M4," Nate said. "It's got the Aimpoint for night fighting and full auto. If you weren't infantry, I wouldn't dare give it to you, but I think you can handle it."

"It'll stay on semi most likely. Rock-n-roll's only good for certain situations."

Nate seemed reassured. "Good. I thought you understood the score."

"Why don't you keep a couple magazines and the AR?" Deni asked. "Tie it to your pack."

"No. I'm weighed down enough as it is. The M14 and revolver is what I need. And now I have the ammo for the job." He handed her flashlight back. "We'll leave the AR with the bike." Nate started walking.

She followed, carrying the M4. "So you're going to shoot up their vehicles with that AP stuff."

"Yep."

"Yep hell. How are you going to get within range? They'll have men stretched out along both sides of the road in the woods for half a mile or more."

Nate stopped and let her catch up so he could take his full canteen from a side pouch on her back. "You'll be there watching by back." He took a long pull, the first drink in many hours. "I trust you."

She coughed. "Yeah, you trust me all right; you just can't stand the thought of me being hurt."

"Bullshit."

"You deny it?"

"I can't say as I like the idea. Look, I wanted to make damn sure you understood that I don't expect you to stay. And I wanted to make damn sure you understand we both will probably die somewhere along this dirt road." He shrugged his shoulders. "You seem to understand and you're still here."

"I guess I just don't have anywhere else to go." Deni looked away, into the dark.

He continued. "And you came back. That says it all. Now let's get to killing some of those bastards." He checked the Aimpoint on his rifle.

She tilted her head in the dark, the carbine resting on her right hip. "Oh, so it's like that now? Good, let's kick some ass. They've been raping and pillaging, they deserve it."

Nate took his pack off and found a relatively dry place to sit. "Now that we have that settled, let's eat."

"Eat!"

"We need calories and this will be the last chance we'll have for a day or two. It depends on how long we live."

Deni sat beside him and took her pack off too. "Gee, you're full of cheer tonight." She held one of the cans of food out. "Got a can opener?"

~~~~~~~~~~~

Nate whispered. "I think we're close, but we'll have to wait until false dawn so we can see well enough to find it."

Deni tried to penetrate the dark, searching for a large pine tree. "It won't take them long to figure out the fire is coming from the tallest tree around."

"Long enough for me to take out a half dozen trucks, Nate said. "They won't be able to tell how far away or exactly what direction until the fourth or fifth shot."

"They have patrols out, you know." Deni kept her voice low. "A team could be nearby just when you start shooting."

"That's your job: keep them off me. It won't take me long to ruin five or six radiators."

The pitch of her voice rose. "Twelve hundred yards?"

"Exactly twelve hundred and thirty yards. It better be anyway, or I won't hit a thing."

"How much punch does a 7.62 have at that range? I know it can kill a man at long range...but."

"Enough. Men have been killed at twenty-four hundred yards with the 7.62. A radiator isn't that hard to puncture. The trouble will be in hitting them. Armor piercing ammo isn't as accurate as National Match. I'm going to use the anti-armor stuff in case I hit an engine block."

They sat in silence for fifteen minutes and watched the graying dawn materialize.

Nate stood and searched the woods, getting his bearings. He pulled a compass out from under his shirt where it hung from a string around his neck. "This way," he said. "Stay alert."

She got up and followed, her carbine at low ready, eyes sweeping the woods.

After ten minutes, Nate pointed.

Deni nodded.

The big tree was only fifteen yards away.

Nate sat down and attached steel spikes on the instep of his boots with leather straps. He looked up at Deni. "I knew we might be doing a little sniping from trees, so I brought my pole climbing rig."

"Uh, do you climb poles often? Worked for the power company once?"

"Naw," he said, "My father did for a while decades ago, when crop prices were so low he couldn't make a living farming. Hated it. Quit as soon as he could go back to farming. I've been using this rig for hunting deer from a tree stand for years."

Nate rigged up a rope harness that went around the tree trunk and his waist, around both legs and looped back under his crotch on both sides, creating a seat made of rope. He leaned closer to the tree, giving the rope slack, and flipped the other end of the loop up higher on the trunk. Then he jumped up and dug both spikes into the pine bark. He was only six inches above ground, but he started taking small steps up the tree, each time leaning into the trunk for a split second just enough to allow him to flip the loop up a few inches on the backside of the tree trunk. Then he immediately leaned back against the rope to drive the spikes in. The whole process started all over again, when he moved first one boot, and then the other a few inches higher up the tree, leaning out and digging the spikes in before leaning in for a second just enough to flip the rope a little higher on the tree trunk.

Near the top of the ancient pine, Nate sat on a thick limb, just able to see the bridge and several trucks parked on the far end. The men had been working feverously and they were nearly finished with the crude, but effective repairs. The posts Sam pulled away from the beams they supported had been pulled back in place with a truck and heavy logs attached to them for beams. More logs had been laid across the beams for decking. Sometime later in the day, they might be driving the first trucks across.

Fog lifted lazily up from the river in the dew-drenched morning. Nate draped a rope over another limb above him and off to his side, the free end reached to the forest floor. The other end was tied around his chest just under his arms with a knot that would not slip and allow the loop to tighten on his chest and restrict his breathing. Then he untied and removed the harness he had used to climb up with and let it fall to the ground where Deni stuffed it in his pack. The spikes were removed and also dropped to Deni. He planned to use the limb like a pulley while he let the rope slip through his hands when he rapidly descended. Even though it would be wrapped around his body once for friction and to take nearly all of his weight, he knew his hands would be burned since he had no gloves, and he planned to get down fast. The longer he stayed in the tree, the more danger they both would be in.

What he had never done before was shoot at such long range from a tree. He knew the first shot would be a guess. There was no way to know exactly where his rounds would hit. Normally, he always shot from prone at long range and from his natural point of aim. Shooting from an awkward position means the rifle would not shoot to its normal sight settings. The first shot or two would be a guess—and he had no spotter to tell him where those first shots hit.

Deni kept her eyes on the surrounding woods and waited anxiously, not wasting time looking up at Nate. Her job was to protect him while he was in the tree, and she would do it to the best of her ability.

Observing the treetops and how the fog still gathered in low places near the river told Nate there was no wind to push his bullets off target. He knew that would change as the sun rose and heated the atmosphere. His back sight was at its highest setting, but he would still have to aim high.

Nate leaned his left shoulder against the pine tree's trunk, rested his left hand on a convenient limb, and took careful aim at a pickup's radiator. The result of his first shot surprised him. A pickup's left front tire deflated. Dirt flew where the bullet struck. He was trying for the radiator by aiming at the windshield. He aimed higher and more to the right. The left headlight shattered. He couldn't see such a small object at that range, so he looked through his binoculars to confirm his suspicions.

After adjusting windage on his back sight, he tried again. Echoes of his shot reverberated back from the river valley as firing from men on the bridge roared. Looking through his binoculars rewarded Nate with the sight of radiator fluid pouring onto the ground. He let the binoculars hang from his neck and shot out three more radiators, missing only twice more.

Men scurried off the bridge or took cover behind vehicles. Heads bobbed about, looking for the sniper. Nate's shots were impossible to locate because the river valley and its tall trees created an echo effect, making it seem shots were coming from all directions. Some men fired blindly into the woods.

Nate fired into two more radiators and then into the side of a two-ton flatbed truck parked one hundred yards farther down the road and partway up on the river valley's upward slope. He hoped to damage the engine. There was a load piled high on the back and covered with a canvas tarpaulin. He shot into it. *Maybe I'll hit a gas can.* With such a large target, he squeezed off round after round. His last shot was followed by a large explosion. The truck disappeared in a fireball.

Shocked, Nate stared at the scene. A gradual smile spread across his face. *Dynamite? Blasting caps?* He stuffed his binoculars under his shirt out of the way, slung the rifle across his back, and dropped off the limb, falling at a fast rate until near the forest floor, then braking, landing on his butt.

Deni glanced his way just long enough to see if he got down unhurt. She then resumed her vigil, watching the woods for threats.

In fewer than fifteen seconds, Nate had the rope off him and pulled out of the tree and in his pack. He ran to her. While grabbing a fresh magazine out of his load-bearing harness, he said, "We got lucky! That explosion blew a crater in the road on the other side." He slammed the magazine in his rifle and stashed the nearly empty one in a pouch. "Time to make tracks."

Deni smiled too. "What happened?"

Nate still had not resumed his normal levelheaded demeanor. "I shot up a load on the back of a flatbed truck and it blew up. There's a crater all the way across the road. It'll take them forever to fill it with shovels."

Deni's eyes lit up. "Holly shit! I wonder where they got the explosives."

Nate shrugged. "Time to retreat. We'll backslap sometime when we're not being hunted."

She gave him a wry smile and tilted her head. "Okay, party pooper, let's go."

They moved fast for one hundred yards, and then slowed to hunting speed. A group of men moved in but Nate and Deni heard them coming and veered off. By noon, they were waiting five miles down the road.

Deni sat with her back against a sycamore, keeping her eyes busy searching that side of the woods. "What now? If that crater's as big as you say, they won't try to fill it. Probably they'll cut enough trees down to allow them to drive around."

"Yep," Nate said. "But we bought ourselves some time. There are giant cypress trees on both sides of the road there, and they might not have a chainsaw big enough to handle trees that big. They can still cut them down, but they will have to cut one piece out at a time in wedges until they work all the way through. That will take time. Then they have to get those big tree trunks out of the way. That means more cutting through those giant trees. We might be lucky enough their saws' chains are dull and they have no files to sharpen them. Can't bank on anything but the fact we have a little more time now. And that's more than we had at sunrise this morning."

Deni turned her head even though she could not see Nate where he sat on the other side of the sycamore. "I was thinking we should have ambushed the bunch that came hunting us."

"No," Nate said, "ambush works a lot better when it's a complete surprise. They knew we were in the area and were on full alert. Safer to get them later when they're not so ready for us."

"Yeah. You're right. I'm too gung ho sometimes."

Nate got up and stepped around to her side of the tree. "I'm glad I have you with me." He held his hand out to help her up. "I guess I have more actual combat experience than you—and more training in jungle fighting."

She stood and slid into her pack straps. "You Rangers are sent to Panama, so I guess the Army taught you a few things."

"Real combat taught me more." Nate looked her in the eye. "Now, I'm going to teach you something about booby traps."

"Oh?" She watched him cut a small oak limb off.

Nate said, "That hickory over there—cut some branches off. We need sticks one half to three quarters thick and at least a foot long."

"Punji sticks?" Deni did not waste time waiting for an answer. She walked to the hickory tree.

They were forced to search for more trees to find enough branches the right thickness and low enough to reach. After two hours, they had a large pile of sticks sharpened on both ends.

"My knife's dull." Deni got a stone out of her pack and sat down to sharpen it. "And I need a rest."

"It's going to get dull again," Nate said. "We're going to be digging in the road tonight, and that clay is dry and hard packed."

She looked up at him, a smile on her face. "The tires."

"They can't have many spares with them." Nate bent down, wrapped a cord around one bundle of sticks, and tied it off. "We're going to be busy tonight."

"You know," Deni said. "Even if we can stop all of their vehicles, some of them may keep coming on foot."

"That's possible." Nate tied a bundle of sticks to his pack. "They damn sure want to cross here for some reason. If they're running from someone, I wish they would get here already."

Deni nodded. "Why don't you use my stone while I bundle the rest of the sticks, and tie them to my pack?"

Nate sat down to sharpen his knife. He kept searching the woods while he worked. "I think we should put these in the bottom of shallower washouts. They're not as likely to notice the fresh dirt where we dig. Also, when the tires fall in the gullies, it will make the sticks more likely to puncture them.

I'm talking about washouts about a foot deep and not much wider. There's no shortage of them, so we can put quite a few out by false dawn."

"What about putting some along the side of the road back in the woods to cripple a few in those hunter patrols?" Deni finished tying the sticks to her pack.

Nate's face hardened. "I've got other ideas for them."

Deni cocked her head and smiled. "Yeah? I can't wait."

Chapter 11

"What are you looking for?" Deni asked. "It'll be dark soon."

Nate rummaged through a pile of scrap lumber someone had dumped back in the woods, just off the dirt road. It must have been dumped sometime before the plague. Most of the boards were rotted from months of rain and termites, but a few were pressure treated and still solid.

"Firing pins," Nate answered. "Keep your attention on our surroundings. They're hunting us right now."

"Don't worry, I'm on guard." Deni searched the woods. "Just asked a question is all."

"You'll find out later when you help me set the traps," Nate said. He put four 2X4 boards that had nails poking out one end under a pine tree by his pack. There were four shorter 4X4 scraps that someone had cut off fence posts already lying by the pack where he had left them. "Keep your eyes working while I improvise."

As soon as it was full dark, they placed punji sticks across the road in a shallow washout. They covered the sticks with a mat of pine boughs cut from saplings and then put a thin layer of dirt over that. The result of their work made the washout look like level road and no sign of the sticks could be seen. The next afternoon summer shower would make the fresh earth look the same as the surrounding road.

A little past midnight, they set to work back in the woods, setting booby traps.

"Let me show you," Nate said. He twisted his small pocketknife, drilling a hole in the 4X4. "Use the small blade and the hole will be a little smaller than a .308 bullet. Careful you don't let the blade swing closed and cut your fingers."

Deni rolled her eyes in the dark. "I'm not a *total* klutz."

"Didn't say you were." Nate handed her his knife. "Make it as deep as you can with the short blade. Do the other pieces the same, about four inches from the end."

"Can't see a damn thing in the dark." Tired, dirty, and sick of dealing with danger, Deni was becoming irritable.

"Feel," Nate said. "Your fingers can do the work of your eyes. It's just like reloading a gun in the dark."

"Don't let me bother you," she said. "My arm hurts, and I'm growing more pissed at those bastards every hour. We could be taking regular baths, eating well, and sleeping in a bed if not for those assholes."

"You're doing fine. Focus on surviving another day, and do that every day. Maybe we'll make it. Either way, they already know they fucked with the wrong people when they shot at us and killed our friend."

She snickered. "That's the first time I heard you cuss like that."

"You're not the only one that's pissed." Nate went looking for hickory branches to cut.

Two hours before false dawn, Nate and Deni had completed drilling larger holes from the other side of the 4X4s, in line with the smaller holes. The larger hole would be the chamber for a rifle round, the smaller hole, the "barrel" for the bullet. Both had bleeding blisters from twisting Nate's pocketknife into wood.

Nate had to push hard with both hands to get the .308 rounds seated in the holes. "Perfect," he said. "As long as I can get them all the way in, the tighter the better."

"I don't think that wood is going to withstand the pressure," Deni said.

"It won't." Blood ran from his raw palm onto the last round as he pushed it in with one hand pushing over the other. "Not over fifty thousand pounds per square inch, but it will hold together long enough to send that bullet on its way with enough energy to kill a man if it hits in the right place. The wood fragments will wound also."

Deni smiled. "Oh. You Rangers are devious bastards."

He smiled back in the dark. "Yep, and I'm as pissed as you."

With just a hint of light showing in the eastern sky, Nate constructed the last trigger with string and sticks while Deni lashed a 4X4 to a tree waist high, using one quarter inch thick vine Nate cut earlier. She did the best she could to aim the rifle bullet where it would take out a man's guts.

Nate then worked on the "hammer," made from the last 2X4. The nail on its end would be the firing pin, a springy length of hickory branch the mainspring that would drive the hammer with nail/firing pin into the primer of the rifle round.

"Okay." Nate stood in the predawn glow and cocked the trap, holding the 2X4 back. "Hold this while I set this thing."

Deni held the board back against the power of a bent hickory limb. She watched nervously, waiting for him to tell her to complete the most dangerous part.

Nate walked into the trap's kill zone and set the trigger. He had to hold everything in place while she let the board move toward the rifle round enough to take up all slack in the cord and trigger device.

"Okay, let it move a little." Nate watched the cord tighten and the trigger he held in place take some of the pressure. "Hold it there." He backed away, out of danger. "Slowly let it go."

They held their breath.

When the trigger held, Nate said, "Let's camouflage it and set the rest of those punji sticks. We're running out of time."

~~~~~~~~~~~~

Nate could just hear the chainsaws at work as he scanned the bridge and the road beyond through binoculars. He lay in brush by the dirt road watching a dozen men lean against a cypress log ten feet in diameter, straining to make it roll. It was not moving. A much smaller pine tree had been cut into ten-foot lengths and rolled into the massive crater left by the explosion.

Nate was exhausted, and he knew Deni was dead on her feet. He wanted to go deep into the woods and find a place for both of them to sleep. What he was about to do would make rest an impossibility for a long time. *No rest for the weary.*

Nate took careful aim, killing a man standing guard on the near end of the bridge. He fired three more rounds at the radiator of a pickup and quickly crawled back into the woods. They would be coming for them. He must be ready.

Firing from down the road closer to the bridge told him a patrol had walked into Deni's ambush. *So they were closer than I thought.* Nate heard her coming on the run, swinging around one of the traps as planned. A large group of men was chasing her.

A man's screaming echoed in the woods. Morning mist dulled the sharpness of his high-pitched voice, but it still cut into Nate's soul. He reminded himself what kind of men he and Deni were killing and what they would do to Deni and the others if they had half a chance. One of Nate's booby traps had just put a sharp two-foot-long stake into his gut.

Deni's face was rigid with stress as she ran past Nate. She raised her left hand and showed him five fingers twice, telling him there were ten men coming. He nodded, his eyes searching her for signs she was wounded. He found none.

She kept running, making as much noise as possible.

Another of their traps was triggered, this one powered by a rifle round. Its dull report told Nate they would be on him in seconds. Screaming told him the trap did its job.

From thirty yards away, a voice yelled out, "Stop! Let the little bitch go. She'll just lead us into more booby traps."

Another man yelled, "Someone put one in that bastard's head. I'm tired of hearing it."

Nate had already located the first man. He put his sights on the man's head and squeezed the trigger. Then he swung on another man's stomach—all of him he could see through the undergrowth of the forest. Nate was disappointed to find the man had already moved and disappeared behind brush.

Snapping brush and crunching leaves told Nate the men were seeking cover just where he hoped. More screaming, this time from two men, echoed in the forest.

"Punji sticks!" a man yelled.

Nate backed off and made his retreat.

Gunshots roared behind him as he made his way to where Deni was waiting.

Deni was keyed up. Her desire to live kept her senses on high alert. She saw movement before Nate was close enough to see her standing still back in shade and thick brush.

When Nate came close enough, easing his way through the woods, flowing like a ghost so slowly he did not appear to be moving at all, he saw her pointing her carbine at him.

One step and he was behind a pine tree.

She knew it was him and had already lowered her weapon, but Nate had disappeared.

Deni searched the woods, breath catching as if it were torturous to fill her burning lungs, afraid the movement would betray her, the sound prevent her ears from detecting danger stalking closer. She was not sure how far behind Nate the killers were.

Then she saw him. Nate had come closer without her seeing or hearing a thing, despite her best efforts.

Nate's attention was on something off to her left. His eyes were hawkish, the eyes of a predator. Deni knew he was hunting and danger was only yards away.

Dropping to a squat and turning to look behind her, she prepared to take on all threats.

Her motion attracted attention. A man aimed a carbine at her. Nate threw his rifle up and fired as soon as the butt touched his shoulder. The man dropped.

Automatic fire erupted twenty yards from Deni. She caught movement from spent rounds ejected onto brush. Someone was firing at Nate. It took her fewer than two seconds to locate the shooter and fire three rounds. The shooting stopped.

Deni dropped to the ground and fast-crawled ten yards. Automatic fire sprayed the area she had just left. She kept crawling until her right shoulder slammed against a scrub oak.

Nate's rifle cracked the temporary silence. Three rapid shots, then one more.

Crunching of leaves told Deni more men were maneuvering closer.

Nate's rifle spoke, first a double tap, then rapid-fire. He was answered with a roar of automatic fire from several directions.

Deni needed to support Nate with her covering fire, but could not see while lying on the ground, so she sat up. That was the last thing she remembered.

Nate knew they were in trouble. Another group had come up on them from behind. Deni and he were between them and the first group. He wondered why Deni stopped shooting. There were plenty of targets.

Gunfire filled Nate's ears. No longer was it rapid pops, it had become a solid roar, growing in volume. Nate reloaded and fired into them, guessing their location in the forest's thick underbrush. Then he ran to another position, seeking out cover and trying to work closer to Deni.

Already twice wounded, he may have tried to escape, but that meant leaving Deni. *No! Not as long as there is a chance that she still lives.* He had little hope of saving her. She probably was dead or nearly so, and he could do little for a serious wound. However, he would not leave her to them as long as she still breathed. He owed her that.

Nate ran while bent over, keeping as low as possible. In seconds, he had enough trees between him and the hail of bullets to be safe. He ran in a straight line until they followed, firing at him.

He ran faster, and continued to run until they were so far behind the shooting waned. Turning in a wide arc, he worked around, back toward Deni. They ran on, in a straight line.

To be quiet, Nate was forced to slow to hunting speed. She was not far, but it took him many minutes to find her. Well hid in thick brush, half a dozen men must have run by her when they went after Nate.

There she was, lying in her own blood.

Nate gently rolled her over and checked for a pulse. His breath caught. He laid his right hand on her chest. It rose slowly but steady.

Ripping his pack off, he pulled out what little medical supplies he had. A quick check for wounds told him she had taken a hit to the head, but otherwise was not hurt, except for the old wound on her arm. The head wound was a glancing blow, leaving her skull exposed, a slab of flesh hung down above her right temple. He feared brain damage. Her brain could be swelling in her skull as she lay there.

Nate put on his last pair of surgical gloves. First, he cut her hair away and cleaned the wound with the last of his antibiotic. Then he swathed her head in gauze, holding the loose flesh in place as he made the first wrap. Nate planned to suture it the first chance he got. He had to get her out of there before they both were killed.

When he first threw her across his shoulders, she seemed surprisingly light and small. However, three miles later, his body was reminding him he was not in his twenties anymore. He once carried a wounded soldier much heavier than her from sunup to dark through jungle, but that was a lifetime ago. A life he had left behind, or so he thought, until the world went to hell.

Another four miles and Nate had to rest. Gently, he put her down under an ancient oak.

She was breathing still. Worried he might be carrying a dead woman, that discovery was a relief. Her head had bled for nearly an hour, dripping down his right leg at times. When it stopped, he didn't know whether to be glad or stop carrying her. He hated to remove the gauze and start it bleeding again, but the wound had to be stitched up, and he wanted to do it while she was still unconscious.

He had no surgical gloves left, so before starting the task, he washed his hands as best he could, using most of a canteen of water and some bar soap that he kept in a plastic bag in his pack. Where her hair would hide the scar, he used a larger gauge needle and Dexon thread for its strength. There was no telling what she may be going through if she ever woke. There was more fighting to do, and he wanted the sutures to be strong enough where the wound was deepest. He used a finer needle and thread where the scar would show. A hemostat in his modest medical kit was put to use holding the half-circle needles. He knew it is nearly impossible to hold a bloody needle with bare fingers while pushing it through flesh and kept the hemostat in his medical kit for that purpose as much as clamping off a blood vessel. After he finished closing the wound, he bandaged it and lifted her to his shoulder again.

After two hours of screaming muscles, Nate just managed to get them both to the motorcycle they left by the road. *How do you ride double with an unconscious woman?* It would be dark soon, and then he would find out.

Deni lay in the woods, while Nate kick started the Harley. After giving the motor time to warm up, he carried her onto the road and sat her on the seat, held her up, and sat behind her. Nate prayed none of the men were near while he used rope to strap her legs to his, leaving her feet on top of his boots. Then he tied her upper body to his, keeping the top of her head leaning against his chin. He kept thinking he would feel a bullet slamming into his back at any moment. They were an easy target out on the open road, even in the dark.

At first, he had to use both hands, letting Deni's head dangle. She could not breathe well with her neck like that, so as soon as he had the Harley in third gear, he held her head up with his left hand. He held her head the whole way. Several washouts caused him trouble. He was forced to carry her around one and then retie her in front all over again. She never showed any signs of waking.

Nate was worried she may never wake again.

The trail of brush, which Deni ran over when she rode around the mound of dirt in the driveway, led Nate until they came out onto the drive. Nate gunned it and they were soon home.

He left Deni lying by the Harley and took a quick look around, rifle in hand. Finding no sign anyone had been around since Deni's trip; he pumped water and took a long drink. After filling both his and Deni's canteens, he hurriedly fed and watered the chickens and cow.

Days of going on little to no sleep and dealing with the stress of combat had left Nate so tired, he could no longer think well enough to carry out complex tasks. His movements were involuntary, just animal instinct. He wanted to lie in his bed and pass out, but there was still one thought burning in his head: Get Deni to the bunker. Get her to help.

Once more, Nate got her back on the bike and headed for the river and a canoe hidden in the swamp.

~~~~~~~~~~~

Where in the hell is that creek? Nate asked himself. The night was overcast, and he could see little, as he paddled upriver keeping to the shore, out of the main current. Deni lay in the bottom of the canoe, still unconscious.

A quarter mile farther and he realized he had missed it. He turned back, letting the current catch him with full force. Sometime past midnight, he recognized a fallen cypress that jutted into the river. *How in the hell did I not see it the first time?* Nate turned the canoe into thick cattails and entered the creek, paddling with all the strength he had left.

~~~~~~~~~~~

Brian mopped sweat from his forehead and kept vigil, searching the dark. He could see nothing *but* dark on this night. He kept his eyes constantly working anyway. This was his watch, and no one would come up on the bunker without him knowing. The past months had taught him what responsibility really is, even more so than his father's gentle lessons.

A rough voice came bellowing from out of the black. "Brian, Ben, don't shoot, I'm coming in."

Brian snatched his shotgun up to his right shoulder and prepared to shoot out of the loophole. "Everyone wake up! Grab your guns."

Ben scrambled to his feet, shotgun in hand. Martha was asleep beside him. She grabbed a carbine and was awake nearly as fast.

Cindy took longer to wake but made it to her assigned loophole before her parents, carbine pointing into the dark.

"How many?" Ben asked.

"It's my father, but he sounds different." Brian yelled out of his loophole, "Are you hurt?"

Nate answered. "No, but Deni is. I'm carrying her in. Open up. It's safe. There's no one out here but Deni and me."

Brian ran and unbolted the door. He gasped when he saw his father and Deni. They were both covered in dried blood.

Ben hung his shotgun on a gun rack, so he could help Nate get Deni to a mattress.

Brian closed and bolted the steel door.

Martha had a kerosene lamp lit in seconds. She looked up after putting the match out and saw Deni. "Oh God. Cindy, get the fist aid supplies out."

Brian's worried eyes went from Deni to his father. He watched Nate take his pack off. He could not tell if Nate hesitated when he moved because of tired muscles or the wounds. "Dad, you're hurt too."

Nate shook his head. I'm okay. Who's on watch?"

"Me," Brian said.

"Then get back on duty." Before Brian moved, Nate said, "Wait." He walked across the small room and held his son. "I'm okay."

"Yeah, you're always okay. As reliable as a hammer." Brian grabbed his shotgun. "I guess Sam is gone."

Everyone stopped whatever they were doing. Even Caroline and Carrie, who had woken to stand sleepy-eyed, were hit by the news.

Nate's jaw clenched. "Dead. They caught us tearing down the bridge and started shooting right off. I yelled for him to back the Cat away, but he kept working on the bridge."

"I think he was a good friend," Brian said. He glanced at Deni lying on the mattress. "We've had it easy while you two did all the fighting."

Nate's face changed and he raised his chin. A light that was not there before shined. He suddenly was not as tired. "We could not stop them completely. They will be coming."

Caroline and Carrie stood out of the way with colorless faces, not saying anything, just listening.

Martha said, "We will deal with what comes when it gets here. What about her head? Have you done everything that can be done?"

"Yes, no need to bother it for now. I stitched it up after cleaning it. She has a superficial wound on her arm that needs cleaning though. You might want to check her over for more wounds."

Cindy pulled on a blanket hanging from a rod until Deni and Martha had privacy. "We'll clean her up and check her." She disappeared behind the blanket.

Ben grabbed a pail and pumped water from the hand pump on the floor.

Brian glanced from the loophole to his father. "You need to sit down and take your shirt off so someone can look at your wounds too."

Nate gave him a tired smile. "Have you taken to ordering your dad around?"

Brian's eyes went back to looking at the black night. "I didn't mean it that way."

"Just kidding." Nate pulled his bloody shirt off.

Brian spoke without taking his eyes off what little he could see outside. "What about it. Does she have a chance? A head wound is bad." He smeared his face.

"I like her too, Brian." Nate knew the others were listening. "The bullet glanced off her hard skull and ripped some flesh loose. Infection and brain damage from swelling is the main danger. We won't know whether she'll still be Deni or not until she comes to—if, she comes to. I think she has a good chance from what I saw of the wound. She's been out a long time now though."

"We'll take care of her," Brian said, "as long as she's still alive."

Ben asked Nate, "I'll bet she impressed you some out there, didn't she?"

"And then some," Nate answered without taking his eyes off Brian. "I never fought with any better. Her showing up at the farm was one of the best things that happened since the world went to hell. Brian and I've been lucky to have the caliber of friends we've met lately."

Caroline said, "If you want, you can go outside and clean up. I'll pump water and hand a bucket out the door for you. There's soap and a rag and towel outside too, just to the left of the door."

Nate stood. "I'm dead tired, but I'll sleep better clean than filthy." He noticed she seemed to have come out of her shell since he last saw her.

"And you need those wounds cleaned too," Brian added.

"That's true." Nate nearly fell over when he bent down to untie his boots.

Carrie spoke up, surprising everyone. "I'll fix something for you to eat while you're outside."

When Nate came back in, his hair still wet, he was shirtless and in extra jeans, he had in his pack.

Martha was waiting for him. She had a lamp on a table covered with medical supplies and a chair nearby. "Sit here," she said.

Martha had to sew Nate's wounds, using three dozen stitches, a dozen on one wound alone.

"We're going to run out and be reduced to sewing thread or fishing line if this keeps up," Ben said.

Martha gave her husband a sharp look. "If this keeps up, we're going to run out of friends. You're looking at a living miracle."

Nate's eyes flashed to Brian. "I'm here, and I'm not hurt bad."

"You're going back, aren't you?" Brian's voice echoed in the concrete bunker.

Nate looked down at nothing. "I'm going to eat and rest for a few hours."

"Then you're leaving." Brian faced his father squarely. "Even though a few hours from now you will still be so tired you can barely move. And this time you will be fighting them alone. I remember how you said a two-man team is ten times more likely to survive a gunfight than one man. You barely made it back. Now you're going alone."

"Like I said, I am going to eat and then take a nap." Nate checked to see if a bandage would stay in place. He looked at Martha. "Put some duct tape on that. I don't want it falling off."

"At least take Ben with you if you won't let me go." Brian showed no sign of crying. His voice did not crack.

"If it's woods fighting, my shotgun will work fine," Ben said.

Nate kept his eyes on Brian. "No. You have a family to take care of. Brian is a man now. He can make it without me if it comes to that. But I swear I intend to be back here soon."

Brian inhaled through his nose, his lips drawn tight. His chest rose and then fell as he stared at his father. "Nothing I can do about it. You're bigger than me." He turned and looked out the loophole.

No one said anything while Nate had his first real food since he left the farm days ago.

Ben found him a T-shirt to wear. It was white.

Nate threw it back at him. "I need something green or at least dark."

Brian jerked his head around. He said nothing, but his eyes told Nate he knew.

Nate stood when Ben brought him a T-shirt a size too small, but it was dark green. "Brian, I need you to go to the cave and get an IV kit for Deni." He slid the shirt on. "Take Martha with you so she can get other things Deni will need. Might as well fill a pack with food and ammo while you're there."

As soon as Brian and Martha left, Nate put on clean socks and his wet, dirty boots. He stuffed food and rifle ammunition in his pack and filled his canteens. Ben handed him an olive drab military surplus jacket. Nate hung his compass from his neck and then put on the jacket and his boonie hat.

"Tell Brian, I promise I'll be back in a few days." Nate picked his rifle off the gun rack and unbolted the door.

Cindy, who was keeping watch, her carbine in hand, said, "I can't see much but I don't think anyone's out there."

Ben waited until Nate was in the doorway. "You keep that promise."

Chapter 12

Nate rushed to the canoe as fast as darkness would allow. He paddled with a rage. A renewed force within drove him on, despite his fatigue.

Before false dawn, he was twenty miles downriver.

The morning was three hours old, when Nate found the chainsaw and gas can, he had hidden so many days ago. There was no one around since they were hunting Deni and him on the other side of the river. He left the saw and headed for the bridge with just enough gas to do what he needed.

Deep in the swamp, not far from the river, Nate found a hiding place to rest. They would have to step on him by accident to see him where he slept.

Something yanked Nate out of his slumber. Voices. He held his rifle across his chest and listened.

At first, he could not understand their words, but they came closer and he could hear the conversation.

Nate heard what sounded like a teenage boy. "I think we should turn back. If they catch us—"

"It's too late for that," a man sounding much older said. "You know what happened to Shaun Twillager when they caught him away from his post. Never liked the bastard. Seemed to be kind of a pansy. But it wasn't pretty watching him die." He hawked up something out of his throat. "Goddamn smokes. Wish I had one right now though."

"It ain't cigarettes I miss," the teen said.

"This is a hard bunch, boy. Too hard for me. And I know you ain't got the stomach for their ways. I saw you throwing up when we raided that last town. I ain't never even took nothing that wasn't mine in my life before the shit hit the fan. But I got to eat. Taking what you gotta have to survive is one thing, but they go way too far. No. We got to get the hell away from that bunch before it's too late."

"I figured if I didn't join them, they would kill me," the teen said.

"You figured right. There's some truth to the saying about safety in numbers, but that bunch is too rough for me. And I always thought *I* was a rough old cob." They were close enough now Nate could hear the man spit. "Boy, that murdering bunch of animals could make Hitler's SS puke."

They walked by no more than fifteen yards from Nate. He let them go.

Nate slept until sundown. Then he ate a quick meal of powdered soup reconstituted with cold water. By the time it was good and dark, he had already made his first kill. The old Ka-Bar was bloody when he slid it back in its sheath.

There was another sentinel to take out before Nate could burn the truck. Of all the trucks parked in the road, it had the heaviest load on it. Nate hoped whatever was stacked so high under that tarpaulin would explode.

Before Nate could work his way closer, the last sentinel grabbed his belt buckle and trotted into the woods. Taking advantage of the opportunity, Nate ran to the rear of the truck, pulled the tarpaulin aside, and splashed gas on the crates. He didn't have time to read the labels, but they reminded him of military crates like those he had seen years ago.

Nate lit a safety match and tossed it. There was no need to look when the fire caught with a small explosion of its own, he just ran faster.

A powerful shock wave slammed Nate face first into the mud. Searing heat burned his skin. He lay there until the heat receded some before pushing up from the mud and running to the river.

It took Nate ten minutes to find a place to hide his pack and rifle. He needed to be able to find them when he returned. A mossy windfall jutting out from the other side of the river was good enough. He could see that while swimming downstream.

Even without his pack and rifle, he was weighed down with a heavy revolver and pockets full of ammunition for it. Swimming in the tea-colored warm water, he approached the bridge. Shouting echoed from down the road, feet drummed the wood planks above him.

Slime growing on the braces attached to a bridge piling made for tenuous footing, but Nate managed to climb up and slide under a railing. He lay there, searching for danger and getting his bearings.

A sliver of moon came out from behind clouds. Nate slid along a timber the bridge's designer must have intended to be a curb of sorts. It provided him with a narrow ribbon of shade that he used to hide in as best he could.

All of the vehicles Nate shot up had been pushed off the bridge and dropped into the river. They had no way to repair the shot up radiators and few spare tires, so the trucks were useless to them. There were more pickups parked in the dirt road, but not on the bridge. Nate hoped to see another large truck loaded with something under a tarpaulin, but there were only empty pickups for transporting men.

Racing against time, Nate ran to the first pickup and looked in. There was no key in the ignition. He ran to the second truck, looked in, snatched the door open, and slid behind the wheel. The starter groaned and the engine sputtered, then caught. In seconds, he was racing for the repair, hoping it was not strong enough yet to hold the pickup's weight. He slowed to three miles an hour just before reaching the flimsy patch in the bridge and jumped out, rolling to the edge and under the railing.

Shouts and gunshots reached Nate's ears just as he slid feet-first off the bridge, holding on just long enough to swing his body out to miss a heavy beam below. When he came up, the current had carried him against one of the pickups. It was lying on its side, and something on its undercarriage snagged his shirt. He pulled loose, losing several inches of skin a quarter inch wide. He saw another pickup's back bumper poking out of the water nearer to shore, the front end disappearing into a deep hole. It was a convenient place to hide while he took his bearings.

Splintered logs floating downriver gave him an idea. He swam under water and came up in the flotsam, keeping his head just high enough to breathe through his nose.

Shouts and blind shooting sounded like music to his ears. He was still in danger. They would be hunting him hard all night, and he still had to get his rifle and pack before evading them. But he just bought several more days of time. How could he not feel better than he had since Deni was shot? The bastards. He was past resisting the urge to hate them.

His smug smile faded. What next?

Since it's obvious, I'm trying to stop them from crossing the river and advancing down the road, they will expect me to be on that side of the river. It's where Deni and I have done most of the fighting.

Nate crawled out of the river, dripping more than water: his old wounds were bleeding again. He knew that scratch he suffered from the truck in the water was actually a deep gash. Thinning rivulets of blood ran down his stomach. Taking his pack and rifle, he moved on. His plans included attacking them from the far rear of their caravan of cutthroats.

Morning came and Nate moved closer to his target. Peering through brush, he could see the road and the last of their vehicles parked across it to form a roadblock. They had their rear position well guarded. *Yep, they're expecting trouble from behind. Who? What force could take them on toe-to-toe? There is no sheriff department, no state police. Vigilantes seeking revenge? How could civilians possibly gather up enough men for that? I doubt if there are more than a few thousand men left alive in this part of the county.*

A sudden flurry of shots forced him to leave those questions unanswered.

A woman screamed. A child cried. Nate maneuvered so he could see to shoot.

Hate hardened Nate's face as he watched two men fire rounds into the driver of a pickup before he could get it turned around in the road. A man and his wife and daughter had driven around a curve and into the killers' trap.

Several men dragged the man's bloody body out of a diesel powered Dodge, its windshield shattered. They dropped him in the dirt. One man shot him in the head, though it appeared he was already gone. Then they dragged the screaming woman out and dropped her in the road. Her little girl, she was about three years old, ran up, and bit one of the men on his hand, when he yanked the woman up by her hair. He took the girl by her upper right arm and flung her against a pine tree. She lay unconscious in a ditch.

Nate feared she would drown, as the ditch was half-full of water. He started firing immediately. The man who threw the little girl was the first to die. In a hurry to help her, Nate fired until his rifle clicked on an empty chamber. Normally, he would have repositioned after two or three shots, but he wanted to kill them as fast as possible.

While Nate ducked behind a tree to reload, the mother tried to run for the girl. One of the men shot her in the back. She fell on her daughter. Nate ran across the road, firing. The little girl would certainly drown with her dead mother holding her under water.

A bullet spun Nate around and he dropped his rifle. He reached for his revolver and aimed with one hand. A man fell. Nate shot him again. Dirt flew behind the man's torso when the big bullet went through.

Struggling to rise, Nate looked up and saw another man fifty yards away running down the road toward him, rifle in both hands, swinging wildly. The man stopped and raised his rifle to shoot. Nate lay on his stomach, aimed, and squeezed the trigger. The man was dead before he hit the ground.

After pulling the mother off her, Nate found the girl's head was not under water after all. He pushed on her chest. She was not breathing. He continued to push down on her chest until he was afraid he would break ribs. She would not breathe.

Nate checked the mother. She was dead.

Rage made Nate's hands shake as he reloaded the revolver. He walked back to his rifle and picked it up. His right arm seemed weak and would not do what he wanted without extreme effort to will it to move.

A sound from behind caught his attention. He swung around, ready to shoot. The girl was coughing. Her chest racked. Nate ran to her and turned her on her side. "Breathe, little girl." He picked her up and laid her on the pickup's seat. He noticed her eyes were half closed and without life.

Motion down the road alerted him to danger. A wounded man tried to crawl to his rifle. Nate walked to him.

The man looked up, his face defiant, hard. "What are you crying about, asshole? I'm the one that's dying." He coughed up blood.

"Yes you are," Nate said. He raised his revolver. No need to waste a rifle bullet.

The man stared at Nate. "What's that little girl to you?"

Nate shot him in the head. "A little girl," he said to no one. He used the revolver to shoot up the radiators of every vehicle but the pickup the girl was in.

When he walked back to the truck, the little girl was crying and trying to sit up. "I want my mommy."

A bullet slammed into the headrest above her. She cried louder.

Nate got the truck in reverse and its back tires spinning. Dirt billowed out of the rear fenders as he backed around the curve at forty miles an hour. He continued down the road in reverse, the diesel engine screaming, for another mile. Then he backed into a jeep trail until the truck was stuck in mud.

The girl sat in the cab looking around, crying for her mother.

A quick search of the truck's cab produced nothing useful other than a container of water that he left. *How did they survive this long without weapons? What have they been eating?*

Nate searched the back. There was a tarpaulin covering a long mound of something. He pulled it aside. With an involuntary move to cover his mouth, he stepped back, his eyes wide. All the signs of the killer disease that had just wiped out ninety-five percent of the world's population were on a dead elderly woman. He pulled the tarpaulin back over her.

They were being hunted, and any moment, pickups filled with armed men would come racing down the road. The killers could not miss the tracks where he turned off onto the jeep trial.

Nate grabbed the girl and ran into the woods. He had to get far enough away they could not hear her crying. She pounded at his head and left side of his face with both fists. "Let me go! I want my mommy."

Nate heard them bouncing down the dirt road, engines roaring. He surged forward, bullying through thick brush. His right arm was still weak, but he willed his hand to hold the rifle tighter. "Close your eyes, girl." He could not protect her face since both hands were occupied. "Turn your face the other way and close your eyes." She would not listen. The little girl kept hitting him and screaming for her mother.

Nate was too out of breath to keep talking. When he broke through to an open meadow, he skirted it and ran faster. There was no stopping and he knew it. With her crying, he dare not let them get within two hundred yards.

~~~~~~~~~~~

Brian opened his eyes. Something had awakened him. He blinked and peered into the dark of the bunker. He guessed it to be 2AM. Cindy was on security and looking out the north loophole. He could just make out movement where she was. She moved her head to search her field of view.

There it was again. Brian sat up.

Deni was moaning. He jumped off the mattress and ran to her, nearly stepping on Ben. "Deni. You're awake!"

"My head hurts," Deni said.

Cindy nearly yelled, "Hey, Deni's awake!"

In seconds, everyone was scurrying out of bed. Brian lit a kerosene lamp.

Martha pulled the curtain aside and Deni looked up to see smiling faces glowing in the yellow lamplight.

She touched her head gingerly. "Where am I?"

"At Mel's bunker," Martha answered. "You've been unconscious for days."

Deni blinked, looking up at them. "What happened?"

"You were shot." Martha got down on her knees and put her left arm across Deni's shoulders to steady her. "Nate stitched your head up and carried you all the way here."

Deni reached up to touch her head.

"Careful." Martha pulled her hand down. "It seems to be healing okay. Most of the scar will be covered by your hair." She smiled with happiness. "And you're awake."

"Are you hungry or thirsty?" Brian asked. He seemed more relieved than the others did.

"Uh, I guess," Deni said. "Help me stand. I want to sit in a chair."

Ben rushed to her.

Before he could help her up, Martha said, "I don't think she should move yet. We don't know exactly how…"

Deni broke the awkward silence. "I'm not dizzy, and I can see okay." She looked at Brian. "I may be crazy though."

"Why do you say that?" Martha asked.

"I've never seen Brian smile so much."

Cindy broke in. "What, you didn't know he likes you? We're all happy to see you are better. We didn't know if you would ever wake."

Ben and Brian helped her to a chair.

Cindy put a glass of water on the small table.

Deni took a long drink. She looked around the dimly lit room. "So this is the bunker."

"Yep. Mel's place," Brian said.

Deni's face changed. "Nate! Where is he?" She looked at Brian. Her face told everyone she was already remembering the killers at the bridge.

Brian's jaw set. "After he carried you here, he ate, cleaned up, and left to stop those men." Brian turned and looked into a dark corner. "He was hurt, but he wouldn't stay."

"You should have stopped him." Deni tried to stand, but seemed to weaken and sat back down.

"He's bigger than me," Brian said, "and I've learned not to argue with him so much. He's got enough to worry about."

"I would rather you argued this time." Deni tried to stand again."

Martha grabbed Deni's shoulders. "Stop that. You should be lying down."

"He's out there alone! There are hundreds of them." Deni looked at Ben. "And we are sitting around jacking our jaws."

"You just woke up after being shot in the head." Brian's voice rose, not unlike his father's. "Calm down and think. You can't walk across this room yet, and I've learned it's better to do what he says. He's usually right. And when he's wrong he's still my dad and the boss." Brian walked to a shelf stacked with cans of freeze-dried food. "You feel like breakfast or dinner?"

Ben and Martha glanced at each other with tight-lipped smiles.

Deni's eyes gleamed. "For some reason I have a craving for ham and eggs."

"I'll make it," Caroline said. She had been staying out of the way, but seemed as happy as the others to see Deni awake and talking. She lit the gas stove. There was still a little gas left, and they dared not use the wood stove, because smoke could be seen by anyone close by.

Brian put a can of scrambled eggs on the table and filled a small pot with water from the hand pump, guessing accurately how much water to use.

"Cindy," Brian said, "Maybe you should finish your watch. The next one's mine." He turned the lamp down. "If you can see anything out there with this lamp on."

Carrie woke up. Rubbing her eyes, she walked to their side of the bunker and said, "I'm hungry." She did not show any recognition of the fact Deni was awake.

Brian looked out a loophole, his eyes distant.

Chapter 13

Nate could not get the little girl to stop crying. She wanted her parents. She was afraid of him. He tried many times to console her and ease her fears, but wasn't successful. He couldn't get her to eat anything, but did get her to stop crying long enough to drink some water.

She appeared to have been eating lately, but she was thin. Nate wondered where her family came from.

Nate also wondered if he was doing the right thing. The sickness killed the old woman, and that meant it was probably being carried by the girl. He could be bringing death to Brian and the others. Despite the danger, there was no thought of leaving her.

As exhausted as he was, he picked her and his rifle up and ran. He planned to shake them off his trail and then turn upriver. With the canoe he had left hidden, he could take her to the creek and within a mile of the bunker. She needed to be with women and Tommy. Perhaps then, she would feel safer.

His right arm still bothered him. It felt numb and weak. Fine motor movements were possible only with extreme willpower. It had taken all he had to hold steady while aiming the revolver at those men in the dirt road. He discovered he had not been hit by a bullet. Instead, a bullet had slammed into his pack from the right side and yanked it so hard the right shoulder strap cut into his flesh and caused nerve damage in his shoulder. The rifle was a heavy caliber magnum of some kind, more suitable for large bears, than men. The bullet hitting a full canteen that exploded in his pack gave the impact more force.

It grew darker with sunset. Nate kept moving fast, taking advantage of the dying light.

By the time twilight faded into night, she had finally cried herself to sleep. Exhaustion overcame terror and grief. She slept in his left arm, her head leaning against his cheek, hot and sweaty in the humid river swamp. Heavy brush slowed his progress, and he could not see well in the shade of the jungle canopy where not even starlight penetrated. Mosquitoes managed to keep up, because of his slower pace, and buzzed around them both. Nate could not keep them off her. His other hand carried the rifle.

The canoe had to be close. Nate could not be sure, but he thought it was not much farther. Exhausted, he moved on.

The girl woke up and immediately started crying and fighting Nate, wanting down. He had not found the canoe yet, and now he had her to deal with. She was afraid in the dark, and Nate knew she had to be tired of being carried. He certainly was tired of carrying her.

"Don't be afraid little baby girl," Nate said. He used to call his own daughter that when she was about her age.

She cried.

"What is your name?"

Nate got what he expected for an answer.

She cried.

"Do you want a drink?"

"I want my mommy."

"I'm sorry. She is not here."

She cried.

Hell. This will go on all night. He was starting to remember all those sleepless nights when his children were babies. He was patient then, and he would be patient with her. What else can you do? Losing your cool with a child this small makes you more immature than the kid. Little kids cry sometimes. It's the way it is, no matter how annoying it can be, and in this case dangerous. This little girl had good reason to wail, and he would not hold it against her or blame her for his headache. She damn sure had good reason to be unhappy with the world and no reason at all to trust him. After all, didn't he take her away from her parents and into this dark swamp? She probably couldn't comprehend that both her parents were dead. She did know he was the one who took her away from all she knew and loved.

"I wish you would eat and drink while we're resting," Nate said. "Later we will go on a boat ride."

"No! I want my mommy!"

Nate sighed. "If you're not going to eat or drink, we might as well go on to that boat." He slung the rifle over his right shoulder and held her in his arms so they both would be more comfortable.

She slapped at his face, kicked, and cried.

It was not easy finding the canoe. He had to turn back downriver and cover old ground because he missed it the first time.

He put her down on her feet. "Just stay there a second." He took his pack off and sat it on the ground. "Sit on this while I get the boat ready."

She took off at top speed.

Nate caught her within three steps. "Whoa, whoa, whoa. Little baby, I'm trying to help you."

She cried.

"If you run off and get lost in this swamp you will die. Now sit on the pack and don't move."

The tone of his voice must have had an affect. She sat there not making a sound, while he got the canoe ready and in the water.

"Okay. Stand up, little girl. I have to put the pack in." Nate took her by her hand. Together, they walked the short distance. He let her hand go and tied the pack to an aluminum strut on the front seat so it could not fall out if the canoe turned over. Just as he finished, an owl hooted in a tree above her. She ran to him and wrapped her arms around his leg.

"It's just an owl, little baby girl." He bent down and picked her up. "I won't let anything hurt you. Are you starting to realize I'm the only friend you have at the moment?"

She said nothing, but she was not crying.

"I know I'm ugly, dirty and I stink, but I promise you that I'm not mean like those other men."

He put her in the bottom of the canoe.

"Just lie still and try to get some sleep. We're going to a better place where there are kids. One little boy is about your age."

"How old is he?" She asked.

Nate smiled in the dark. "About your age. Maybe a little older."

She did not say anything else, and she did not cry.

Eleven miles upriver, she woke, and asked for a drink. Nate stopped paddling and gave her water.

She went back to sleep.

It was dangerous, but when the sun came up Nate kept paddling. He wanted to get her to the bunker as soon as possible, and it was unlikely any of the killers were this far upriver.

Paddling was difficult at first because of his numb right arm. As the hours flowed by, his arm seemed to be getting better. Perhaps the exercise was helping. Nate hoped so. He might have to shoot at any time.

She sat up in the canoe. Nate wished she would lie in the bottom to keep her center of gravity low. Now that the sun was up, she enjoyed watching the trees on both sides flow by as Nate worked to overcome the river's current, staying close to shore and in any eddies he came to, avoiding the full force of the flow.

Nate kept searching both banks for trouble. He didn't like traveling by canoe in daylight, but it was unlikely any of the killers would be this far from the bridge. There could be others around though, and he knew from experience that you never knew what strangers were like. He hated thinking the worst of people. Despite his feelings, he really had no choice. To do otherwise could be fatal.

As the day wore on, Nate became more anxious, his eyes were constantly on the shoreline. Just around the next bend, he would be pulling in to shore. They were close to his farm.

"Do you want to tell me your name now?" Nate tried to hide is worry, keeping his voice soft.

She shook her head.

"Okay. You don't have to. You can tell me later. You have been quiet. That's good. We both need to be as quiet as possible." He drove the bow of the canoe onto a sand bar with a powerful stroke of the paddle. "Just stay like you are and I'll get you."

He waded in the shallow water and picked her up. "There we go." He put her down on shore. "Just stay there for a minute, while I take care of the canoe."

Nate pulled the canoe into brush and hid it. When he walked back to her, he had his pack on and his rifle in hand.

"We're going to my house where we can eat and clean up and rest."

Her eyes brightened a little. "The little boy there?"

"No. Tommy is at another house. We'll be going there later today. I have some clothes for you that belonged to my little girl. We will pick that up before we go to the other house."

"Where is your little girl?"

Nate picked her up. "I'll carry you most of the way, and then you can walk." He waited until he had carried her up the steep bluff before answering. "Her name was Beth. She got sick. She's in heaven now."

"Oh." She looked up at the sky, but not seeing much of it through the scrim of treetops. "My Grandma is in heaven, but she's really in the truck. Mommy said it's her insides that's in heaven."

Nate kept walking.

"Is Mommy and Daddy in heaven too?"

"Yes." *Might as well get it over with. She saw it. She knows anyway. Just doesn't want to let them go yet.*

She blinked and looked up at the sky again.

Nate put the rifle against a pine and held her with both arms. "I'm sorry, but you're not alone. Now, you have me, and soon you will have a lot of people to take care of you."

"They never come back?"

"No. Never."

Nate did not know what to think of her silence. She did not say another word all the way upslope and out of the river valley. He hoped she would remain silent until he was sure no one was around.

She sat quietly under a magnolia while he eased close enough to the edge of his field to see the house and part of the driveway. There was no sign of anyone.

Scanning the scene with binoculars gave no clue of danger. The cow was in the pasture, her udder swollen. He would have to take the time to milk her. Both she and the chickens needed feeding. The cow could graze in the pasture, but the chickens had only the feed and water Deni left when she came for the ammo. The little girl complicated everything and made the situation more dangerous.

He backed away from the clearing. She was still where he left her, playing with a twig. She smiled up at him when he came back.

"Okay," he said. "We have a little more walking to do. I need you to be quiet and not say anything or cry. Will you do that for me?"

She nodded.

"Good."

It took Nate more than an hour to work his way around the farm while staying in cover, searching every inch of the exterior of the house and barn for any sign that someone had been there since Deni. He stopped every ten feet or so to scan the ground for tracks and check the woods around him for movement. There was nothing, no sign anyone had been there.

Nate left her in the woods one more time and unlocked the front door. A quick search confirmed no one had been inside.

Nearing the pine stump, he left her sitting on, Nate said, "We can go on into my house now." He stopped in his tracks and jerked his head around in a panic. She was not where he left her.

He ran to the stump, eyes searching in desperation. "Little girl, where are you?"

Movement in thick brush twenty yards away prompted an automatic reflex. He snapped his rifle up, shouldered and ready to shoot. The movement was low. He kept the rifle's muzzle high.

When he saw blond hair, he forced his way through thorns. There she was, looking up at him, pointing. "Big doggie was here. He ran away when you came."

Nate looked where she was pointing. An area six feet long and four feet wide had been rooted up by a hog.

"How did you get through all those thorns?" Nate picked her up. "You don't have a scratch on you." His own hands were bleeding. "Must have crawled under it."

"I'm hungry," she said.

"Good. So am I, but I really wish you would tell me your name, because I don't like eating with strangers."

She tilted her head and gave him a look as if she were wondering if she should let her secret out. "Synthia."

"Synthia is your name?"

She nodded.

"That's a pretty name for a pretty girl." He carried her into the house. "My name is Nate." After putting her on a couch, he said, "I suppose you couldn't tell me if we're friends yet."

She yawned, squirmed until her feet were on the couch and she was on her back, and closed her eyes.

"I thought so," Nate whispered.

When Nate came back in to check on her after milking, feeding, and watering the cow, he found her still asleep. He then went to the barn to feed and water the chickens. While in the barn, he searched for several items. First, he grabbed a spool of insulated double-strand wire and six plates of glass twelve inches square. He took those items in the house. In Brian's bedroom, he opened a desk drawer and got out notebook paper and masking tape. He returned to the living room where he taped a sheet of paper on each plate of glass and stuffed the wire in his backpack and wrapped the glass in an extra shirt, putting it in the middle of his pack where it would be protected somewhat.

Searching the hall closet netted him a bag of wooden clothespins. He took those into his bedroom and got a steel box out of the closet where it sat on the floor. There, he found an eight-pound can of Bullseye gunpowder, the fastest burning powder he had. They did not have time to get all of his reloading supplies hidden in the woods and the powder was left behind. It was two-thirds full.

Next, he grabbed four rechargeable nine volt and four one and a half volt batteries that were still in the charger being powered by a solar panel on the roof of the house.

Nate checked on Synthia. She was still asleep. Then he headed back out to the barn with the clothespins and gunpowder.

Using a hand-cranked brace, he drilled holes in half a dozen clothespins where the ends touch each other under spring pressure. Then he got a small propane torch off a shelf, and soldered wire to the heads of a dozen eight-penny nails. When the nails cooled, he cut them so they would just go through the clothespins, leaving the heads on the inside. All it took was a small hammer and punch to tap them in all the way.

He found eight feet of two-inch pipe behind the barn and used a hacksaw to cut six eight-inch-long pieces. Back in the barn, he put his vice and pipe-threader to work, and then threaded both ends of every piece.

Where did Brian put that stuff?

Nate climbed a ladder and searched a high shelf. He finally found a cobweb-covered, stained cardboard box and took it down. When Brian was ten, his hobby was flying remote-controlled model planes. Nate grabbed all the glow plugs in the box and put them in a plastic bag, leaving it on the floor. Brian also played with rockets back then. Nate found what he was looking for and took the bag and other items to his workbench.

He counted four electric glow plugs and three rocket fuel igniters.

It took an hour to install the improvised igniters, or blasting caps. Finishing the job only took a few more minutes. He had three glow plugs left over.

Nate carried everything to the house. He emptied his pack and put the heavy pipe in the bottom along with the wire, putting the glass on top, still wrapped in a spare shirt.

I wish I had thought of this a long time ago. I could have made a couple of bigger bombs and blown that bridge and this would have been over the first night.

Synthia was still asleep when he walked by the couch and down the hall to Beth's room. All of Beth's clothes would be too big for her. They had to do anyway. He grabbed the most utilitarian items and stuffed them in his now full backpack. In the closet, he found two relatively new pairs of shoes, one, he put in the pack, the other he put beside pants, and a T-shirt.

Nate started out the door. He stopped to wipe his face before going down the hall. Seeing his little girl's clothes and giving them to Synthia meant more to him than he thought it would.

After taking a bath in the barn and changing clothes, Nate checked the tub of water he had filled with the hand pump in front of the house and left in the sun. He decided it was as warm as it was going to get.

"Time to wake up, Synthia." Nate shook her gently.

She opened her eyes. "I'm hungry."

"We'll eat in a few minutes, but first you've got to have a bath and clean clothes." Nate was more concerned with the disease that killed her grandmother than her hygiene. He wanted to reduce the danger of bringing the sickness to the others, and that was why he took the time to clean himself up. After her bath, he would bury her old clothes. Nate knew if she carried the disease, it would be inside her, but he couldn't even think of leaving her alone to die. What is the point of surviving if the price is your humanity? He knew Brian would agree.

She shivered in the water while Nate worked as fast as he could.

"Close your eyes. I have to wash your hair. This lye soap will sting."

Synthia kept watching him until some soap ran down her forehead into her eyes.

He had to pour a bucket over her head to stop her from crying. "Is that better now?"

She still cried.

"We're done." He soon had her dried off and dressed.

"We can eat now, if you stop crying." Nate carried her in the house and sat her at the table.

Nate heated water on the stove and reconstituted freeze-dried spaghetti. Some saltine crackers were left and a small packet of freeze-dried applesauce, which he put in a coffee cup with warm water.

"After you eat the spaghetti, you can have this whole cup of applesauce."

She stretched her body and leaned over to look into the cup. Her eyes flashed to him. "Is it good?"

"You bet it is, but I'm giving it all to you, because I feel bad about getting soap in your eyes."

She smiled. "That's okay. I always cry when I get soap in my eyes." She already had her face smeared with spaghetti sauce. "You're really not a mean man. At least, you're not mean to little girls." She shoveled another forkful into her mouth.

"No. I'm never mean to little girls. It's a rule I have."

Her bowl was nearly empty. "I'm not afraid of you."

"Good. There's no need to be." He refilled her bowel. "Eat some crackers. It's the closest thing to bread we've got."

Nate kept looking outside while she ate the applesauce. After checking out the front window and seeing no danger, he closed the shutter and then put his pack on and leaned his rifle against the table.

"Let me clean your face and then we'll go." Nate wet a rag and wiped the spaghetti sauce off. "There, now I can see you."

A rumble in the distance spurred Nate into action. He picked her up, grabbed his rifle, and ran for the front door. His hand shook as he fished a key out of his pocket and turned the deadbolt. The rumbling was getting closer. It sounded like several Harleys coming down his drive.

You've hurt her your last time. No victims today, bastards.

Nate ran around to the back of the house just as three men on Harleys rode up.

Chapter 14

Brian looked out the loophole. His mind did not see what his eyes were seeing. He was looking inward.

Deni noticed something on Brian's face when he turned to look down at a topographic chart he had in his hand. "Your father is okay."

Brian's eyes flashed to her. "You don't know any more than I do."

She came closer and put her left hand on his shoulder. Looking down at the map, she said, "The worst thing you can do is go after him. He wants you here—all of us here—so we will be safe."

Looking out the loophole again, Brian said, "He's out there alone."

"If anyone goes, it will be me." Deni put the palm of her hand on his face and turned him to her. "I'm the soldier. Your job is to protect our friends here."

"But I don't think you're well yet. You don't even know if you can shoot, or if you can walk very far."

Deni stepped back. "Well, in that case, why don't I just grab my pack and carbine and patrol the area and we'll both find out how far I can walk?"

Martha broke in. "It's too soon."

"You know," Deni put her hands up as if to tell them to back off, "I don't need anyone's permission." She bent over to pick up her pack. To steady herself, she had to put her hand against a wall. Everyone noticed.

"You're still dizzy, Deni." Martha sounded like she was talking to one of her children.

"I'm not going far," Deni sad. "It will be good for me."

Ben was sleeping after pulling a four-hour security shift. He got up from his sleeping bag on the floor. "Let's both go for a walk. I'm going stir crazy in this coffin."

"Don't call it that," Martha said.

Ben smiled at the tone of her voice. "We've all been cooped up in here for so long we're going to be at each other's throat soon. Let us go for a walk and have a look to see if anyone's been snooping around."

"Tomorrow a couple more can go on patrol," Brian said. "We need to know what's going on out there anyway." He looked out the loophole. "I want to check out the farm."

Ben and Martha gave each other a worried glance.

Deni shook her head but said nothing.

~~~~~~~~~~~~

Nate put Synthia under a wide oak that must have been more than one hundred years old. "Okay, little baby girl. I need you to sit here and do not go anywhere until I get back."

Synthia looked up at him suspiciously. "Where are you going?"

"I have to go shoot my rifle a few times. You may hear the shots, but I'm just going to test it."

She gave him an expression that told him she did not believe what he said.

"It will be a while, but I will be back. Just stay right here and do not walk away, not even a little. I promise I'll be back. And then we can go to the other house."

Her eyes rounded. "But if you don't come back."

"I will." Nate took his pack off and set it by her. "See, I'll have to come back for my stuff anyway. It's got my food and water in it."

She looked up at him, bewildered.

Nate got down on his knees and held her. She nearly disappeared in his massive arms. "I will be coming back for you, not my pack. I just want you to take care of it for a while. I won't be gone long." He stood. Okay?"

She nodded.

Nate ran for the house. He planned to waste no time on these killers.

He heard shooting before he was close enough to see the house. Keeping low and behind cover, Nate made his way closer until he could peer out from the edge of the tree line and across the bean field.

They were shooting the front door apart. Finding Nate's Grandfather had built doors too solid to kick down; their frustration forced them to waste bullets.

Two shot at the door while one kept watch with his carbine ready. The killers' three motorcycles stood in the front yard.

Nate adjusted the back sight on his rifle. It was an easy shot, but he had to be quick or the last man would have time to run for cover. If that happened, Nate would have to leave one of them alive. He was not going to leave Synthia alone the amount of time it would take to maneuver into position to kill him.

It took Nate two minutes to get into his natural point of aim and set up his shooting sling so he could shoot from prone. It took him two seconds to kill all three men.

After the last shot, Nate crawled deeper into the woods.

Working around behind the house and coming across to the driveway, Nate kept his rifle shouldered and ready. He looked down the drive and searched the woods on both sides while staying hid. They could have had a man over watching for security, and he was not just going to walk out into the front yard until he was sure there were no more killers around.

Evidently, this bunch had no military trained men among them. He found no sign of anyone else. Nate was beginning to think there were cliques within the larger group of killers, some military trained, others not. They probably just fell together, because they felt more secure in a large group.

Rushing to the motorbikes, he kick started one and rode it into the woods as far as he could before it got too thick for him to go farther. Then he ran back, rode another bike into the woods, and hid it.

Searching the bodies produced three AR15 carbines, some loose ammunition, seven thirty-round magazines, and one Browning 9mm pistol with one extra magazine. There was some money and personal items such as small knives, matches, and bloodstained wedding bands. He dropped the rings in the dirt. *You bastards cut these off your victims.* Nate carried the guns, ammunition, and knives into the woods and piled leaves over them.

Nate then ran into the barn and got a rope. Running to the dead men, he piled one on the other and tied them together. He left ten feet of slack in the rope when he tied the end to the back of the Harley.

One last look down the drive, and Nate slung his rifle across his back, jumped on the bike, and cranked it. Its engine roared, when he revved it up, but coughed when he let it idle. Nate managed to keep it running by twisting the throttle and never letting it idle down again. In first gear, he pulled the dead men across the field, flattening cornstalks that had already been picked clean of corn, and down to the river swamp.

These old Harleys have a lot of torque. Even with bad gas, it's pulling these bastards like a two-wheeled tractor. Nate didn't bother to look back at the dead men as he dragged them as far as he could into the swamp. The Harley finally got stuck in deep mud, so he got off and left it there. He used the rope to pull the bodies, one at a time, the rest of the way down to the river. He left them for alligator food and ran for Synthia.

Nate was out of breath when he reached the oak tree he left her under.

She was gone.

"Synthia!" Nate searched the area, his eyes flitting from one spot to another.

A crunch of leaves drew his attention. His eyes caught movement behind a bush, low to the ground.

"I'm here." Synthia came around the bush into view.

Nate rushed to her and picked her up.

"I heard guns, so I hid," she said.

"Okay. We have to go for another boat ride." Nate set her down long enough to put his pack on. He grabbed her and his rifle and took off for the river.

Neither of them spoke until they were in the canoe.

Nate paddled against the current. "I told you to stay where you were. I said you would hear me shooting, so that shouldn't have scared you."

Synthia gave him a stern, serious look. "I took care of your pack like you said. There it is." She kicked at it where Nate tied it to a strut for safety against loss.

Nate chuckled. "Yeah, okay. We don't need to get into a fuss about it. Why don't you lie down? It will be a while, and you might as well rest."

She squirmed until she was comfortable in the bottom of the canoe, yawned, took one last look at the treetops flowing over her where they hung out over the river, and closed her eyes.

The rugged features on Nate's face softened. *You scared the hell of out me.*

Synthia was still asleep when Nate turned into the mouth of the creek. The canoe was light on her end, even with Nate's pack in the middle, so the bow was nearly out of the water, but Nate's weight forced the rear of the canoe deep. When his end scraped across a submerged log, jolting them, Synthia woke. She seemed afraid at first. Her eyes flashed around, taking in what she could see from the bottom of the canoe. However, when she looked back and saw Nate, she rubbed her eyes and sat up, smiling.

"We'll be walking again soon," Nate said. "It won't be much farther after that."

They came around a sharp bend, startling an otter. It slid into the creek and took off, pushing a bow wave ahead of it.

Synthia pointed and started to stand.

"Hey. Get back down. You'll turn the canoe over or fall out." Nate pointed the canoe toward shore.

She ignored him. Standing on her knees, she held onto the bow gunnels, searching for the otter. "What was that?"

"An otter."

She looked over her left shoulder at Nate. "Where did it go?"

"Up the creek. It can swim faster than I can paddle. It's gone." He put the paddle down and rubbed his right arm.

Exercise seemed to be good for it. The numbness was fading. "Get back down. You can see plenty well enough while you are sitting."

She ignored him, too engrossed in this new world she was discovering. Her head could not be still, turning one way and then the other, her eyes drinking in the swamp jungle around her.

Nate deftly maneuvered around or over many logs. The creek narrowed as they made their way, and more logs and weeds choked the water flow.

A half mile further revealed another new creature she had never seen. A snapper turtle took off in the shallow water, leaving a cloud of mud in its wake. More than two feet across its back, it was one of the largest Nate had ever seen.

She giggled and pointed, looking back at Nate, as if to ask, if he had seen it.

"That was a big turtle, wasn't it?" He forgot to warn her to sit down.

She nodded, and then resumed searching the water, leaning over the bow.

Nate decided that was enough. He eased the canoe onto the bank where it slopped upward. It was muddy there, but seemed solid enough. Everywhere else, the creek had cut into the earth, leaving a drop-off one foot or more high.

"Sit down while I try to push the canoe further onto dry land." The water was only six inches deep, and Nate readied to push off from the bottom with his paddle.

As soon as she sat down again, he shoved. In less than five minutes, he had them both on dry land and the canoe hid by a rotted cypress stump, turned bottom side up to shed rain.

He lifted her. "You're getting heavier every time I pick you up."

"I'm getting bigger," she said, her arms around his neck.

"We have a little walk ahead of us, but we're almost there now. I could have paddled closer before we started walking, but I couldn't get you to stay sitting down. I was afraid you were going to turn the canoe over."

"I wanted to see."

Nate noticed she was still looking around for more animals. "Well, now you can see everything I can. Can't you, kiddo?"

Half an hour later, Nate slowed to hunting speed. A squirrel barked from a tall pine, telling him something had disturbed it. They were too far away to be the object of the squirrel's scolding. Now, he slowly lowered to his knees.

Synthia pointed. "Look."

"Sshh." Nate set her on her feet. Then he put his fingers to his lips and whispered in her ear. "Don't make any noise."

Her eyes grew wide. She nodded, looking around.

Nate whispered, "Do not move. Just sit here and be very still. I'll be back in a few minutes."

The look on her face compelled Nate to hold her for a second. "Everything is okay. No one is going to hurt you. Just be still. Don't move. I'll be back soon."

She nodded, her little chest heaving. She touched the knot on the back of her head, which was the result of her being thrown against a tree by one of the men who killed her parents.

Nate pulled her hand away from the gash. *Goddamn it. Little kids should not have to go through this.*

"Lie here behind this log," he whispered.

Nate moved away, flowing through the woods, his rifle ready.

There was no one, but there were two sets of tracks.

Nate examined them. One was smaller than the other was. He could tell they were moving slow, staying in cover. He noticed something about the smaller track that seemed familiar. Tension on his face eased.

After determining their direction of travel, Nate swung around, moving fast enough to get ahead of them. He had to hurry. Synthia would not wait long before wondering off.

~~~~~~~~~~

"I told you I heard something back there," Brian whispered.

"Best not to go looking for trouble," Ben said. "I think it was just the squirrel anyway."

Brian turned to scan their back trail. "It was no squirrel."

Nate watched from behind a thick hickory. "Brian, it's your long-lost father, don't shoot."

Brian swung around, shotgun at the low ready. Ben dove behind a limestone rock, and then peered over it, his shotgun shouldered.

"I'm coming over. Don't shoot me." Nate stepped out in the open.

Ben and Brian lowered their guns, a look of relief and surprise on their face.

"What took you so long?" Brian asked.

"Circumstances beyond my control," Nate said. "We don't have time for that now. I left a little girl back there and I have to get to her before she wonders off."

"A little girl?" Brian seemed more surprised by that information than finding his father in the woods. "Where did you get her?"

"They were selling children at a fruit stand on the side of the road."

Ben snickered. "Everything's okay around here. We're just out patrolling and stretching our legs."

"So, there's no one else around as far as you know?" Nate looked Brian over.

Brian shook his head.

"No one," Ben said. "Deni was with me earlier, but she got tired pretty fast. So I took Brian to finish patrolling the area."

"How is she?" Nate asked. "I was afraid she might never wake."

"She's okay." Brian's eyes lit up. "I mean she's not stupid or anything. I think she still has headaches and she's still dizzy sometimes. But she tries to hide it."

"Yeah. I think she'll be okay," Ben said.

"I wish she hadn't been hurt." Brian looked up at his father. "Her being a soldier, you would think she wouldn't be easy to shoot."

Nate walked closer and put his hand on Brian's shoulder, then knocked his hat off.

Brian picked it up and put it back on. "What I mean is with her training it must have been blind luck on their part."

"They're not all idiot thugs," Nate said. Some of them are military or ex-military, and some are probably just trying to survive in a lawless land. There are different types in that bunch. All fallen together, trying to survive. The problem is some of them are animals and many of the rest are just going along with the barbarity, holding their nose and stomach. I saw two who had seen more than they could stand. They parted ways with that bunch, headed into the swamp as fast as they could. As far as Deni getting shot goes, we have been kicking at rattlesnakes. You do that long enough, you're going to get bit. And don't ever think anyone is bulletproof."

"I don't. I guess I didn't say it right." Brian pointed over his shoulder. "I heard something back there." He looked at Ben. "And it was no squirrel."

"It was probably Synthia." Nate walked past them. "Come on. I don't want to leave her alone any longer than necessary. She saw her parents killed and has been through too much already. I don't want her to think I abandoned her."

Brian followed behind his father. "She doesn't know you well enough then."

Ben smiled while looking around, searching for danger, following behind Brian. "He does have a habit of taking in strays, doesn't he?"

"So far, I'm glad he did." Brian tried to see his father's reaction from behind. "But I don't have any idea what use a little girl is going to be to the group."

Nate just walked faster. He smiled but said nothing.

Chapter 15

"Admiring your handiwork?" Deni stood still while Nate held her hair out of the way so he could check her wound.

"Most of the scar is hidden by your hair." Nate stood back and looked away, averting his eyes. "I'm just glad you seem to be okay. There's no sign of any infection, and the stitches can come out in about a week."

"Does it hurt?" Brian asked.

"No," Nate said. He was grateful for the distraction. "You just snip them and pull 'em out with tweezers. Doesn't hurt at all."

Deni's eyes flashed from Brian's to Nate's. "You guys! Both of you feel sorry for me. And you, Nate, feel guilty. You didn't shoot me. You saved my life—and carried me miles. So stop it—both of you."

Martha placed a pot of reconstituted freeze-dried soup on a small table. "She's been dizzy, and I would bet her vision is blurred at times." Her eyes met Deni's. "She won't admit it, though."

"I'm getting better every day," Deni said. "There's nothing that can be done for me anyway. Everything that can be done has. And I am grateful to all of you. I am lucky to be alive."

"Dad was pissed when he brought you here," Brian said. "He didn't stay long, just took off to go kill more of the bastards."

"Brian…" The tone of Nate's voice changed.

"I can tell when you're pissed," Brian said, "and you were pissed that night. That's why I didn't even try to stop you."

"What happened at the bridge since you've been gone?" Ben asked.

Nate realized he was trying to change the subject.

Synthia stopped looking at a picture book with Tommy where they sat on a rolled up sleeping bag and listened in.

"Well." Nate opened a military surplus ammunition can and got out items to clean his rifle and pistol. "Synthia and I were in the house eating when three goons rode up on Harleys. I heard them coming, because of their loud mufflers, and we had time to run for the woods before they got down the driveway."

Caroline was cleaning clothes in a bucket of water from the hand pump. When she heard what Nate said, she stopped. "They're at the farm already?"

Carrie sat in a corner. She began to breathe faster as she waited to hear what Nate had to say.

"Only those three on bikes." Nate noticed Carrie's reaction. "I managed to destroy their bridge repairs and set them back several days. They won't be getting any four-wheeled vehicles across for a while." He glanced at Deni. "Deni may have told you they managed to get a few bikes across. I used one to get her to the farm when she was unconscious. Anyway, those three must have been scouting ahead. Maybe, they left the main group for good. Who knows? All I know is they were pumping bullets into my front door when I shot them. I hid the bikes in the woods and dumped the bodies in the river."

"Three more we don't have to worry about," Brian said. "How many more did you get at the bridge?"

"I don't know," Nate said. "A few, but there are still hundreds of them. We can't take them on face-to-face." Nate put his rifle down and walked over to Synthia. "But we're safe here. They will never find us."

Synthia stood and held her arms up.

Nate bent down and lifted her. She hugged his neck.

"Looks like I've got another little sis," Brian said.

Caroline spoke. "If they do find us here, it's not going to be fun."

"They don't have time to be walking around in the woods this far from nowhere," Nate said. "I still think they're running from someone. And that someone must be a large, well armed group of people."

"The Guard," Deni said. She rubbed her aching head. "Either the ANG or regular Army."

"Or the Marines," Nate added.

"Or vigilantes," Ben said. "Get enough common folk together and mad enough and they can be a force capable of dealing with even that bunch of killers."

Nate shrugged.

Caroline took Synthia out of Nate's arms. "I'll keep her calm. You need to finish cleaning your guns. You'll soon need them again."

Cindy had been listening while trying to sleep after pulling a four-hour security shift. "If it's the National Guard, your friend, Mel, may be with them."

"That would be great," Brian said. "But I doubt he's still alive."

Nate went back to field stripping his rifle so he could clean it. "I don't think they'll find this place. It's the farm that I'm worried about." He looked at the others and settled his gaze on Brian. "I'm not giving up on the farm yet. They're not going to raid it without taking more casualties. Mel's supplies won't last forever. We need that farm to feed ourselves."

"I'm ready for another fight," Deni said.

Brian stood between her and Nate. "No you're not. You need more time. I doubt you could even walk to the farm, much less the bridge." He turned to his father. "Ben or me would be more help than her. She's not ready yet."

Nate gave him a hard look.

Brian looked apologetic. "Mr. Neely insisted I call him Ben."

"Yes I did," Ben said. "And I also think Deni is not ready to go back out there and fight those bastards. I'll go."

"Three people have a lot better chance than two," Brian said.

"Well." Nate pushed a cleaning rod down his rifle's barrel. "We could slow them down by cutting trees across the road. We have to hurry though. It will take time and the more places we drop trees, the better. Space them a mile or so apart."

"Only the tallest pines would work," Brian said. "And it will take one from each side of the road to reach all the way across even then."

Nate put a clean patch on the rod. "And you two will have to use the two-man crosscut saw. We don't have any gas left for the chainsaw. You're going to have to work fast. In fact, we need to leave as soon as possible."

"You need to rest first," Brian said.

"If we're going to do it, we need to do it now. They're coming as soon as that bridge is repaired again." Nate was already putting his cleaned rifle back together. "We might just have enough time—if we hurry." He slammed a fresh magazine in, pulled the bolt back, and released it, loading the chamber.

"Just what are you going to be doing while Brian and I are cutting trees down?" Ben asked.

Nate unloaded his revolver and started cleaning it. "Sniping at them when they stop to remove the trees. I can double the time it takes for them to get going again if I kill one or two at each roadblock."

"They will get wise to that fast and send people out in the woods on both sides of the road," Ben said.

"Sure they will. That's why I'm only going to be able to kill one or two, maybe three, at each roadblock." Nate pushed a patch on the end of a cleaning rod into all six cylinders of his revolver, one at a time. "You guys will be doing all the work. I will have it easy."

Brian snickered. "Yeah, right. I think I'd rather cut down trees than get shot at." He grabbed his backpack. Then he pumped water into a pitcher so he could fill all of his canteens. "Ben, bring your canteens over here and I'll fill them."

Martha and Cindy were already selecting packages of freeze-dried food they could take with them.

When Brian grabbed his shotgun, Nate said, "Take your rifle this time. And plenty of ammo."

Brian nodded and stuffed his pockets with 30/30 rounds. "I guess you think I might get to shoot down the road some too."

Nate reloaded his cleaned revolver. "Before this is over, we're all going to be sick of shooting."

Caroline, who had been standing by Carrie, holding Synthia, spoke up. "I can push on one end of that saw."

"You don't push it, you pull it," Brian said.

"Whatever." Caroline kept her eyes on Nate. "Pull it then. I can help cut trees while one of you rests or stands guard."

"With your injuries...are you sure you can walk far?" Martha asked.

"I'm sure I can walk as far and fast as Ben." Caroline searched Nate's face. Nate would be the one to decide.

Nate loaded more ammunition and food in his pack. Brian handed him full canteens and Nate put them in also. When Nate stood and put the pack on. He said, "I don't think you should go."

"Why not?" Caroline asked.

Nate thought for a moment. "I need to talk to you alone." He grabbed his rifle and opened the door.

Caroline followed him outside. "What?"

Nate closed the door. He spoke low so the others could not hear. "Several times I have woken in the middle of the night to find you standing over Brian. What is that about?"

Caroline looked Nate in the eye, though it was dark and they could not see each other very well. "I would never hurt Brian."

"That's reassuring. But it does not answer my question." Nate heard her sigh in the dark.

"It's Carrie," Caroline said. "She keeps asking me to check on him."

"What? Why?"

"She had a younger brother. Brian reminds her of him." Caroline stopped talking.

"So?"

"She has opened up to me a little. A lot more than she has the rest of you, anyway." Caroline hesitated. "She made me promise not to tell anyone. So, please don't let her know I said anything."

"I won't, but you need to explain a lot better than you have so far."

"She has it in her head you're going to abuse Brian. And—"

"What!" Nate's voice was loud enough those inside heard.

"I know. It's crazy. If anything you're…I'm sorry. Her father killed her brother a couple years ago. She was in a foster home when the plague hit, and like I said, Brian reminds her of her brother. I told her a hundred times, but…she's been through a lot."

"Both of you have."

"You have to believe me. I would never hurt anyone here. And I don't think Carrie would either."

"But you can't be certain of that."

"No, but I know I would never…"

"Okay." Nate opened the door. He stood aside and waited for Caroline to walk inside.

Everyone but Tommy and Synthia was standing in silence, waiting for them to return.

Nate cleared his throat. "We need all the help we can get. Caroline wants to go, so she's coming with us."

Caroline smiled. "Good."

"Do you think you could find your way back here if anything happens to the rest of us?" Ben asked.

Caroline blinked and seemed to be thinking. "Just don't let them take me alive. I don't intend to come back without you."

Brian pulled items out of a pile until he found a backpack and a two-quart canteen. He filled the canteen while Martha loaded the pack with food.

Caroline stuffed the canteen in and put the pack on. She found the shoulder straps were adjusted too long.

Brian hesitated, and then adjusted them for her. "That okay?"

Caroline nodded. It was the first time she had let a male touch her since Nate cut the chain off her wrists before Martha and Cindy cleaned her wounds.

Brian stepped back. "You're just as much a part of this group as any one of us." He shook his head. "No one is ever going to hurt you again."

Nate walked over to the rack where extra carbines hung and looked over an AR15. He handed it and a loaded magazine to Caroline. "Load it."

She timidly slid the magazine in.

"Take it back out," Nate said. "Load it again, but this time, slam it in. You won't hurt it. You need to make sure you seat it all the way home."

She did as he said, taking little time to find the release button.

"Now make sure it's on safe, and then load the chamber. You've seen us do it."

Caroline turned the carbine so she could read where the "S" and "F" was, flipping the safety switch so safe. Then she pulled the bolt back all the way and let it go. She kept the muzzle pointed up.

"Now it's ready to go," Nate said. "All you have to do is flip the safety lever with your thumb, aim, and fire by pulling the trigger. Never point it at anyone you do not want to kill." He pointed at the door where no one was near. "Keep you trigger finger straight against the receiver and away from the trigger. Aim at the door by looking through the back sight and centering the front sight in the little peephole."

Caroline shouldered it and aimed. "I've shot a gun before. I'm no crack shot, though."

"You don't have to be," Nate said. "A man is a big target all the way out past one hundred yards. The main thing is to always look through that back sight and use the front sight. Center it in the peephole and on a man's chest. Then squeeze the trigger. Keep your head and make sure of your target." He stuffed two more magazines in side pockets on her pack. "No man can get his hands on you as long as you have that in your hands and you keep your head. You've got ninety rounds. Make them count and they'll not be wanting to get close to you."

She nodded. "I can carry more."

Nate smiled. He stuffed two more magazines in her pack.

Ben spoke up. "Maybe Brian should take an AR too. I'll stick with my shotgun myself."

"No," Brian said, "I'm used to my lever-action. I can do pretty well with it."

"He can hit a running buck or a charging boar," Nate said. "It's not as fast as a semi auto, but it's hits that count." He looked around at everyone. "We should go now. We'll have to go to the farm and get the saw on the way."

Nate started out the door.

Synthia ran grabbing Nate's legs and cried, "Don't go." She looked up at him, her eyes filled with terror.

"The people here will take care of you." Nate patted her back. "Don't cry. I'll be back soon."

Cindy pulled her away and picked her up. "He will be back, Synthia. They all will."

Synthia cried.

Tommy reached up and touched Synthia's leg. She slapped at him. He grabbed her hand and held it. "Don't be afraid."

Nate was the last one out. "Bolt this door," he said.

Martha nodded. "Take care."

Deni rushed to Nate and held him. "You should let me go."

Nate pushed her away. "Not this time."

They left with the sound of Synthia's wailing in their ears, fading as it gave way to distance.

~~~~~~~~~~

Nate looked across his field, staying behind cover. "That place means more to me every day we spend in that damn bunker." There didn't seem to be anyone around. The house was untouched. "I'll go get the saw. Brian, you keep watch with your rifle."

"It's two hundred yards. I can't do much good with my shotgun from here," Ben said.

"I guess you and Caroline should come with me and feed and water the chickens, while I do the same with the cow," Nate said. "Brian can keep them off us if some of them show up. We need to hurry though. Got to get to work on the road as soon as possible."

"Dad," Brian said, "you ever think about how if everyone would just work on taking care of themselves and helping one another rather than stealing stuff we would all be better off? I mean. As bad as it is, we could get by okay if it wasn't for those who act like animals."

Nate stood. "I think about that all the time, Brian. Keep your eyes open."

Caroline said, "If they come, don't think twice about killing them. Some men are animals. They must be killed before they hurt more people. There *is* a difference between animals and people. Those that are coming are animals."

Ben, Caroline, and Nate ran for the house. When they got to the barn, Nate opened one of the double doors and started filling the wheelbarrow with hay.

Ben grabbed a bucket and poured feed from a bag for the chickens. He handed it to Caroline, who ran to the coop and filled a feeding trough, then poured the rest out on the ground.

When Ben ran past Nate who was looking for the saw, he yelled over his shoulder, "You're putting a lot of responsibility on Brian."

"I have no choice." Nate leaned the saw against the barn wall outside. I wish it were not so, but it is."

"Yeah, I know, but killing is not going to be easy at his age." Ben raised his voice so Nate could hear him as he pumped water.

Nate stopped by the pump on the way to the pasture. He had hay stacked high on the wheelbarrow. "This lawlessness is going to last years. At first, I thought it would be better by now. I was wrong. There's more killing to come if we're going to survive long enough to see this country rebuild. And I'm more worried about him getting shot than him having to live with killing a man."

"By the time you get back," Ben said, "I'll have water for you to bring to the cow."

Caroline took one of the full buckets and hurried back into the barn as fast as her damaged body would allow her. The chickens needed more water.

Nate took two loads of hay out to the pasture and rushed back, stopping at the pump.

Ben but four buckets of water in the wheelbarrow. "I'll take this out there. You two grab the saw and head back to Brian. You can do more to protect me over there with your rifles anyway."

Nate nodded and headed for the woods.

Caroline followed. She kept looking toward the driveway.

Nate jumped over the windfall Brian was using for cover and dropped to his knees beside him. "Keep your eyes on the driveway," Nate told Brian. "That's where trouble is most likely to come from. I'll watch the far tree line."

Caroline had not reached them yet. She limped along as fast as possible.

Brian had his rifle shouldered, resting on the log. "I don't want you worrying about me. I promise I'll be careful. You keep your mind on what you have to do when it starts."

Nate cleared his throat. "We'll talk more about how we're going to do this when we start building the first roadblock. I want to explain why I'm putting you at risk—what has changed."

"I know what has changed," Brian said. "You have more people to take care of now. It's not just us. We need that farm to feed everyone. Mel's stuff won't last long with so many mouths to feed."

Nate's chest rose and held. He looked at his son, his eyes bright.

"Ben's got the wheelbarrow in the barn and the barn door closed," Caroline said. She got down beside them, wincing in pain.

"You okay?" Nate asked.

"I'm fine," she said. "If I can't go on, I'll let you know. Just leave me and keep going. At the very least, I can watch your back from wherever I have to stop."

All three watched for trouble as Ben ran toward them.

Ben stepped over the log, huffing. He picked up the long saw and looked at the others. "Well, let's get this show on the road."

Nate led them into the woods.

~~~~~~~~~~~~

"We're about eight miles from the bridge," Nate said, "and this pine tree is about as tall as they get. Might as well cut this one and that one on the other side. Together, they'll reach all the way across." He grabbed the saw out of Ben's hands. "Let me show you how to do it so you can control the direction a tree falls."

"You already showed me where to make the first cut, so I might as well take the other end of the saw this time so they can watch," Brian said.

The pine tree was three feet across, but they were not tired yet and had the tree down and across the road in fifteen minutes.

Ben nodded. "So you cut a wedge out first. You cut it nearly halfway across the trunk and pointing in the direction you want the tree to fall. Then you make the cut on the back a little higher."

Caroline looked on, taking in the information.

"That's it," Nate said. "Just be careful you don't cut too far with the first and second cut when you're cutting out the wedge. The tree can start to lean before you're ready and pin the saw in. If that happens, you're through. You'll never get the saw back out unless you're very lucky. Also, don't choose a tree that's leaning away from the road. It will likely fall the wrong way no matter what you do, and if the tree is already leaning heavily toward the road, just cut the back and forget about the wedge. It will fall the way it's leaning anyway."

"On the way here," Brian said, "I saw where rain washed the road out partway. In a couple places, there was a big tree handy on the far side of the road. What I mean is, we can cut that tree and let the washout do the rest of our work on that side of the road."

Nate nodded. "Good. That will give you enough extra time to build a few more roadblocks."

Ben took the saw out of Nate's hands. "Time to cut the other tree."

Nate turned to Brian and Caroline. "You two over watch from here."

They took off on a run, crossing the road and disappearing into the woods.

It was a smaller tree than the first, and Nate and Ben had it down in less than ten minutes. It fell across the road, the two trees' tops overlapping in the middle.

"Perfect," Nate said.

They ran back to Brian and Caroline. This time they were behind concealment partway because of the downed trees.

"There's a tree big enough right over there," Brian said. He pointed a quarter mile down the road. "There's no reason why the second one can't be close enough we can help you if there's trouble."

Nate looked down the road toward the bridge. "Okay. That's about the right range for me to set up anyway." He gave Brian and Ben both a stern look, as was his habit when he was serious. "But after that, the roadblocks will be a mile or more apart."

"I'll see to it," Ben said.

They started walking. "Caroline and I will cut the next one," Nate said. "You three will have lead-heavy arms by the time this day is over. And tomorrow will be even worse."

"Then you'll set up for sniping," Brian added.

"Yes," Nate said. "All I can do is slow them down and kill a small number."

"This is really a desperate move," Ben said.

Nate stopped walking. The others stopped also.

"You're right, Ben," Nate said. "If the people chasing them don't show up in time, those killers will still get to the farm. There is no way we can stop them. All we're doing is slowing them down."

"We could get lucky and they run out of gas for their chainsaws," Brian said. He looked away. "Yeah, I know: We can't rely on luck."

"In a way, I am relying on luck. It's all we've got left," Nate said.

Everyone listened to what he had to say.

"The chance of the US Cavalry riding around the bend with bugles trumpeting like an old movie is slim to none." He looked back at the others. "But it's all we have. And this last desperate effort is my way of telling those bastards if they beat me it won't be because I gave up."

Ben nodded. "They've already paid a price, but we will extract more blood before they take what we've worked all summer and you and Brian have worked all your life for."

Caroline looked down the road. "The more we kill now the fewer people they hurt later." She blinked. "Carrie will never be the same. I'll never be the same." Hate showed on her face. "And those coming now are the same kind."

Chapter 16

Nate shot the one standing on the hood of a pickup. He was looking around with binoculars, searching the tree line on each side of the road. The range was five hundred yards. They had not gotten their chainsaws cranked yet, but one was already working on smaller limbs near the top of the downed trees with an ax. The sun had risen, but the day was less than an hour old.

There was a frenzy of activity with Nate's first shot. Men streamed into the woods by the dozen. They knew someone with a rifle would be waiting and had already vacated the vehicles and lain down in the ditch on both sides of the road, ready to shoot. Nate planned to pick off the ones too stupid to stay behind cover.

Nate quickly killed two more and then took off on a run. He had set up something he had told none of the others about and needed time to get into position before the killers cleared the trees out of the way.

They were coming, slow, and careful, painted on their right side by the midmorning sun. The ground was still wet from a late night rain, and mist was just starting to rise with the growing heat of the day.

Nate watched them come around a curve in the dirt road. Four men walked ahead, looking for tire hazards. *So, the spikes Deni and I placed must have worked.* A flatbed truck led the long train of a ragged collection of vehicles, mostly pickups and larger trucks. There were no motorcycles. The flatbed truck in the lead overflowed with men, all pointing rifles outward.

Nate was gratified of the obvious results of his earlier work. *They don't know what to expect next. Good. Fear is slowing them down as much as the roadblocks.*

Nate aimed for a patch of white ten feet high in a pine tree four hundred yards from where he lay. It was one of the glass plates with white paper taped to it. Wire ran from nails on a clothespin clipped to the glass plate to a nine-volt battery, and then to one of the pipe bombs that were buried where they would have to drive on the near side of the road to avoid a deep rain-cut gully. The only thing keeping the nails apart and thus preventing the electrical circuit from igniting the bomb was the glass.

From the prone position and in a tight shooting sling, Nate sharpened his sight picture and held his breath.

He squeezed the trigger when the flatbed truck passed over the pipe bomb.

None of the killers heard his shot. The explosion overpowered all sound and deafened them, leaving their ears ringing.

There was no time to look at his handiwork. Nate aimed at another square of white in a tree, one hundred yards farther than the first, just before the curve in the dirt road. He pulled the trigger and another explosion shook the ground. Even where Nate was lying, he could feel the shock wave, though it was not as strong as he had felt in combat. His bombs were not made with military explosives and so they were not as powerful as what he was used to. He wished he had some C4 and blasting caps, but had to make do with what he had.

Nate took a second to check the results. The pickup was still upright, but it was billowing black smoke. Bodies were hanging over the truck's side. Two tires were burning on one side and the windshield shattered. He checked the first truck and found it too in flames. Bodies lay on the flatbed and the road. The road was blotched red in more places than he cared to count. A few men lay dying; others struggled to push up from the ground and crawl or stand.

Several more met death delivered by a bullet from Nate's rifle. Not wanting to push his luck too far, Nate crawled into the woods. He could hear their blind firing the first quarter mile as he ran.

Nate did not think he would have enough time to set up another bomb or two before the next roadblock, so he ran past that one and set up nearly a mile farther down the road.

He was wrong. It took them several hours to clear the flatbed truck and the pickup out of the way. Other vehicles were damaged from fragments of metal also. When they finally were able to move again, they traveled even slower than before. Despite their losses, they had more men than room in their dwindling number of stolen vehicles, because many of the trucks were loaded with stolen supplies, so more had to walk.

The sun was starting to fall in the west by the time Nate saw them again.

There was a reason they were traveling slower and Nate knew what that reason was. Men were in the woods, traveling on both sides of the road and were probably half a mile ahead of the caravan. A man cannot walk as fast in thick woods as he can down a road. The need to allow those patrolling both sides of the road to keep ahead had slowed the entire entourage.

Their woodsmanship was not so great, and they were not traveling quiet the way Nate was trained to patrol. Nate could hear them coming as he headed deeper into the woods.

He let them pass.

When the woods became quiet, Nate eased back to the edge of the woods and lay down. At his shot, another explosion resulted, and another pickup went up in flames. He took off at top speed and headed deep into the woods, swinging around to avoid the patrols and get ahead of them again.

Out of breath from a two-mile jog through thick woods, Nate buried another bomb, this one on the edge of the road where they were less likely to notice the different colored dirt left by his digging. He ran the wire to a nearby tree, burying it with dirt by the road and leaves farther back into the woods. He then placed another glass plate high enough that he could see it at extreme rifle range. It could not be seen by anyone until they had passed the tree, by then it would be too late. He clipped the clothespin on the edge of the glass and tied the wires to the leads he had soldered on the nail heads. Then he climbed down, careful not to snag the wire and pull the clothespin off the glass.

Nate settled into a hiding place seven hundred yards from the white spot in the tree. He could see the tree from that distance, but not the white square. *If Ben, Brian, and*

Caroline have been working as hard as they could, they probably have built about six roadblocks by now, maybe seven. He glassed the road with his binoculars.

Nothing.

A glance at the sun told Nate there might be enough time for one more bomb after this one, before darkness made it impossible to see the white paper in a tree. There are other ways to trigger a bomb, but he did not have enough wire for most of those methods.

He came up with another plan. Working as fast as possible, Nate stretched wire across twenty yards at waist level, starting just back from the road, going deeper into the woods. On one end, was the battery and bomb, on the other, a small twig clipped between the jaws of a clothespin. The clothespin was tied to a tree. If someone walked into the wire, it would pull the twig out of the clothespin, completing the circuit and igniting the powder in the bomb.

Time to get out of the patrol's way.

Back from the road one hundred yards, Nate listened for any sign of movement in the woods. He heard none. He did hear the explosion and the screams afterward.

Nate had set the woods bomb father down the road, so he knew most of the caravan was past the roadside bomb, more important to him, he knew the patrol had passed also.

In ten minutes, Nate was lying prone, close enough to the road to see, and aiming for the white square. The caravan had stopped and most of the men had vacated the vehicles. There was a large gathering on the right side of the road—too far from his bomb. However, there was a smaller crowd on the left side and well within the kill zone. He squeezed the trigger. The carnage was instant and horrible.

Nate was heading into the woods before the echo faded.

Working feverously in the last moments of the dying afternoon, Nate set another bomb. This one was designed to be tripped by those removing one of the trees Brian and friends had cut across the road. He set the bomb itself back from the roadblock so it would damage a vehicle as well as wound men. He filled his boonie hat with dry sand and covered the wires with it, pouring it out in a stream as he walked along. It took four hatfuls to do the job.

~~~~~~~~~~~~~

"I heard something," Brian whispered.

Ben and Caroline stopped chewing. They were eating while Brian provided security.

Everyone searched the dark woods with their eyes, keeping all senses sharp, ready for trouble.

"Don't shoot. It's your father." Nate came closer and materialized out of the dark. "I'm so tired I can't even sneak up on you guys."

"Are you okay?" Brian asked.

"Not a scratch." Nate sat on a log, bending backwards, stretching his aching back muscles.

"We heard explosions," Ben said.

"That was my bombs. They're at least two dozen short of men compared to yesterday." Nate opened a canteen and put it to his mouth. The dull rumble of an explosion from miles down the road got everyone's attention. Nate stopped drinking. "That would be my last one."

"Where in the hell did you get the bombs?" Brian asked.

Nate put his canteen down. "Made them. There's no time to explain how. I destroyed a few of their trucks too." Nate looked up at them. They stood looking back in the dark. All he could see was their silhouette. "They're going to catch up with us if you guys don't get busy cutting trees."

"We stopped to eat," Brian said. "They did that is. I was pulling security. I haven't eaten yet."

Nate got out a package of food. "Well, stop jabbering and eat. I'll man the other end of the saw when you're done."

"What do you think they're up to?" Ben asked. "They have to be reacting to your tactics."

"They are sending killer teams farther down the road than before." Nate poured water in a plastic package of powdered soup. "We have to put down a couple roadblocks pronto and get some miles between us and them."

The saw was leaning again a tree near Caroline. She reached over and grabbed it. "We have a big ponderosa pine picked out right over there."

Brian said, "Let's get started."

"You haven't eaten yet," Ben said. "Wait a minute and I'll go with her." He gulped down his food.

"Be careful," Nate said. "They might be closer than I think. Don't just saunter out there like you're on a Sunday stroll."

"Right." Ben headed for the road with Caroline following, his shotgun ready.

Nate took a quick drink to clear his throat. "Brian and I will be there in a few minutes."

Brian leaned against a tree, eating spaghetti out of a plastic pouch. "Bombs? You're full of surprises. Why didn't you show me how to make bombs a long time ago?"

"No way." Nate shook his head in the dark. "It's a felony to even play with explosives without federal permits. That stuff is too dangerous for a boy your age anyway. I would never have made bombs under normal circumstances."

"Dangerous?" Brian asked. "What do you call what we're doing? They could be here any time, and I can't even see my rifle sights in this dark. At least you have the Aimpoint on your rifle."

"I felt you were right when you said you are better off with a carbine you're used to. Otherwise, I would have had you take one of the ARs."

"If we get back, I want to practice with one of the full auto M4s." Brian threw his empty food pouch down.

"No. You don't need a full auto weapon. It takes a lot of training and practice to handle one properly." Nate finished eating. He picked Brian's litter up and put it under a rotten log along with his and the pouches left by Ben and Caroline.

"Why did you do that?" Brian watched. "They will know we've been here because of the roadblock."

"Force of habit. It's best not to leave any clues behind for the enemy. They can determine our number and the fact we have freeze-dried supplies. The less they know about us the better."

"You want them to think we're going hungry?" Brian asked.

"I don't want them knowing a damn thing about us. Just learning we have freeze-dried food may encourage them to raid our farm, looking for a big cache of food, instead of passing on by."

"You think they'll do that? I mean go on by the farm."

Nate walked toward the road. "I have no way of knowing. That's the problem. If we knew for sure they would go on by, we could stop all this and wish them a fast trip out of this county."

"Yeah," Brian said as he followed his father.

"And those three gang bangers on Harleys didn't go on by," Nate added.

"Yeah," Brian said. "We can't chance it."

"Brian, you know we can't stop them, just slow them down."

"Maybe the cavalry *will* come around the bend. If not, at least they will know how we feel about them trespassing on our land and stealing our stuff."

They could hear the others sawing, as they approached.

"I'm afraid they may have revenge on their mind now," Nate said. "If the cavalry *doesn't* show up in time, our farm is gone. And we better not be there when they arrive."

Brian stopped walking. "What are we going to do if we lose everything but Mel's place?"

Ben and Caroline stopped sawing.

"We can still farm the land," Ben said. "Nate made sure we put away those seeds and buried them in jars. So we can plant another crop."

"I guess we can get by." Brian sounded defeated. "It will not be fun pulling that old plow of Grandpa's."

"What plow?" Ben asked.

Nate answered. "I buried it just before we met, when Brian and I were planning on moving to Mel's bunker, because we didn't have enough people to guard the farm until you and your family came along. I put it in one of those large, heavy plastic contractor's garbage bags before burying it, so I doubt it's even rusted much."

"Oh." Ben pulled the saw away from the tree. "Stand back, Caroline. This things about to fall."

Groaning from splitting wood told them all Ben was right. The three-foot-wide pine fell two thirds of the way across the road.

Nate used his binoculars to glass the road in both directions. He could see better in the dark with his binoculars because of their light gathering capacity. "Okay, stay low and close to the tree. It will hide our silhouette and provide cover on one side."

Been led the way. Caroline followed, then Brian. They all bent over as they walked.

Nate caught movement down the road. It was in the opposite direction from where they were expecting trouble. "On your bellies!"

Everyone got down, their heads swiveling, searching for trouble.

A vehicle of some kind was coming from the direction of the farm with no headlights on. All they could see was a shape in the dark. The sound of an engine running roughly came to their ears and grew louder. Either the muffler was rusted out, or it had no muffler at all.

"Stay low and roll over the log." Nate's voice did not mask his worry.

They all were on the other side in less than a second.

"Crawl back this way," Nate whispered.

The coughing, spitting, and rattling of the engine grew louder.

Everyone followed Nate as he crawled back to where they came from, keeping behind the tree trunk. When they got far enough into the woods, everyone stood.

Nate used his binoculars to scan the road in both directions. "I don't see anyone else, just that one car."

Ben let out a lung full of air. "Where the hell did they come from?"

"I doubt they're with the others," Brian said.

Nate lowered his binoculars. "I doubt that too. I'm wondering how they got that car past the ditch I cut across the road and the mound of dirt beside it. There hasn't been time enough since we were there for them to have filled that ditch in with shovels unless there's a lot more than a car full of them."

Caroline stood in the dark and said nothing.

Brian spoke. "I think we should get away from this tree we cut down. Move down the road, closer to the farm."

"Yeah." Nate spoke under his breath. He was ready to do just that. "Keep spaced apart some but don't get separated from me. Stay as quiet as possible. If any shooting starts, hit the dirt. Listen for my commands and do what I say."

They headed deeper into the woods. All were expecting trouble.

Chapter 17

Nate heard music and singing. He stood in the dark and could not believe his ears.

He had led the others in a wide arc to avoid the new arrivals. However, Nate did not walk far enough before heading back to the road. This gang was much larger than he thought. He realized it must include hundreds of vehicles. They were still too far from the road to see anything, but they could hear.

The others moved closer.

"Sounds like they're having a party." Brian sounded incredulous.

"Yeah. There's a hell of a lot of them too," Ben said. "They sound drunk."

Caroline breathed fast and loud. "We should go back to the bunker. There are too many of them."

Nate pulled his compass out of the top of his shirt where it hung from a string around his neck. "You guys, sit tight and stay alert. I want to learn more about this bunch of music lovers before we start moving again. We have to cross the road to get home, and I want to know what we're up against. I'll be back in about fifteen minutes."

The glow of many fires lit the scene that Nate watched from the edge of woods. He bent over low and crept down an overgrown ditch that paralleled the dirt road to get a better look. Two dozen people gathered around a big truck, each had a bottle or can in their hand. *I don't believe it.* Nate shook his head. It was a beer delivery truck, its company logo only half-legible under a thick layer of grime. Everyone enjoyed a warm beer in the hot night. Others were boiling a big pot of corn on the cob right in the middle of the road. Both men and women, even a few children, were lined up, waiting for their turn to pile food on their plate. A boy about Brian's age was staggering around, trying to dance to the music, with a bottle swinging in his hand. One pickup had a tailgate loaded with Mason jars filled with vegetables. Nate's suspicion that their big meal was compliments of his farm was confirmed, when he saw tools from the barn on one truck parked near a fire with its tailgate open, and three chickens on a long spit, over a smaller fire near the pot of corn. A teenage girl rotated it slowly.

Nate trained his binoculars farther down the road and saw the form of a cow in the back of a two-ton truck. Farther back but still in the light of the fires, there was the long trailer he took off the men who had captured and tortured Caroline and Carrie. All the barrels of diesel fuel were on it.

Shit!

His blood surged when he thought of those who depended on that farm, depended on him. No fresh milk for Tommy and Synthia. No eggs for breakfast. All the food they had canned and stored away gone. An entire summer's work; an entire growing season lost. Many of their farming tools gone. More than likely the home stripped and burned to the ground.

He had tried so hard to take care of his little group. He was Brian's father. He had failed him. Failed them all. Not since his wife and daughter died, had he felt so low.

Then, there was nothing to hate. You can't hate a disease. He looked through his binoculars again. There were no small children, at least none he could see, but there were children from eleven or so up. His urge to shoot into the crowd and kill as many as he could cooled.

Nate backed away, wondering how he was going to tell the others.

~~~~~~~~~~

"I feel like killing somebody," Ben said. "All that work—and we're still going to go hungry anyway."

Caroline held the carbine Nate gave her tighter. "What do you expect? The world is full of assholes. They're called men."

"Jeez." Brian shook his head and said, "My father is a man. What has he done to you?"

"There are a few exceptions." Caroline turned away and looked into the dark woods.

Brian shook his head again.

"Well, there's no point in risking ourselves now. There is nothing to fight for." Nate headed north so they could get past the mob on the road and cross over.

Nothing was said for more than an hour.

When they were at the road again, Nate scanned both directions with his binoculars. He tried to penetrate the dark and seek out any danger. He saw no sign of people. What he did see was a dip in the road. He backed away, deeper into the woods, and headed down the road toward the low spot.

Nate left the others in the woods and took another look. He realized the low place would hide them only at longer distance. Anyone within one hundred yards, could see them even if they kept bent over as they crossed. He did not think anyone was within miles of them, but it made him nervous.

A hill, just seventy-five yards north, made it impossible to see if there was danger farther down the road. Nate went back to the others. "Stay here while I check the other side of that hill. Not likely to be anyone, but I'll check anyway."

"Okay," Brian said.

The other two just nodded in the dark.

Nate glassed the dirt road from the crest of the hill. He didn't see anything, so he backed down the slope and started for the woods. A sound he could not believe he was hearing, froze him in his tracks. Just as he hit the dirt, a helicopter flew over low and fast. After waiting to see if more helicopters were coming and hearing none, he got up and ran into the woods.

Heavy machinegun fire erupted.

Nate ran, heading back to the others. Sporadic rifle fire came from down the road, to be drowned out by some more heavy machinegun fire.

Nate bulled through brush until he arrived out of breath.

"What the hell is going on?" Ben asked.

In the distance, they could hear the helicopter's blades chopping the air as it turned and maneuvered for another strafing run.

The ground reverberated, a dull rumble rolled over them. Fuel tanks in vehicles and the drums of diesel fuel were exploding. Even at such a long distance, flashes of light, glaring orange and red, ruined their night vision. They stood, blinking.

Nate thought he could hear screaming, but wondered if he was not imagining it. He had seen civilians, women, and children, slaughtered from the air before.

"Looks like a lone military chopper is attacking the partiers." Nate looked to the north, expecting more helicopters. "It appeared to be an old Huey. Damn things are antiques, but they still fly. With enough maintenance, you can keep aircraft going forever. Those Hueys are tough. Probably the more advanced aircraft have been grounded for lack of spare parts."

"The Guard?" Brian searched the sky.

"Who cares, as long as they kill the bastards," Caroline said.

Nate looked at her, seeing little in the dark and quietly said, "There are children in that group."

She said nothing.

"If it's the Guard, they must have orders to get really tough on the gangs of killers and looters. How do they even know who they're killing?" Brian looked at his father's form in the dark.

"You're right," Nate said. "But they probably have been following their trail of destruction and death. So they are pretty certain they have a gang of brigands down there. Still, under normal circumstances, no chopper crew would be given the green light to attack civilians like that." He did not speak for several seconds and then said, "The first sign of any government—and this is what we see. What a bad omen. Things must be pretty damn crazy out there."

"Things haven't been so sane where I've been either," Caroline said.

"I know." Nate was thinking. His voice was just heard by the others. He spoke louder. "We can't cross here. It's too dangerous. They can see us down here with infrared. And they obviously are not careful about whom they kill." He walked past them, heading deeper into the woods. "Stay on my six and stay quiet." He turned to look back. "Brian, get up here behind me and stay with me unless I tell you otherwise."

Brian quickened his pace and moved up the line. "Back to the bunker, huh?"

"Yes," Nate said.

Ben pushed a scrub oak limb out of his way and held it for Caroline. "We sure have had a turn of bad luck lately."

"It can get a lot worse," Caroline said. She walked by in her strange limping way, not looking at him. Her injuries were showing more and more as she put ever more miles under her feet. She did not complain or ask to rest. She would never complain about pain again.

For the next two hours, all four were quiet. Nate turned to the road, keeping a slow pace to avoid walking into an ambush. He did not have to turn much. The road swung around more to the east there and came across their path. Time was getting short. Nate wanted to be across the road before sunrise.

After leaving them behind in the woods, Nate glassed the road. Just a hint of graying of the night told him they needed to get across soon, but there was still time. He recognized the stretch of road he was looking at. A deep washout cut into over half the width of the road. It was not much farther.

It took a few minutes for Nate to make it back to the others and instructed, "We need to go a little more east." He did not stop, just kept walking by them.

"What's wrong with here?" Brian asked.

"There's a gully just a little farther," Nate said. "We'll cross there."

No one said anything else.

Once again, Nate left them in the woods and approached the road just close enough to glass both directions. He saw no sign of danger, so he went back to get the others.

"I'll go first. Once I'm across, all of you run at the same time, spaced ten yards apart. Keep low so you won't be above the gully. When you get to where the gully gets shallow and ends, run like hell, keeping low."

They all nodded, but said nothing. Nate got the feeling they were too depressed to speak.

After making it across without any trouble, Nate led them toward the farm. He wanted to see what damage the raiders left behind.

"Look at that." Ben kept hid in the woods with the others and looked out across the field. "They didn't burn the house and barn. It's hard to believe."

"They stripped the field of everything edible, though," Brian said. "You can bet they took everything in the house and barn."

Nate glassed the scene. "The tractor looks untouched. They probably tried to crank it, but I took the battery and fuel pump out. They're buried. Trouble is—we don't have any fuel for it now that they took it all." He trained the binoculars on the house. "Front door's beat down. We can repair that." He stiffened. "Everyone get down! There's someone in the house."

Brian shouldered his rifle and aimed it at the house.

Nate glanced at him. "Don't shoot. If there's any shooting, it will be me that does it. Keep watch to the left of us while I watch the house." He put his binoculars to his eyes. "See anything, let me know."

"Okay, Dad. I wasn't going to shoot, just getting ready in case I had to."

"Nothing wrong with being ready," Nate said.

"Nothing wrong with shooting either," Caroline said. "Those bastards need killing. There are now a couple little kids who're going to go hungry because of them. And there's no telling how many people they've raped and murdered."

Nate lowered his binoculars. "Caroline, I fully admit there are assholes that need a damn good killing bad, but we don't know who's in the house yet. I understand the reason for your hatred, but not every man in this screwed up world needs killing." He glassed the house again.

"Just nine out of ten." Caroline turned away from Ben because he was looking at her with pity in his eyes.

Nate held the binoculars steady and stared hard through them. "It's a woman." Someone inside was dragging something heavy to the front door where light slanted in and allowed Nate to catch a suggestion of movement. The person moved closer to the open doorway.

Nate smiled. "She's got a bandage on her head. Now, who do you think that might be?"

Brian and Ben spoke in unison, "Deni."

Caroline blinked. "What the hell is she doing here?"

"At the moment, she's dragging a dead man out the front door," Nate said.

Deni appeared, back first, struggling with deadweight, and emerged from the house and onto the front porch.

"Damn, she's careless," Caroline said. "We could shoot her right now. Wonder if it had been one of them instead of us out here?"

"Well, let that be a lesson to you all," Nate said. "Let your guard down once, and all the other times you were careful will be for naught. Security is a twenty-four seven thing, not nine to five."

"It's not a fun way to live, Dad."

"Someday this will all be over," Nate said. "Everything but the rebuilding. The idea is to survive until then."

Brian looked up from kneeling behind a rock and spoke to his father. "We will make it—as long as we have you."

Nate's Adam's apple moved up his throat. "We'll make It, but now that we've lost so much, it won't be easy."

Ben looked at Brian. "It's about time you said out loud what you've been thinking about your father. We would all be dead, including you, if not for him. Of course, you're his son, and it's not surprising to anyone he will do whatever he can to protect his son. But he has done the same for the rest of us. And that is way beyond being a decent man. Your father is a lot more than that."

"Yeah, he's my father."

Caroline pointed toward the house. "Look. She's still dizzy. She should have stayed in the bunker."

They watched as Deni leaned again the house, catching her breath and steadying herself.

Nate glassed the far tree line. "I still don't see anyone else." He handed the binoculars to Ben. "Keep glassing the entire area. You will have to spot for Brian."

Brian read his mind. He stood on his knees and handed Nate a handful of 30/30 rounds. Nate and Brian traded rifles.

Nate took his pack off and then his load-bearing harness, containing six extra twenty round magazines for the M14. "Sights are set so you can aim for the center of his chest and hit him somewhere, no matter if the range is as far as you can see from here or up close. So just aim and squeeze."

Brian nodded. "I'm glad you let me shoot your rifle over the years so I could learn to hit with it."

"The longest range will be the driveway," Nate said. "It's two hundred yards." Nate watched Deni walk into the barn, carrying an M4 carbine they took off one of the dead men by the bridge. "The field's so grown over with cornstalks, you can't see toward the river, so the range won't be any more than two hundred."

"I don't think there's anyone around but Deni," Ben said. He glassed the driveway. "Deni sure doesn't seem to be worried."

"Yeah," Nate said. "But someone could show up anytime. There are certainly plenty of them down the road. Two different gangs. That chopper didn't get them all."

Caroline moved closer to the edge of the woods, so she could see better. She stood behind a pine tree, keeping the carbine ready, scanning with her eyes. "If they come back, there's going to be more of them sent to hell."

"All right." Nate levered Brian's rifle open, just enough to see a round in the chamber. "Caroline, keep watch on your back as much as the house. Someone could come up on you guys from behind. I'll go around to the right and get close enough that Deni can hear me yell." He headed into the woods.

By the time Nate was close enough, Deni had a motorcycle rolled out of the barn and was trying to crank it.

Nate yelled at her. "Deni!"

She stopped and snatched her carbine off her shoulder, a puzzled look on her face.

Nate yelled her name once more and stood, exposing his upper body.

Deni saw him and waved. "It's safe. There's no one around."

Nate walked across the clearing with Brian's rifle in the low ready position.

"Where are the others?" Deni asked.

"They're keeping watch." Nate glanced at the dead man. "Any more?"

"Two more in the house," she sighed. "I was too late. They got everything worth stealing. Those three were drunk. I just walked in and they woke up. When they grabbed for their guns, I shot them."

"You just walked in?" Nate's face hardened.

"No. Of course not!" Deni looked back at him. "If it was that way, *I* would be dead, not them."

"The thing is you shouldn't be here. You're not well yet." Nate headed for the house. "I'll get the other dead meat out. You think there might be some rope left?"

Deni put the kickstand down and got off the Harley. "There's wire." She staggered to the barn door. When she got inside, she leaned against a post and blinked. She shook her head. "God, don't let me be a burden." Somehow, she gathered herself and walked to the back, behind where the shovels and hoes were kept, now empty racks, and found a roll of barbwire.

Nate piled the other two bodies on the one Deni dragged out and tied them together with the wire. He tied the loose end to the Harley. "I don't know if this wire will hold."

"Those bastards sure like Harleys, don't they?" Deni looked at the dead men. "There are two more bikes in the barn."

"If you're going to steal, you might as well steal what you like." Nate checked to make sure the gas valve was closed. "All the gas that's left is going bad by now. Won't be long only diesels will be running. That'll be the end of motorbikes until society rebuilds."

"Damn shame we lost that diesel fuel." Deni looked at the dead men with hate in her eyes. "That fuel would have kept your tractor running for years and helped feed us all."

"It's all burned now." Nate was letting the carburetor drain. He saw that it was flooded. The gas that leaked through the air filter smelled stale. "What does the house look like inside?"

"Surprisingly, it's not that bad. They took anything of use though." She touched the ragged scar on her head. "That easy chair is ruined, soaked with stinky blood, and there's a couple stains on the floor. There is no bucket around to bring water in, and no mop."

"By the time we get to move back in, that blood will be nothing but stains. The easy chair, we'll throw out." Nate looked at the broken door. "Help me close the doorway somehow to keep animals out."

They managed to jam the door in and use a fencepost Nate found behind the barn to prop it up.

"It will keep *some* animals out anyway." Nat looked their handiwork over. "My grandfather built this place. Of course they don't give a damn about any of that."

She noticed the look in his eyes. "It won't keep the two legged kind out. And they'll be back." Deni motioned with her head. "Looking for them."

Nate headed for the motorbike, not allowing himself to dwell on old memories or let the bastards get to him. His son and friends were safe, that's all that really mattered. "Maybe, maybe not. They were attacked from the air. A lot of them were killed."

"Oh…I forgot to tell you. I heard a chopper last night."

"Yeah," Nate said. "That's the one that killed a bunch of them in the road." He turned to her. "Do you think you can ride one of the bikes?"

"Sure," she said, none too convincingly.

Nate gave her a sideward glance.

"If you can get the damn thing to run, I can damn sure ride it." She held her chin up.

Nate smiled. "Okay."

It took some time, but Nate managed to get two of the bikes to sputter to life. They both ran so rough on the old gas, Deni and Nate had to keep them revved up, not allowing them to idle down for long.

The noise of the motors kept them from hearing the pickups coming down the drive.

Chapter 18

It was Brian shooting the M14 that alerted Nate and Deni. He killed the first man who had shouldered a rifle and aimed it at Nate.

Caroline cut loose with the carbine, pumping bullets into the windshield of the first pickup. After six rounds, she moved her aim to the back. There were men jumping out while the truck was still moving. Many were hit before their boots touched ground. This was her chance, and she made all effort to kill as many as she could. Only an empty magazine slowed her. Her movements fluid and smooth, but with amazing speed, in seconds, she had a fresh magazine in and was killing again.

Ben glanced her way and saw no emotion at all, just cold death.

Brian fired with deliberate precision, keeping them off Nate and Deni foremost in mind. He put a round into the first driver, though Caroline had already hit him, and then put two in the second. One truck hit the tractor's front-end loader blade, the other slammed into a pine tree.

Ben could do nothing but watch. The range was too great for his shotgun. He looked Caroline's way again and saw tears running down her face. She fired into them until they were all behind cover.

All shooting stopped.

Brian could not see his father or Deni. They had sped away, cutting through the cornstalks heading down to the river. He could hear the motors roaring and tires spinning.

The barbwire had come loose when Nate twisted the throttle open, leaving the bodies on the edge of what was left of the butter beans. The wire had nearly cut the body on the bottom into pieces.

Brian heard the engines cut off. "They must have made it to the trees."

The men started shooting again. They had no targets, and they were just shooting blindly.

Ben bent down and grabbed Nate's pack. "Let's go. We can meet them halfway to the river if we hurry."

Caroline took aim and fired. A man shooting from behind a firewood pile fell. "You go. I'm having too much fun to stop now."

"You're going to run out of ammo fast the way you're shooting," Brian hissed.

Ben crawled to her. "There are other people here besides you. What is more important, your friends who care so much they would die for you, or your hate?"

She stopped firing and looked at Ben. Then she looked at Brian. "What are you waiting for? Let's get the hell out of here."

Nate and Deni did not make it to the woods as Brian had thought.

Deni lost control and tumbled, the bike rolling over her. Nate's attention was on Deni for a second. He did not see an area rooted out by hogs and went over the handlebars. Brian's carbine barrel was plugged with mud and the buttstock broken. The carbine flew into a mud puddle, and Nate had no time to worry about it.

Stunned, but unhurt, Nate rushed to Deni and pulled the bike off her chest. He found her conscious and in pain.

When Deni coughed up blood, Nate turned white. He felt until he found two broken ribs on her left side. *Oh God, don't let it be her lungs.*

She tried to speak and motioned with her right arm, telling him to leave her.

Nate looked around for her carbine but it was nowhere. He saw men running toward them. He lay down and pulled his revolver. They had made it into the cornfield just far enough the men could not see Deni or him yet, but he could see them, because they were standing. There were two narrow shooting lanes left by the bikes when they rode through. He had no idea how many more were coming at him that he could not see. Those he could see, he planned to kill. Deni would not be left behind, not as long as her heart was beating.

The range was one hundred fifty yards. Nate pulled the hammer back to shoot single action and steadied his aim, resting his hands on a clump of dried dirt. The revolver roared and recoiled. A man fell. He aimed and fired. Another man fell. He aimed again. That man fell before he pulled the trigger. Nate looked over and saw Deni on her stomach, her carbine shouldered. It had been hidden under her. She fired again. Nate did not see if she hit her target. He rushed to her, wondering how in the hell she was able to fight in her condition.

Firing started up from the woods again, closer this time, and Nate knew Brian and the others would keep the men pinned down. He picked Deni up and carried her in his arms through the cornstalks; afraid to throw her over his shoulders, because it might cause the broken ribs to puncture her lungs—if that had not already happened.

Nate ran as fast as he could. Brush yielded to his body as he plowed through, snapping limbs. He wanted to be with Brian, and there was nothing he would not go around or through to reach him.

When Nate saw Caroline shooting from behind an oak, he put Deni down in a depression where she would be safe and took her rifle from her hands. She had somehow managed to hold on to it. She was breathing fast shallow breaths, but barely conscious. Her eyes were unfocused and half closed. Nate prayed he was not watching her die.

With a spare magazine in one hand, and Deni's carbine in the other, Nate ran to support Brian and the others.

They were coming in straight on. Caroline and Brian made them pay for their stupidity.

Nate saw a few men from a third pickup staying back, maneuvering around to attack from the right, where they would be uphill and behind cover.

Ben made his way to a better position to meet them with his shotgun as soon as they were within range.

"Stay put," Nate yelled.

Ben could not hear over the gunfire. He kept sneaking away.

Nate snatched Brian to his feet. "Go to Deni. She's just a little ways downhill."

Brian nodded, and grabbed Nate's backpack off the ground as he ran by it.

Bullets ripped into trees around them.

Nate caught Caroline's attention. "Stay with Brian and Deni. Protect them."

There was a look of pleading in his eyes.

"I will," she said, and ran after Brian, her injuries showing by way of her limp but not her speed.

A shotgun roared from uphill. Three more quick shots from Ben's shotgun reached Nate's ears and then silence, except for the men's shooting where Ben was, and the men in the field firing sporadically in his direction.

Nate heard no more of Ben's shotgun.

Oh hell, Ben!

His decision to run toward death was instant, without hesitation or regret. Nate held the carbine at assault level, on full auto. He expected a desperate close quarters struggle for his life.

The sporadic shooting from the field did not cloak Nate's rush through thick weeds. A man stood over Ben, watching him die. Nate sprayed bullets into him just as he turned to the sound of his charge.

Everyone but Ben was dead, and Ben was dying. Nate knew it. Ben knew it.

Nate knelt beside him and saw the wounds. *Damn it!* "I will do my best to take care of your family."

Ben blinked. He could not speak. In a few seconds, his eyes were blank.

Nate checked to be sure.

He was not breathing.

Nate slung Ben's shotgun on his back and pulled his wedding band off, pocketing it, stood, turned, and ran. Ben was past help. There was the living to worry about.

Brian yanked Caroline's carbine barrel up. "That's Dad coming."

Nate could see no one close, though shooting from the field continued. He fell to his knees beside Deni. She was unconscious, but breathing. He slid into his pack, leaving Ben's shotgun on his back. The straps were too short with the shotgun between the pack and his back. He loosened them one inch, while checking Deni's pulse with his left hand.

"We've got to go," Nate said. "Now."

Brian looked at his father. "Ben?"

Nate did not have time to worry about Brian's feelings. "I did all I could. We must go now." He lifted Deni.

Brian hung Deni's carbine on his shoulder. "Where?"

"The swamp, downhill," Nate said. "And the river."

Caroline shot at something only she saw.

They took off as fast as Nate could carry Deni.

~~~~~~~~~~

Covered with sweat and out of breath, Nate had to rest. The river reflected gray and mirror-smooth ten yards in front of them. He put Deni down by a log so she would have cover on one side and the river on the other.

She seemed worse.

Brian wet a handkerchief and wiped her face. He touched her forehead. "I thought she would be overheated, but she feels cold." His eyes met Nate's.

Nate's heart jumped into his throat. *How can I tell him she is probably dying?*

"There's nothing we can do." Brian smeared his face.

"No," Nate said. "But she is not dead yet. Keep thinking. Maybe we will all make it."

"Ben didn't." Brian did not look at him.

"He is past helping. Deni is not. We are not." Nate's voice rose. "This is the worst time to quit on me."

Brian stood and looked his father in the eye. "I won't quit on you—ever."

Nate nodded. "Okay. I believe you." He lifted Deni. "Let's go."

Caroline had been watching their back trail. "I think we may have lost them." She kept scanning the woods. "But how are we going to get her back to the bunker?"

"First, we get more breathing room." Nate walked downriver. The others followed, looking over their shoulders.

~~~~~~~~~~~

Sunlight slanted down through a canopy of treetops. Morning had become afternoon, and Nate had carried Deni without rest. Afternoon had begun to die, fade into evening. Still, he carried her, feeling her slow, shallow breathing on his neck where her head rested on his shoulders, rolling with his steady gait, unsupported by her neck muscles.

Nate saw that Brian and Caroline were calmer now that danger seemed to be far behind. Finally, he put Deni down in the middle of a jumble of windfalls. Nate looked the scene over and saw logs lying crossways, one on top of the other, offered protection from bullets. "We'll rest here."

Brian knelt by Deni and helped Nate get her in a comfortable position. He moved closer and brushed dirt off her face. "I would pray…but it never worked before."

Nate grimaced as he pulled his screaming shoulders back and took his pack off. "She's lived this long. Maybe it's not as bad as I thought."

Caroline had been watching their back trail. She came closer, looking down at Deni. "You guys watch for trouble while I examine her." She knelt down and took her pack off, laying the carbine on top of it, out of the mud. "I was a nurse before the world went to hell," she said, without taking her eyes off Deni. She began to unbutton Deni's shirt.

Brian's eyes flashed to his father, then Caroline. "What the hell! Why didn't you tell us that before?" He threw his hands up. "I mean like weeks, months ago. How about when Deni needed your help when she was shot in the head."

"Brian." Nate's voice rose. "You're not considering everything." He pointed at a place where three logs crisscrossed, forming a three-cornered bunker of sorts. "Take my rifle and spare mags. Sit down in those logs. Keep low and watch for movement in the woods."

Brian said nothing, just did what his father said.

Nate caught his attention. Brian looked at him, still angry. Nate motioned for him to put his boonie hat on. He wanted Brian to hide his head as much as possible.

"She has broken ribs," Caroline said.

Nate turned and saw Caroline pressing her hands on Deni's chest on each side, feeling.

Caroline bent down close, listening to Deni breathe. Then she moved to Deni's chest, pressing her ear against it, listening.

"Her lungs?" Nate asked.

Caroline almost smiled. "She's bruised bad inside I bet, but there is no hole in her lungs."

Brian saw his father's face. He blinked and turned away.

"Did she cough up blood?" Caroline asked.

Nate nodded.

"Scared you, didn't it?" Caroline smiled for the second time in months.

Nate swallowed.

"She might have spinal injuries. No way to tell. Maybe a concussion. She might make it. She might not." Caroline checked Deni's arms for broken bones.

"We knew that already," Brian said, his voice higher pitched than it was a few moments before. He smeared his face. "She's the toughest girl I ever knew," he looked over at Caroline, "except maybe you."

"She's tough all right," Caroline said. "And stubborn. I don't think she'll let those assholes kill her. She's got fight in her yet."

Nate reloaded his revolver and holstered it. He saw the Kimber 1911 pistol in a holster on Deni's belt and decided he needed it more than her at the moment.

Caroline felt the fingers on Deni's left hand. "I need to splint her fingers. They're broken."

"You need sticks about the thickness of a pencil." Nate got a medical kit out of his pack. "Here." He handed Caroline a roll of gauze and tape. "I'll cut some sticks." He reached down and unbuckled Deni's pistol belt to slide off the holster.

Caroline's glare could have turned him into stone.

Nate slid Deni's magazine pouch off also. He buckled her belt and looked at Caroline, stood, and stared back at her, shook his head and walked away. When he returned, he had moved his revolver back on his hip to make room for Deni's pistol on his right side and had the magazine pouch on his left. He carried thin sticks for splints. He handed one of them to Caroline.

"You're going to be so loaded down with guns you can't move." Caroline put a stick next to one of Deni's fingers. She held it where the cut should be. "That long," she said. "Make it as smooth as possible on the end."

Nate took his time, carefully rounding the edge with a small pocketknife. His Ka-Bar was too large for such a delicate job. He handed it to her when finished.

"Make the next one a half inch shorter," she said.

Nate cut it and left her to splint Deni's fingers while he made a mental inventory of their ammunition supplies, going through all the magazine pouches.

Caroline spoke while she wrapped a finger with gauze to protect it from abrasion before taping the splint on. "Looks like you're getting ready for a one-man war. I think your main responsibility is to get Brian out of this."

"We're pretty much out of it already," Nate said. "Those cowards aren't coming out here after us. There's nothing out here to steal but our guns."

She gave him her cold stare. "There are two women out here."

Nate stared back. "They have women with them. And not every man is so depraved…"

"I realize you're not like them," she interrupted, "but most men are."

"Your husband? Was he like them?" Nate stood. "I don't blame you for not trusting men. But don't ever think Brian is not foremost on my mind." He walked to the river and looked around. After a few minutes, he walked to Brian.

"Are you planning on carrying Deni the whole way?" Brian asked.

"No." Nate reached out. "Let me see the rifle."

Brian handed it to him.

Nate checked the magazine and found it nearly empty. "Go to Deni's and my packs and get our loose rounds. Reload all the M14 and AR mags. This one is nearly empty and so are many others."

Brian stood but did not head for the packs. "What are you planning?"

Nate saw Brian's face looking up at him, but he did not see the boy he had been seeing every day for so many years he could not remember what it was like not be a father. "I want your advice before I decide."

Brian blinked. "Now?"

Nate's face softened. "Think on it first. Let me know what you come up with."

Brian took a few steps, and then looked back. He walked to Deni and watched Caroline finishing the last finger splint.

What Caroline saw in Brian's eyes made her stop working. "I like her too. And I will do everything I can to help her."

Chapter 19

Nate slept for two hours. He woke and found it was already dark. Caroline was asleep next to Deni. Brian stood watch.

"I haven't seen or heard a thing," Brian said. "You really think they won't come after us? They've got to be pissed."

"They're pissed all right." Nate took a drink from his canteen. "There's a place downstream where we can wade across. Then we can make our way upriver and cross again near the creek and walk back to the bunker."

"Make a stretcher to carry Deni?"

"Yes, but," Nate smashed a mosquito on his face, "I would rather use the livestock water tank to float her most of the way like we did with our supplies that time."

"It's too open in the pasture where it is." Brian's voice changed pitch. "Don't risk it. We can carry her."

"Yes, we can carry her, but she'll have a lot smoother ride in that tank floating upriver. It's not us I'm worried about."

"There's no way you can get that tank without getting killed. It's in the middle of the pasture." Brian lowered his voice again, looking around in the dark. "We can carry her without shaking her much."

"She was bleeding inside. I did not have any choice when I carried her before. But I knew it might kill her."

"You've had to make all kinds of decisions like that." Brian stopped when a garfish splashed in the river. "You've done the best you could. It wasn't your fault. Deni getting hurt and Ben killed."

"No, it wasn't anyone's fault." Nate checked the Aimpoint sight on Deni's M4. "Get some sleep. You will have to stand watch again later tonight."

"You're going to do it."

"I'm afraid she will die if I don't." Nate spoke with no emotion.

"How?" Brian asked. "How the hell are you going to go out there in the open and drag that thing across the pasture and then down to the river without getting shot?"

"I'm going to reason with them."

"Whaaat?" Brian jumped up from the log he sat on. "You asked me for ideas earlier today, now you tell me you're going to…what makes you think they will suddenly act like sane people?"

Brian woke Caroline.

She grabbed her carbine and sat up, ready to shoot. "What is it?"

"Go back to sleep," Nate said. "Everything is okay."

"Sleep hell." Caroline rubbed mosquito bites on her neck. "You two fighting?"

"We don't fight. We're just talking." Nate walked over and checked Deni. She was asleep—or unconscious. "You might as well join us if you won't go back to sleep."

They both sat down on the same log Brian had been sitting on before he stood.

"Sit down, Brian," Nate said, "and let me explain what I have in mind."

Brian sat down. "Well?"

"First of all," Nate said, "there is nothing left at the farm for them to steal. They may have come back to burn the place, but I think they just decided to spend the night there. It was our bad luck they didn't show up a few minutes later. If they had, Ben would still be alive and Deni unhurt. They probably reversed course when the chopper attacked and are heading down the road."

"Then they will probably leave tomorrow," Brian said. "So wait and then get the tank."

"We'll see if they leave in the morning. But if they don't, I'm going to leverage the chopper attack in our favor. I'm going to tell them there will be another attack if they don't leave the county."

"Just walk in and talk to them?" Brian snorted.

"Something like that," Nate said.

"And they will believe you?" Brian shook his head.

"They will if I can make it convincing. Tell them I have a friend—make it sister—in the Army, and the air assault was punishment for raiding the farm."

Caroline spoke up. "You know the jargon, chain of command, and other things. There are a few military types in their group. Maybe you can make them have enough doubts about whether you are lying or not that they will not want to take the chance."

"That's the idea," Nate said. "They have to move on anyway. There's nothing to eat at the farm. They already took it all."

"And I guess you're going to help them decide to move on by showing them how dangerous it is to stay," Brian said. "I mean besides the chopper coming back."

"I just want to get close enough to one to talk." Nate lied. "Caroline, check Deni's pockets. She may have her military ID on her. I can use it to help convince them I have the ability to call in another air strike. I don't have my VA card with me. It wouldn't do any good anyway. It just proves I *was* in the Army."

She stood. "Okay."

After Caroline left, Nate looked at Brian in the dark. "I'm going to need your watch."

"Watch? Okay." He took his wristwatch off and handed it to Nate. It was a Christmas gift from his mother. "What do you need it for?"

"It would take too long to explain." Nate put it in his pocket. It was too small to fit on his arm.

"Yeah, right."

Nate laughed. "It will take too long, because I'm about to leave."

"Shit." Brian spoke so low Nate barely heard him.

"I guess you've earned the right to cuss a little." Nate heard Caroline walking up. He wanted to say something, and he would rather say it to Brian alone. But this would be his last chance before he left. "Brian…I want to tell you something. I have raised you in my own way. It meshed well with your mother's gentleness, but it's different from what she thought I was doing."

Brian looked at his silhouette in the dark.

"I believe in raising children like an oak. If I had beaten you down every time you opened your mouth, it would have stunted your spirit. When an oak is just a seedling, a man can step on it and break its back, maybe kill it, maybe leave it crooked, deformed, and never able to grow as strong and straight as it could have. So when it's little, it needs to be protected and treated gently. As it grows, it can take on more wind, go longer without water, and take on the hazards of the world. An oak that's been treated right when small will grow strong. Oaks grow slow, but they're tough. I believe in raising children that way." Nate put his pack on. "Since the plague, you've been growing into an oak. I took you with me on this trip, because I had to. I didn't like it. But I was not taking a boy with me. I was taking a man. At least ninety percent of one. All that is missing is a few more years."

Nate turned the reticle brightness in the Aimpoint on Deni's M4 down so it would not drown out any targets in the dark. He looked through the sight while aiming at some brush.

Brian said nothing.

"This isn't some kind of a good-bye speech, Brian," Nate said. "I'll be back sometime tomorrow. I just wanted you to know I am proud to be your father. I must have not messed up too much in raising you. Your mother was a lot of help though."

No one said anything for several seconds.

Caroline had been staying back, now she came closer. "She had it on her."

Nate put Deni's military ID in a shirt pocket.

"Just come back," Brian said. "I don't see why you don't take me with you."

Nate stood there in the dark. "Someone needs to stay here and help Deni and Caroline."

"Yeah, right. Caroline is tougher than me."

Nate smiled in the dark and cleared his throat and said, "It will take two people to get Deni home."

"Okay," Brian said. "Just get home yourself."

"I will see you both tomorrow." Nate disappeared in the night.

Caroline came closer and put her right arm over Brian's shoulder. Brian responded by touching her hand. She stiffened and pulled it away.

"I'm sorry." Brian stepped away from her.

"No. I am sorry." She hugged him and then stepped back. "That was my fault. I just wanted to tell you I think your father will be okay."

"He's got something planned he's not telling us." Brian walked over to a log and sat down with Nate's rifle across his lap. He did not say another word.

~~~~~~~~~~~~~

All seemed quiet at the farm, but it was crowded with sleeping people. Nate could see no movement. The house and barn were not able to contain everyone, so many slept in tents or under tarpaulins in the yard. There were vehicles parked everywhere. The driveway was choked with trucks and pickups of all types and sizes, and the line of vehicles stretched into the county road for another half mile. People were sleeping under many of them. *It looks like a scene from Mad Max.*

Nate used his binoculars to search for sentries. There were not many. He expected more back in the woods he could not see. Eight men in sleeping bags near the edge of the woods all lined in a row, slept. Nate lowered his binoculars and backed away, deeper into the woods.

Nate circled the farm and headed for the road.

Sneaking past two sentries, Nate ran to a line of trucks parked in the middle of the dirt road. On the back of one truck, he pulled a tarpaulin aside and saw cardboard boxes of canned goods piled high. Another truck contained many items taken from his farm. Mason jars of vegetables and meats, the result of many hours of hot, sweaty work in his kitchen, filled a two-ton truck. He punctured all four tires of the three trucks. Then he crawled under them and cut their radiator hose.

Looking down the line of trucks revealed no sign of Nate's cow. More than likely, it had been killed in the helicopter attack. They would have eaten it by now, anyway. He moved down the column of trucks in the dark of the moonless night and ducked under a truck loaded with barrels of diesel fuel. In less than five minutes, he had the radiator hose cut and all four tires flat. *Maybe it will work, maybe it won't. We need that fuel.*

Four trucks down, Nate placed one of the two bombs he had left in his pack, running the wire into the woods. He came back and buried the wire under sand.

Working by feel in the dark, Nate readied a battery, attaching one wire, leaving the other bent back and away from the positive battery terminal.

A sound to his left caused Nate to freeze. When he heard nothing more, he stood in the shade of a dogwood and listened.

A man coughed as he walked down the road, keeping to the edge on Nate's side. Obviously expecting no trouble, his rifle was slung on his back. He jumped across a puddle in the ditch and walked into the woods. He pulled his zipper down and urinated.

Nate waited until he finished, then put his knife under the man's throat, clamping his left hand over the man's mouth. "Don't give me any trouble and I won't kill you. I just want to talk."

The man stiffened.

"Stand real still while I disarm you," Nate whispered. "You can come back for your guns later." He pulled a pistol out of a holster on the man's right hip and let it fall to the ground. He felt a large pocketknife in the man's right front pocket, pulled it out and let it too fall. A slash of Nate's knife cut through the sling and the man's rifle fell to the ground.

Nate whispered in his ear. "We're going for a short walk and then you're going to answer my questions. After that you'll be free to go."

"Why not here?" The man asked.

"Too close to the road. Let's go." Nate gave him a push. "I've got an M4 on you, so move easy and slow."

After nearly one hundred yards, Nate spoke. "Stop there. Back to that tree in front of you. Slide down till your butt's on the ground. Keep your hands over your head."

Nate tied his hands behind the tree and gagged him. "We'll have that talk when I get back. I've got to get on the radio and see if a chopper is available." He kicked the man's boots. "Last time they tore you bastards a new one, didn't they? Lost a lot of vehicles, huh? Well, you're going to lose more tonight—and a lot more people."

The man's eyes widened.

Rushing through the woods, Nate headed for the farmhouse. He knew where most of the pickets were and felt it safe to make good time. When he got near, he slowed and quietly stalked closer to his prey.

A man stood guard over the west side, near the driveway, hiding in the shade of a large oak. Nate's grandfather planted that tree more than a lifetime ago. Fifteen yards away, the eight men Nate saw before still slept in ignorance.

Nate's M4 hung from its combat sling out of the way to free both hands. He came up on the sentry, breathing through his nose, because he did not want the man to hear him breathing. They stood there with Nate behind the tree and to the right one foot, while Nate waited in the dark for several minutes until the man stepped away from the tree to get a better look down the driveway. Nate rushed in with his knife and cut the man's throat.

Damn it!

The man was able to slip out of Nate's grasp over his mouth and try to yell a warning. He managed only one guttural, blood-soggy groan before dying, but that was enough to wake one of the men sleeping nearby.

One man sat up in his sleeping bag and reached for his rifle. Two others were stirring, but not aware of what woke them.

Nate dropped his knife at his feet.

Deni's pistol—its Government Model 1911 grip a familiar friend—came out in a smooth motion, met his open left hand halfway up, and rose to meet Nate's line of sight as he thumbed the safety down and pushed the gun forward, extending his arms, locking in the Weaver shooting position. He focused on the glow of the front night sight while looking at the man's head—a mere flash image was enough—and squeezed the trigger, swung on the head of the nearest man beside him, fired, and swung to the next. It was over before the third spent shell hit the ground. The farm was silent, except for the echo of Nate's shots, as he reached down to pick up his knife. Leaving the nine dead men where they lay, he took off at top speed.

Fifty yards into the woods, Nate heard the first wild shots as he ran, heading back to the road. *I wish I could have done more, but I'm pushing my luck as it is.* He wanted to take another prisoner and bring him to the first one, so there would be two witnesses to the military "drone attack" he planned to fake. *I guess one will do.*

Stopping at the battery he left by the road, Nate slammed a fresh magazine into the pistol. Then he touched the wire to the battery, setting the bomb off. He pulled what was left of the wire to him and rolled it up, stuffing it in a pocket. Then he ran to his prisoner.

"Okay, asshole," Nate yanked the gag off his prisoner's mouth, "you had to have heard that missile strike." He stepped back. A storm of voices came from the road. Someone shot at imagined threats in the dark. Someone else shot back. In seconds, men were shooting one another in the confusion. More shots came from the farm. The screams of wounded could be heard from the road.

Nate took Deni's military ID out and shoved it in the man's face while holding a lit lighter up to illuminate it. "My liaison with the Army. She called in a drone attack. More of her team are killing your friends now."

The man's eyes rounded.

"I'm just a redneck farmer," Nate said. "But my sister showed up the other day to help out when I radioed her that our farm had been raided. She's the one who sent the chopper." Nate kicked him in the stomach. When the man finally caught his breath, Nate continued. "The only thing keeping the rest of you alive is the fact the Army is stretched thin right now. Deni did get the chopper she asked for by calling in a lot of favors. And tonight, she has managed to get a drone. It's circling overhead right now, waiting for orders from her. What she tells the fire control team depends on what I tell her in just a few minutes after I let you go."

"What are you telling me? What do you want?" Nate had the man's attention.

"I'm telling you that you have only a few minutes to get in those stolen trucks and get out and down the road. The government has had enough of trash like you killing, raping, and stealing from people who have too little as it is."

"We're just taking what we need to survive." The man was almost crying. "We didn't burn your home or destroy anything. We even left things that we had no use for. You have us confused with that other group. They're the ones who are acting like animals. And where *is* the government? I've seen no sign of any since the plague reached our county. Where's the help? When is it coming?"

Nate's voice carried a hard edge. "You go on deceiving yourself and pretend what you're doing is justified. But if you want to live to see the sunrise, you better get down the road and keep driving until you're out of this county. Help's not coming, but death is."

"We can't go that far." The man's chest rose and fell rapidly in agitation. "There are people back there who would attack us if we came back. They have organized into private armies."

"That's your problem," Nate said. "When you leave dead victims in your wake, you also leave enemies."

"We didn't rape or murder anyone. We just take what we have to in order to survive and kill only to defend ourselves."

"You shot first. You stole first. You trespassed on my farm and took what *we* need to survive, condemning children to hunger." Nate pulled his knife. "When I think of the loss of my friends and those children with no parents and going hungry because of you and your kind, I want to forget about giving you a chance to live." He took a step closer.

"I…I'm sorry, but we're just trying to survive. There's no food or anything now."

"Bullshit! There are hundreds of vacant farms in this county alone. Why didn't you find one of the larger ones where the owners died in the plague and move in and work it?" Nate swung his knife, the blade cutting tree bark just above the man's head and taking some hair off the top also. "I know why. You're too damn lazy to work for a living, that's why. You would rather steal."

"We don't know how to farm. And we would starve before the first crop could be harvested."

Nate kicked him in the stomach. "More bullshit. It doesn't take a genius to farm. If you had spent half as much effort in peaceful, productive work as you have raiding other's homes, you would have been much better off. But that would mean you have to get off your ass and work." Nate put his blade to the man's throat. "You stole a whole season of sixteen hour days from us and most of our farming tools, condemning us to hunger, just because you are lazy trash."

"I…uh…I'm sure I can convince them to leave tonight. I'm sorry about taking your stuff. We're just trying to survive."

"You already said that many times. My guess is that most of you tell yourselves that, every day." Nate reached down with the knife to cut the rope that bound his hands behind the tree.

"Please! No!" The man pulled against his restraints, recoiling from the blade.

"Just keep telling yourself that what you're doing is justified and you'll be humming that chant all the way to hell." Nate cut the rope and stood back, holding his pistol on the man. "But do it someplace else. If you're not down the road in fifteen minutes that drone is going to unload all of its missiles on your caravan of thieves."

The man stepped back from Nate, rubbing his wrists. "I'm sure I can talk them into leaving, but we need more time to pack."

"Fifteen minutes. The clock starts now." Nate took Brian's watch out of his pocket and looked at the man. "Fifteen minutes and she's on the radio calling in an airstrike."

The man took off.

Nate ran in the other direction. He circled the farm and headed for the eastern edge of his field. He wanted to watch the farm. There was a tree with an old deer stand in it. He found it in the dark, because it was by a well-worn deer trail and just past a hog wallow.

Climbing to the top and sitting down on the platform, Nate glassed his farm and saw the storm of frantic movement in flashes of truck headlights as people ran from the house and barn to trucks, dragging sleeping gear and packs behind them. Mothers had yawning, half-dressed children by the hand or in their arms. Nate saw that many of the children were smaller than those he saw on the dirt road that night. He was glad he controlled his temper and did not shoot into the crowd. Other trucks, loaded with people and stolen goods, jockeyed for a place in the choked driveway. Horns blew and men yelled obscenities out windows at one another. The clang and slam of fender benders echoed across the field.

Nate sighed. *Just leave, and don't come back.*

Chapter 20

When the last of the trucks sped away, disappearing around a curve in the driveway, Nate climbed down from the tree stand and walked the edge of the field.

He stayed in the shadows of the tree line. A sniper could have been left behind. The moonless night was even without starlight. Clouds had scudded in earlier, and the sky looked like rain. Nate felt it was not likely to rain for many hours, and he did not have hours to waste waiting for the cover of a storm. Even in the dark, he took the time to find a wrinkle in the lay of the land and crawled to the livestock water tank.

Nate had nothing to dip the water out of the tank, and with no cow to drink from it, it was full. He strained to tilt it. It was too heavy. *Oh, the hell with it.* He pulled both his handguns, put them on higher ground along with the carbine, stepped into the tank, and set down. Gallons of water poured over the top. He shoved his body from one end to the other, pushing out many more gallons of water. When he stepped out of the tank, dripping, the tank was left half-full.

The weight was just within his ability to handle, and he overturned the tank.

Motion near the barn prompted Nate to dive for his guns. He grabbed the carbine and kept watch while holstering both revolver and pistol. The pasture had enough tall weeds growing in clumps here and there, along with tall grass, that he could not be seen while lying on the ground.

He watched through binoculars. Someone had a two-gallon can of something in his hand and began to pour its contents onto the barn's wood front wall. Nate could only see the motion in the dark but knew what was happening. He had learned earlier from shooting the carbine that it was set for close range woods fighting and shot low at longer ranges, so he aimed one foot high through the electronic sight of the carbine and fired. The human form fell, then began to crawl. Nate glassed the area, searching for more threats. He found none, so he fired again. The form stopped moving.

I can't stand an arsonist. Nate crawled back to the water tank and began to pull it toward the woods line, keeping as low as possible.

~~~~~~~~~~~~

"Can you tell if she's getting better?" Brian asked Caroline.

Caroline checked Deni's pulse. "Sorry. All I can tell you is that she's still alive. Who knows what's going on inside her as far as bleeding, spinal injuries, or brain damage is concerned. If I had seen the accident, I would have a better idea, but it would still be a guess."

Brian shook his head in the dark. "Jeez. That tells me a lot."

"We're not in an intensive care unit. No doctor could tell you much either. Not without a few million dollars worth of equipment." Caroline was losing patience.

Brian kept watching the woods around them as he talked. "It's not your fault that she's hurt." He looked her way in the dark. "At least you're talking more now."

She did not say anything, and the silence between them became awkward.

A dull metallic sound on the river snapped them both to attention.

Brian moved closer and saw a rectangle object heading for shore.

A voice rose up. "It's your father, Brian. How is Deni?"

"Seems to be the same," Brian answered. "She has not woken."

"Caroline with her?" Nate got out of the water tank while Brian held his end from shore.

"Yeah," Brian said. "She can't tell much about if Deni's going to be okay or not."

Nate pulled the tank farther up on dry land. "I can bet on how you learned that bit of info."

"What?" Brian watched as Nate put a long pole down. "You going to use that to push the tank upstream?"

"No. You and Caroline are." Nate walked by Brian. "Help me get Deni in the tank so we can start her upriver. Time is short. We can't travel on the river in daylight."

"You're back early." Brian tried to look his father over for wounds, but the darkness made it difficult. He could only tell Nate was not limping or favoring an arm.

Nate kept walking. "I didn't wait to see if that thieving bunch were going to leave on their own. Deni doesn't need to be in this swamp any longer. We have to get her to the bunker."

Brian walked behind Nate. "Aren't you going to rest? You haven't slept much in a long time."

"No." Nate stopped by Caroline and Deni.

Brian looked up at his father. "We heard an explosion. Was that you?"

"It was my bomb."

"You don't seem like you're hurt, anyway." Brian looked but still could not see much in the dark.

"I'm not. Nice of you to mention it."

"Hell, Dad. I've been worried the whole time. We already lost Ben…and Deni is…"

Nate held his son for a second and let him go. "I know. I'm okay. Wait until you're a father. Then you will learn about worry." He turned to Caroline. "The mob of thieves have packed up and left."

"What?" Brian nearly yelled.

"So your scheme worked." Caroline stood.

"Well, I scared them enough they took off." Nate gave Brian his watch back. "Whether they stay scared enough to stay gone is a different matter."

"The sorry bastards," Brian blurted. "Ben was a good man. And what about Mrs. Neely? Cindy? Tommy?" He turned his back. "And look at Deni."

Nate moved to Brian's side and put his right hand on his shoulder. "I know. I dread telling Ben's family." He knew words could do little. "You've helped me a lot. Now I need you even more. The other gang of killers will be here soon. I still think they are fleeing something. So that means they are probably still coming this way."

Brian wiped his face. "I can't lose you. I can't."

"I'm doing my best to stay with you. But I can't take care of you and everyone else without your help." Nate gripped Brian's shoulder and shook him. "Now stand up to it and keep your head on straight. I need you. I can't do it without your help."

"Okay." Brian turned and walked to Deni. "How is the best way to carry her to the tank?"

Nate grabbed him by the back of the neck and shook him. "Good. Get your pack." Nate picked up Caroline's pack. "Come down to the river with me."

They came back carrying the water tank, trying not to make too much noise, avoiding cypress knees, weaving between trees.

Caroline helped them put Deni in.

Brian took his boonie hat off and folded it under her head.

Nate carried the front end, Caroline and Brian the back.

When they had the tank floating, Nate said, "Brian, you and Caroline get in. Put the packs on each side of Deni."

Brian got in the front. Caroline sat behind Deni's head.

Nate handed Brian the long pole. "Just keep it out of the way for now."

After putting his handguns behind Caroline on the tank's bottom, and leaning the carbine against the left rear corner so he could reach it fast, Nate put his pack behind Caroline and waded in. He pushed the tank ahead of him and walked along the river bottom.

"Dad, you can't do that the whole way."

Nate pushed the water tank along. "Just keep your eyes and ears open. Watch the right bank."

"It'll be too deep in places," Brian said.

"Quiet."

"You're going to get bitten by a snake."

For the next mile, no one said anything.

When the sun started to come up, Brian looked back and saw that his father was swimming, pushing the tank against the current with a modified sidestroke. He kept out of the main current by staying close so shore, but it had grown too deep for Nate to push off the bottom.

Brian pushed off the bottom with the pole. The tank surged ahead a foot, then the current caught it again and Nate strained to keep the momentum.

When it was light enough to see well Nate spoke up, his voice revealing fatigue. "Head for that sandbar on the right."

Brian pushed with the pole. When they had the tank pulled up on shore and hidden in weeds, Brian turned to his father and looked him over. "Shit, Dad. It's hotter than hell but you're shivering. You've got to eat and sleep."

Nate took his shirt off and wrung it out. "We can't go any farther until dark. It's too dangerous to be on the river in daylight. We're sitting ducks out there." He put his shirt back on and then sat down to take his wet boots off.

"So, you might as well eat and sleep." Brian waited for an argument. There was none.

"Will you get my pack?" Nate poured water out of his boots and left them leaning upside down against a tree to drain.

Brian returned with Nate's pack and carbine.

Nate wrung his wet socks out. "Get my handguns too."

Caroline checked on Deni and then watched the woods for trouble. She waited until Brian was out of hearing range, edged over to Nate, and whispered. "I think Deni is dying."

Nate froze for a second. "Don't say anything to Brian." His face paled, but he kept looking in his pack for dry socks.

Caroline nodded and walked away as Brian came back.

"Why don't you leave your boots off so your feet can dry out?" Brian asked.

"You know why." Nate had lost all interest in eating but got a packet of freeze-dried spaghetti out anyway. "Think about it."

Brian looked around. "We're not that far from our farm now. But I doubt anyone will come out here."

"If they do, I want to have my boots on." Nate poured water from a canteen into the food pouch and left the pouch in the sun.

"I'm going to kill every son of a bitch that does." Brian looked over at the water tank. "She looks worse. What they've done is as bad as the sickness."

Nate gave him a stern look. "Brian, cool it. You can't think straight if you're mad or full of hate."

"You don't hate them?"

"Just keep your head working constructively." Nate put clean socks on and reached for his boots. "You will not survive this if you don't. Remember, I need your help."

Nate forced himself to eat. Then he found a place in shade next to a log. The ground felt wet and cold. His clothes clung to him, but the food had warmed him inside, and he fell asleep in seconds.

Brian stood nearby. "I'm watching, Dad. You can rest now." He held Nate's rifle.

Though he spoke under his breath, Caroline heard him. She looked at the two of them then at Deni, though she could see only the tank because it was too far and the angle was wrong to see in. "I used to pray," she said. "You might want to try that for Deni."

Brian gave her a hard look. "It won't work. Millions of people prayed when the sickness was killing everyone."

"Yeah." Caroline searched the woods for trouble. "I know."

Chapter 21

Nate slept four hours. He woke up angry that Brian had not wakened him sooner. "I need to check the farm out before dark."

"There's still plenty of time for that. It's not far." Brian kept his voice low. Caroline was asleep. "You needed the rest."

"There's no telling what kind of trouble I might run into. I want to be back here and heading upriver by dark thirty."

"What are you going to do?" Brian asked. "See if they burned the house down?"

Nate made sure all his handguns were fully loaded and holstered them. "I disabled a few trucks that were loaded with our stuff. I'm hoping they left some of it behind. They sure took off in a hurry, so unless they came back later, it should still be there. I'm going to try to get it hidden in the woods before someone else shows up." He checked the carbine's chamber and magazine.

"You'll need help for that."

Nate heard something. He raised his fingers to his lips to warn Brian to be quiet and looked toward the river.

Brian heard it this time.

A low moan came from the water tank.

Nate and Brian both were at the tank in three jumps, looking in.

Deni looked up at them with blurry eyes. "You two look worse than I feel."

Nate helped her drink from a canteen.

Deni coughed, looked up at them, and fell back asleep.

Brian stared at her. "Damn." He looked up at his father, his eyes two question marks.

Nate answered his silent question as best he could. "It's a good sign. She was lucid for a few seconds."

Brian blinked and looked away.

"You eat something," Nate said. "Then we'll wake Caroline and go."

Brian turned back to him. He looked up. His face brightened a little. "Okay."

Less than an hour later, Nate and Brian were looking across the pasture at their house and barn.

"They didn't burn it," Brian said.

Nate glassed the scene. He noticed the man he had shot while pouring gas or diesel fuel on the barn was still lying where he died. A rifle still hung from his left shoulder, barrel down. "I've seen enough for now. It doesn't look like anyone's been back since I left. They would have taken that guy's rifle if they had. We'll cut through the woods to the road."

They backed away, keeping low and in cover.

Approaching the road, Nate slowed to one step every thirty seconds and kept all senses on full alert. He motioned for Brian to come closer. "Expect trouble up here, but don't just start shooting at the first person you see. Use your head. You'll know when to shoot."

Brian swallowed and nodded.

"We have to watch each other's back." Nate was relieved to see Brian paying close attention. "If I'm looking to the left, you look to the right. Neither one of us have eyes in the back of our heads. That means you cover the sector behind my line of sight, behind my head. If you do that, I'll automatically cover your blind side."

Brian nodded, his eyes intense. He breathed fast.

"I'm not saying there is sure to be trouble," Nate said. "Just be ready. If I am killed—run back to the others and get Deni to the bunker. You can't do anything for a dead man. Don't get mad, just leave."

"If you're wounded, I'm not leaving you."

"That depends."

Brian recoiled as if his father had just said the stupidest thing he ever heard. "On what? I'm not leaving you wounded."

"You will, if I tell you to. If I'm dying, there is no point in you dying needlessly." Nate put his hand on his son's left shoulder. "I have been giving you more responsibility lately, because you have been acting more like a man. Don't let me down."

Brian's eyes burned into his father. He tilted his head and stared unblinking, his mouth half open in disbelief.

"Let's go." Nate moved on before Brian said anything. "Stay alert."

"No sign of anyone." Nate scanned down the road to his left through binoculars. "The trucks I disabled are still there. They took off fast. Maybe they did not unload much onto other trucks before they left." He turned to find Brian looking down the road in the opposite direction. "See anything?"

"No."

Nate handed Brian his binoculars. "Scan every inch—every inch—of the far tree line for as far as you can. Then scan the near tree line. You have young eyes. Use them. Penetrate deep into the shade and look for anything out of the ordinary—especially movement."

Brian moved the binoculars steadily.

"You're going too fast," Nate said. "And stop to examine anything that looks different. Try to penetrate the dark areas. That's where they will be hiding. Shade is life when you're being hunted in the woods."

When Brian finished on the far side of the road, he scanned the near side. "The angle is wrong. I can't see much on this side."

"Check anyway." Nate looked down the road in the other direction, then the woods behind them. "You still might see something."

"I didn't see any sign of anyone." Brian handed the binoculars back to his father.

"Okay. That hill on my side, almost a half mile from here, is as far as I can see. We'll back off and ease up to the edge there so we can glass the road on the other side. And we'll glass this area again from the top of the hill."

When they were in position, Nate scanned every inch of the woods line down the road on the other side of the hill. He could see no danger. "Here." He handed the binoculars to Brian. "Scan the woods as far as you can."

Ten minutes later Brian said, "Nothing."

"Check the trucks out—and the road. Remember, you may have the rest of your life to find danger out there. You're dead if you fail to see death waiting in ambush, and these *will* be the last moments of your life. So take your time. Taking a few more minutes now could reward you with all the minutes of the rest of your life."

Brian scanned the trucks Nate had disabled the night before. "I can't see anyone hiding in them."

Nate took the binoculars. "There's more to check out than that." He scanned the trucks after Brian crawled back a foot to get out of his way. "Something's amiss," Nate said, without taking the binoculars from his eyes. "I smell a trap." He scanned the road inch by inch. "Fresh dirt in the road. Someone has buried something in two places." He lowered the binoculars. "I couldn't see looking from the other direction because of the road slanting down this way a little and the direction of the sun. Good thing we took the time to check. Those trucks are booby-trapped."

"Then the food's probably not in the trucks anymore." Brian looked at his father with confidence in his eyes.

"Maybe a little for bait," Nate said. "We need to back off and sneak the hell out of here. Chances are there are men and rifles waiting for one of us to show ourselves in that road."

Brian spit. "Damn it! We needed that food. I hate the bastards more every day. They killed Ben and maybe Deni. And now they don't just leave, they still want to finish us off."

"It's possible it may be the other bunch from the bridge," Nate said. "Some of them are military. They would know how to use explosives. They may have come up on the trucks and decided to set up a surprise." He backed from the road. "Let's go."

Down by the river, they turned downstream.

When Nate stopped to listen for danger, Brian came close enough to whisper. "Dad, have you thought about those military guys acting like animals?" He stood there, sweat dripping down his face.

Nate sighed. "Yes. It pisses me off. They're most likely vets, not active duty. But the fact is there are all kinds in the military. Most are the best America—the human race—has ever produced. I guarantee you for every vet that's gone wolf, there are a hundred that's helping people and using their training to protect the vulnerable."

"Yeah. I bet you're right. Most of them are more like you."

Nate's eyes flashed to his son. He moved on, heading downriver.

~~~~~~~~~~~

Caroline held Deni's head up so she could have a drink from the canteen. "Don't move anymore than you have to. You will start bleeding inside again."

Deni coughed. Brown spittle came up. "I'm worried about Nate and Brian."

"It's getting near sundown," Caroline said. "They'll be back soon."

A voice came from the woods. "Nate and Brian coming in."

Caroline jerked her head around in time to see Nate emerge from the wall of green where palmettos grew thick. Brian followed five yards behind.

Caroline stood. "Deni's awake."

Brian ran past his father and smiled down at Deni. "You scared the hell out of us. How are you feeling?"

"Like I've been tackled and stomped by someone as big as your father." Deni saw concern on Brian's face. "I think I'll be okay."

Nate came up and stood beside Brian. "Can you move your arms and legs?"

"Sure." Deni smiled up at him weakly. "Are you worried about losing a farmhand?"

"A friend," Nate said.

"I'm still in the fight." Deni coughed up more brown spittle. "Caroline says you're floating me closer to the bunker. But how are you going to carry me the rest of the way?"

Nate smashed a mosquito on his nose. "I can pole you up the creek, just like we did the supplies that time. With Brian and Caroline out of the tank, it will not take much water to float. I should be able to get you close. We'll carry you the rest of the way in the water tank."

"I can probably walk by the time you get me that far." Deni coughed again.

"Stop that," Caroline said. "Let us take care of you. There's a chance if you do."

Deni started to say something, then her eyelids seemed to grow heavy and she passed out.

Brian clenched his left hand into a fist. "Damn it."

Nate checked the sun. It had sunk behind the trees on the far side of the river. "It will be dark in an hour. I'll walk this side of the river and keep a look out for trouble. Brian, you and Caroline pole the tank. Keep close to this side so no one can see you from upriver. There's not likely to be any of them on the other side, but watch that shore also."

"We need another pole," Caroline said.

Nate pulled his knife. "I'll cut one." He left a branch on the bottom end to help keep it from sinking in mud as she pushed off the bottom.

Two hours later, they slinked past the farm. By then it was completely dark. All Nate saw or heard was a hog rooting in mud just ten yards upslope. He was glad to hear it because it was a good sign no human was near.

It took four more hours to pole to the creek. Nate felt they were ninety percent home and far from the killers. He did not let his guard down though.

Brian and Caroline pushed the tank toward shore and Nate pulled the near end up on firmer ground.

Caroline and Brian got out and stretched their backs.

"Keep your eyes and ears working," Nate said. He pushed the tank off and stepped in. "It's going to be slow going in the creek. I can't see logs under water and don't want to be slamming into them, making noise." He kept his voice low. "Probably won't be able to go far in the dark, but I want to get away from the river before we stop and wait for false dawn."

Nate got only a quarter mile before he had to stop. There were too many submerged logs and other obstructions in the creek that he could not see in the dark. He pushed for the creek's bank and stepped out, then pulled the livestock tank nearly all the way out of the water.

Deni had not stirred the whole night. Nate knew she may die and worried as much for Brian as Deni. *He's getting tougher, but he's still just a kid.* He put his hand down near her mouth and nose and was relieved to feel her breath. *God, what a loss it will be. How many like her can the human race afford to lose before all that's left are two-legged animals?* Caroline came closer. *And her. After everything she's been through, the good in her still lives. Both of them remind me of Susan in their own way.*

Caroline checked her pulse. "No change."

"It's not that far," Brian said. "We can carry her the rest of the way."

"No," Nate said. "We'll make too much noise banging that thing against trees in the dark. We could walk right into an ambush. You two rest, while I stand watch. We'll go on up the creek as soon as it's light enough to see. Won't be long now anyway."

Caroline lay down in the wet mud by the tank.

Nate pointed. "Brian, check for snakes first and sleep against that big cypress log. You will be protected on one side at least. And you'll be harder to see."

Brian walked over to the log and slipped out of his pack. In a few minutes he was asleep, Nate's rifle in his hands across his chest.

~~~~~~~~~~

Nate heard them coming. It did not take him long to determine there were two. He was ready to shoot when at the last moment they veered off to their left and headed for the river.

Brian woke and slowly got to his feet. Keeping bent over behind the log. He turned to look toward the water tank and

Caroline. She was sitting up, carbine shouldered, aimed at the sounds of movement in the swamp. All Brian could see was her head and shoulders above the fog that lay low, hugging the earth. He knew the tank was there beside her, but it was shrouded in fog.

When the swamp began to gray with predawn light, Nate finally moved from where he had stood like a statue for half an hour in the shade of a magnolia and walked up to Brian. He put two fingers to his lips and motioned for Brian to go to the tank.

Brian grabbed his pack and headed for Caroline.

Caroline stood and put her pack into the tank by Deni.

Everyone moved deliberately to avoid any noise.

When they carried the water tank the few feet to the creek's edge, Deni woke. They did not know it until she spoke.

Nate put his hand over her mouth. "Shh. Men are hunting us."

Deni nodded. Nate felt her head move and knew she understood.

"They went by about thirty minutes ago," Nate said.

"Where's my M4?" Deni whispered.

"I have it," Nate said. "Brian's lever-action was broken in the bike wreck we both were in. I gave him my rifle. I trained him how to use it. He's never shot an M4, and he might accidentally put it on full auto."

Deni felt in the dark for her holster. "My pistol?"

"I have that too. Sorry, I needed it more than you at the time." Nate patted her on the shoulder. "We're at the creek, and will have you in the bunker in a few hours. Just relax."

Deni sighed. "Sure. Relax. The fact is I think I can walk."

"Don't move. You've been bleeding inside." Nate put his hands on her shoulders. "Don't do anything but lay there."

"I'll do what I want." Deni pushed a hand away.

"Sure, go ahead." Nate was angry. "We've lost Ben already, and we've carried you this far just so you can kill yourself to prove I'm not your boss."

Brian waded in the water and grabbed the edge of the tank. He looked down at her. "Please don't move. We're almost there now. Maybe you will die anyway in the end, but we're trying to give you a chance. You're hurt bad."

"Okay, okay." Deni reached up and touched Brian's hand. "I'm not worth all that. Calm down."

"Worth what?" Brian asked. "All we have is each other."

"You and your father have each other." The sun was up more now, and Deni could see Brian's face. She looked at Nate and saw the same thing.

"You're with us now," Brian said. "Just like Caroline and the rest. Dad and I don't quit on each other and we don't quit on our friends."

"Damn," Deni said, "I thought they broke the mold a couple generations back. Except maybe for a few in the military, like my father."

"What?" Brian asked.

"You and your dad, that's what."

"We've got to go," Nate said.

Brian and Caroline started to get in the water tank.

Nate spoke up. "Brian, put your pack on and stay with me."

Brian did what he was told in silence.

"The less water needed to float that thing the better," Nate said. "Your weight will make it sink deeper."

Brian nodded.

Still wet with dew, the leaves carpeting the woods made little noise as Nate and Brian eased along the creek's edge. Caroline could not pole the water tank more than one half mile an hour, and that suited Nate. The slower they stalked through the woods, the quieter they would be.

Things had grown steadily worse, and now there were killers close to the bunker. Nate wondered if they had not already found it. If they had, the bunker could be under siege. Why did they come out here? Have those at the bridge known about the bunker and Mel's cache all along? Nate tried to keep his mind on detecting danger in the woods, but his thoughts kept racing ahead, finding new dangers waiting in the shadows of tomorrow.

Chapter 22

The creek grew more narrow and shallow the last half mile. Caroline was forced to work harder to seek out a clear path around submerged logs, going around some, scraping over others.

Nate finally motioned for her to head for the creek bank when she got stuck on a log for five minutes.

Close to noon already, and they had to carry Deni in the water tank through the jungle of a Southern swamp. Nate decided it best to leave her at the creek with Caroline while he and Brian checked out the route to the bunker.

Deni did not like Nate's plan. "I can walk, damn it."

"We've been through that." Nate and Brian left Deni and Caroline by the creek. They headed upslope, out of the swamp, watching every direction for trouble.

Nate found himself standing more than walking. He examined every inch of the wall of green before him, seeking out any sign of trouble. Knowing it is impossible to see a whole man in thick woods, he searched for the slightest movement. Assuming a flicker of movement in brush was just a squirrel's tail or the sound of something grating against a palmetto frond, a deer slinking off, could get you killed. The more open areas, usually no more than a few feet wide, received a quick scan; it was the thick brush and darkest of shade that Nate's eyes worked the hardest to penetrate. Few men are foolish enough to stand in the open, painted by sunlight.

Nate could feel it. Men were hunting him. He had been through similar situations many times when in the Army, but then he was with a trained team. They were men he respected, and many were friends he would rather die for than let down. One mistake, one careless second, and a friend could die. Now he had not a team of trained Rangers, but his thirteen-year-old son with him. God, did he wish Brian was somewhere safe.

The sun had risen to its zenith, and Nate believed they were no more than a quarter mile from the bunker. His mind was on how to make sure no one was waiting in ambush close by the bunker itself when he turned and saw Brian squatting, looking under brush, rifle shouldered.

Nate stepped behind a tree to put it between him and the direction Brian was looking. He got down and could see two legs. The pants were caked with mud to the knees. The legs stepped around and faced away, more toward the creek. *He hasn't seen us yet.*

A few seconds passed before Brian looked Nate's way. As soon as he did, Nate hand-signaled for him to stay still. Brian nodded.

The man must have sensed something. He turned in a blur of motion. Too late. Nate struck him with the butt of his Ka-Bar knife, full force. He risked killing him. Better that than not hit him hard enough to put him out and he alarm anyone nearby.

In thirty seconds, Nate had the man tied and gagged. He found a Springfield M1911 .45ACP on the man. Nate took it and the holster. The rifle was a bolt-action in 30/06 caliber with a telescopic sight. Nate took all the man's ammunition and stuffed it in his pack with the pistol, tying the rounds in a dirty sock so they could not rattle. He then tied the rifle outside the pack. There were two spare magazines for the pistol. He tried to stuff them in a left pants pocket but found it too full of 44 magnum rounds. The magazines went into a side pocket on his pack.

Nate took other items, including a six-inch expensive custom-made Randall knife. All went in his pack. The Randall had an inscription on the blade. He knew it well. The knife was a gift from friends when he left the Army.

Nate motioned for Brian to come to him.

Brian made his way silently across the thirty-five yards. He stood there looking at the man on the ground. "What are you going to do with him?" Brian whispered.

"Ask questions," Nate said. "Keep your eyes and ears open."

Brian nodded and resumed scanning the woods around them.

Nate looked around until he found a slough partially filled with black water. He dragged the man slowly, so as not to make noise, and pushed his face in the water. When he lifted it, the man woke up. His coughs were muffled by the wet gag.

Nate checked to see if Brian was watching. He was looking the other way. Nate kicked the man in the stomach.

Brian jerked his head around when the man grunted.

Nate signaled for Brian to go back to keeping watch.

Nate looked down on him with a look calculated to put the fear of death in the man. "There is no need to lie. I found items on you that came from my home. You're a thief and a murderer." Nate held the carbine on him while he pulled the gag off.

"I," the man spit mud out of his mouth, "got that stuff off a dead man. By the time we got to the farm, nothing was left to steal." He looked up at Nate. "What do you want?" He spit again.

"The truth. Did you kill the man you say you got my stuff off of?"

"No. He must have been killed by that chopper attack. We were hit too. They really tore us up. Did more damage than your gang."

"That was my doing," Nate said. "You assholes screwed with the wrong farmer. I wasn't always a farmer, and I've still got friends and family in the military."

The man had an incredulous smile on his face. "Bullshit. The military doesn't work that way. They don't do favors for vets. A general maybe. You don't look old enough to have been a general."

Nate kicked him in the stomach again. This time Brian saw it.

"The military does not normally slaughter American civilians on a county road with airstrikes either. But this isn't normal times." Nate gave the man a closeup look at the sharp edge of his knife. "The government may be weak at the moment, but it's not dead. They've had enough of vultures like your bunch preying on people. And *I've* had enough." Nate put his knife to the man's throat. "You bastards killed my friends. You and the other bunch both. The next sentence that comes out of your mouth determines if you live or die."

"What do you want?"

Nate slid his knife across the man's neck, drawing blood. He wanted him to know he was not bluffing. "What you are doing out here in the woods? Why didn't your band of trash go on down the road?"

The man's wide-open eyes turned to slits. "You didn't know? We all thought you must've known. Why else would you have been keeping us stopped at the bridge?"

"That's two questions, but there's not a single answer in those words." Nate bent down. "I thought we had an understanding. You do not seem to get that I've had enough."

The man saw Nate's knife coming. His eyes rounded, but he had no time to scream before Nate put a hand over his mouth.

Just as the blade entered flesh, Nate heard a gasp. He looked over and saw Brian's pale face. Nate pulled the knife out of the man's shoulder. "We're both running out of time. I'm not going to play with you any longer." He took his hand off the man's mouth so he could speak. "Answer my question."

The man could barely talk. His eyes were wild with fear and pain. "They caught up with us because of you stopping us at the bridge and then the road. We were at one of your roadblocks when they came." The man coughed. "We had to leave our trucks and run for it."

"Who caught up with you, the military?"

The man looked puzzled. "No. The vigilantes. They've been chasing us since we hit a town a couple weeks back." He looked up at Nate. "They ain't playing. We heard they intend to clean this county of what they call brigands. Some of the guys stayed back and thought they would ambush them. We never saw but three of them again. From what they said, the vigilantes must have gotten into a National Guard armory and they took heavy weapons. They even have mortars and grenade launchers. They have a couple armored trucks too."

"So you bastards scattered and ran into the woods?"

The man nodded. "There are hundreds of them. They have some deputies and war vets leading them."

Nate looked at him with hate in his eyes. "And a lot of pissed off citizens. What do you expect when you go animal? You idiots could have gone to work and provided for yourselves instead of murdering, raping, and stealing. Trash like you was sucking America dry before the plague. Now you're showing what welfare leaches really are."

"We have to eat to live." The man looked down at the rope around his ankles.

"You're not going to live long with a belly full of bullets." Nate motioned for Brian to come closer. "How many more of your trash are in this area?"

Then man shrugged. "I haven't seen anyone in hours. I tried to separate from the others on purpose so the vigilantes would go after them and give me a better chance to get away."

Nate noticed for the first time the man did not even have a canteen or backpack with him. He must have taken off fast.

Brian only glanced at the man and then kept looking around for trouble. "Do you believe him?" He asked his father.

"We'll see," Nate said. "Keep your eyes and ears working. There's bound to be more of them around."

"What do we do now?" Brian asked.

"What we don't do is talk about that in front of him." Nate untied the rope binding the man's ankles." Get up and start walking." He pointed back toward Caroline and Deni. "That way."

The man had trouble getting up with his hands tied behind his back, but managed. "What do you want with me? Let me go."

Nate slipped the gag back over his mouth. "Walk."

They reached the creek a mile upstream from Deni and Caroline. Nate led them to the east a little on purpose.

Brian stood by his father, constantly searching the woods.

Nate tapped him on the shoulder. "You go on ahead, slow, and careful. I'll catch up with you before you get to the women."

"You going to let him go?" Brian's eyes burned into Nate.

Nate looked out into the woods, away from his innocent son's eyes. "Go on now. I'll catch up."

Brian faded slowly into the wall of green.

The man tried to run. Nate tripped him and he fell on his face in the mud.

Yeah, you know, don't you? Nate hit him on the back of his head as hard as he could with the butt of his knife handle. While the man lay there out cold, perhaps dead, Nate cut his throat. He untied the man's hands and put the rope in a side pocket of his pack. Then he went to the creek and washed the blood off his knife and hand. He sighed, looked around, stood, and headed for Brian.

Brian's eyes told Nate he knew. They said nothing. Nate walked past him and Brian followed.

Twenty minutes later, Nate signaled for Brian to come closer.

Brian stood beside his father, looking into the woods, pretending to be watching for danger.

Nate reached into a shirt pocket and pulled out a cloth pouch he had taken off the man. He tapped Brian on the shoulder.

Brian looked up at him.

Nate opened the pouch and poured out bloody gold teeth and wedding bands onto his hand for Brian to see. He picked out several thin rings that came off little girls, held them up, and then dropped them into the leaf litter of the swamp. Then he turned his hand over, let the rest rain down, and join the little rings. "He was too close to the bunker," Nate said. "He may have seen it. I couldn't take the risk he would lead more killers to us."

Brian swallowed. "I know. He was different from Synthia. You took the chance on her bringing the sickness to us all because she was innocent. That man was not worth the risk."

Nate stood there looking at his son while his chest rose and fell several times. "If he had not been so close to the bunker I would have let him go, even though he deserved to die. I'm not a judge and jury, and I don't want to be, but I will do anything to protect you and the others."

Brian nodded. "I know."

They both flinched when the swamp roared with gunfire. It came from downstream.

They took off on a run. When the shooting stopped, Nate slowed to a walk and Brian kept pace behind him, his chest heaving.

Several more shots rang out. This time Nate kept his slow pace, easing through the brush.

Brian wanted to rush ahead, but Nate grabbed him by his pack. "No," Nate said. "Stay behind me. Keep your head working."

Another flurry of shots told Nate and Brian they were getting close.

Nate shoved Brian to a four-foot thick cypress log that disappeared into heavy brush. "Stay here and stay down."

Brian started to speak.

"Do what I told you." Nate took off on a run.

After fifty yards, Nate slowed to hunting speed. He had no idea what he was walking into.

A woman's voice came from out of the wall of green. It sounded more like the roar of a beast, but Nate recognized it as Caroline's. "Come and get me, you gutless bastards!"

Crashing in brush telegraphed the rush of someone toward Nate. He had the carbine up and ready.

They saw each other at the same time. Caroline slid in the mud, coming to a halt only long enough to recognize Nate. She rushed at him, crossing the twenty yards between them in seconds, and snatched at a spare magazine in a side pocket of his backpack. "They're coming," she said. "I'm out of ammo." She dropped the empty magazine in her carbine in the mud and slammed Nate's full magazine in.

Nate wanted to ask her about Deni, but two men ran into a narrow opening. He sprayed them with a short burst of full auto fire.

More men were coming at a run. They shot blindly into the brush. Nate jumped for cover behind a wide cypress.

Caroline stood where she was and fired at any movement she saw. In her state of mind, she was as dangerous to Nate as the others.

Nate ran to her and pulled her behind cover. He handed her another magazine. "I want to maneuver around them, but you will have to watch who you shoot."

"You go after Deni," Caroline said. "I tried to lead them away from her when I ran out of ammo."

Nate started to speak. He stopped short when he saw a man come out from behind a tree and aim a rifle at them. The man's head exploded.

Brian continued to shoot at a log near the edge of the creek. Wood flew off with each shot.

Two hands and an M4 came up over the log and sprayed bullets in Brian's direction.

Brian shot. The hands and carbine disappeared.

Nate saw the man's hand take Brian's bullet. He jumped up and rushed the log from the side. The man was still rolling on the ground holding his hand when Nate fired a burst into his chest.

Crashing in the brush, told Nate that at least two men were running away.

Caroline fired at the sound. She ran after them. Her limp was not slowing her.

Nate ran after her with the intention of getting her to come back to Brian with him.

Brian ran downstream.

Nate heard him. *Goddamnit!* He turned and took off after Brian.

Running at top speed, Brian exploded out of thick brush into a small clearing. He heard voices and slowed to creep up on them.

There were two men. They had Deni out of the water tank. She was on her back, swinging a four-inch pocketknife to keep them away.

One of the men was pulling the livestock tank toward the water. "We have no time to play with her. Let's get this thing down to the river and float the hell out of here before they get back and want to fight over who gets a boat ride."

"It won't take long," the other man said. "I'll just shoot her arm off and take that knife. Then we'll have some fun."

They both heard Brian coming, but there was no time to react. Bullets slammed into the man near Deni. The other man jumped into the creek. It was only a foot deep. He dropped his rifle and came up muddy. He threw his hands up. "Don't shoot!"

Nate yelled," I'm coming up behind you Brian."

Brian aimed at the man.

After making sure there was no one else around, Nate fired a short burst into the man as he held his hands up. He slammed a fresh magazine in the carbine and gave Brian a hard look.

Brian ran to Deni. "Did they hurt you?"

"No," Deni said. "Where is Caroline?"

Nate looked around again and saw dead men everywhere he looked. "She went after them."

Deni wiped blood off her cut lip and spit more blood.

"They did hurt you." Brian knelt beside her.

"I saw stars when that one kicked me, but I'm all right." Deni laid her hand on Brian's shoulder. "Give me that bastard's guns and any ammo he has. Then you two go after Caroline. She took one in the side."

Nate grabbed the man's AK47 clone and three magazines. He handed them to Deni and then took the pistol he had in his own pack out and gave her that and two magazines. "You two stay here. I'll go get Caroline."

Semiautomatic fire erupted in the distance.

"Caroline," Deni said. She still lay on the ground, looking into the woods.

"I tried to stop her, but then Brian took off to help you." Nate glared at Brian.

Brian glared back. "And you just *had* to come after me?"

"Okay guys." Deni looked up at Nate. "He did get here just in time."

Coughing from behind Brian, alerted them that the man he shot was still alive.

Brian stood and turned on him, aiming the rifle.

The man opened his eyes. "Help me."

Brian shot him through his heart. "No…freaking…way!"

"Cool it." Nate put his left hand on Brian's shoulder. "Stay with her. I'll go see about Caroline."

"You didn't hear what he said, Dad."

"That's not what I mean. He had to die and would have in a few more minutes. You did him a favor. I mean keep your head on straight."

Nate walked about half a mile when he heard someone coming through the brush. He stepped behind a cedar tree and waited.

Caroline appeared between two trees. She was limping more so than usual.

Nate rushed to her. He helped her to a crooked palm tree, growing horizontally from one of many Indian mounds in the area before turning up toward sunlight. "Sit down." While scanning the wall of green surrounding them, Nate asked, "Are you being pursued?"

"No, those bastards are in hell," Caroline said. "Where are Deni and Brian?"

"Back at the creek. They're okay." Nate cut her pants leg away and saw the wound. "Damn it. Don't walk on that again." He yanked his pack off and pulled out what little medical supplies he had. After ripping a package open, he poured the contents on her wound. "This stuff came from Mel's cave." He pulled her shirt up and examined a wound that entered and exited just under her flesh over a rib. "That one's not bad. The stuff I used on your leg will stop the bleeding." He looked up at her. "But it will have to be surgically removed later."

She rolled her eyes. "Great. Don't use it on my ribs then."

"We are a long ways from the bunker, and now there are two stretcher cases. Your leg was bleeding too much. It had to be stopped."

Caroline's chest heaved. "Well, wrap it up and let's get going."

"Do me a favor: Do not walk on that leg again. I'll go back, and Brian and I will carry Deni here."

"Then what? Carry both of us in that water tank?"

Nate tied the bandage off and stood. "We will carry you one at a time."

"That will take forever."

Nate took a canteen out of Caroline's pack and handed it to her. "We might still make it to the bunker by nightfall." He picked up his carbine. "If you walk on that leg you will bleed to death. Stay here." He ran.

Brian was alert and saw his father at the same time he saw Brian. "Deni's out again." He seemed worried. "Not long after you left, her eyelids looked like they were getting too heavy for her and she went out like a light." He looked behind Nate. "Where is Caroline?"

"She's got a nasty leg wound. We'll have to carry them both." Nate walked over to Deni with Brian following.

They got her in the water tank and started for Caroline.

When they arrived an hour later, Caroline was passed out on the ground.

Nate checked her breathing. "She's out from loss of blood."

"Damn, Dad. My leg got infected from a little .22, and we used all the antibiotics."

"I know." Nate saw ants crawling on her. He brushed them off. "You stay with Deni. I'll carry Caroline about one hundred yards and come back."

"So we're going to do that the whole way?" Before Nate answered, Brian said, "Okay. We can do that."

"We'll have to." Nate picked Caroline up and left Brian standing there.

~~~~~~~~~~

Brian fell. His end of the water tank hit the ground and made a dull metallic sound that reverberated through the darkening forest.

Nate put his end of the tank down and rushed to Brian. "You hurt?"

"No. Goddamnit. I dropped her and made enough noise to let anyone around know we're here though." Brian's clothes were soaked with sweat, and he could barely stand from fatigue.

Deni woke up. "What's wrong?" She gripped the pistol Nate gave her.

"Nothing," Nate and Brian said in chorus.

"Sit down somewhere in cover and rest, Brian," Nate said. "Both of you be quiet in case someone did hear the tank hit that root."

They waited thirty minutes. No one came. The time did give Brian a chance to get his second wind.

Just as it grew too dark to see, they reached Caroline. She was sitting up, her back against a pine tree, and her carbine in her hands.

"Brian," Nate said, "stand watch while the rest of us eat."

"Okay." Brian left his pack by the water tank. He found a magnolia to stand under, taking advantage of its hiding shade.

"That boy has been carrying his own weight all day," Deni said.

"I know." Nate gave her a package of reconstituted soup and some crackers. "After I eat, he does, and then he goes to sleep. We're not going any farther until morning."

Caroline said, "It's not far now. I can walk the rest of the way."

"No!" Nate pointed at her leg. "There were blood vessels spurting. You get them to bleeding again and you're dead. I didn't carry you this far for nothing."

There was silence for several seconds.

"In that case I'm dead anyway," Caroline said. "Unless there's a surgeon around I don't see."

"They're minor blood vessels. But you can bleed out if you try to walk." Nate stopped to think. "They can be sown back together."

"By whom? You?" Caroline asked.

"Maybe." Nate did not seem too sure. "We still have Mel's pain killer. So you will be out of pain, and I'll have plenty of time—if you haven't lost too much blood from walking. You will lose a lot during the operation."

"But we have no antibiotics." Caroline's voice was emotionless.

"People survived surgery before there were antibiotics." Nate lost patience. "Caroline, think of it this way: That leg was ripped up by a man. Are you going to let that asshole kill you? Or are you going to show him you're too tough to let some prick get the best of you?"

There was silence for nearly five seconds. Then Caroline started to laugh. "You know how to screw with my head, don't you?"

"We can't afford to lose you," Nate said.

~~~~~~~~~~~

False dawn came. Nate had stood watch all night. He woke Brian. "Time to get moving. We will be at the bunker in two hours or so."

Brian sat up and looked around. "You should have woken me to stand watch."

Nate woke Caroline. He thought about just picking her up while she was still asleep but thought she would likely wake up and shoot him, thinking he was attacking her.

They were closer to the bunker than Nate thought and arrived less than an hour after sunrise. Nate stood at the door waiting for Martha to unbolt it, dreading telling her and her children about Ben.

Chapter 23

Martha and Cindy had little time to grieve. They went to work helping Caroline while Nate and Brian got Deni comfortable. Their tears and worries about how they could go on without Ben did not slow their efforts to save Caroline's leg and her life.

Tommy sat in a corner with Synthia. He was in a daze, not understanding why his father did not return with the others and his mother and sister were crying.

Carrie, as usual, paid little attention to the world outside her head. She did seem to wonder why Caroline was lying on the table they usually ate on.

Nate explained how the coagulant would have to be removed with a scalpel. He did not mention the damaged blood vessels.

Dead tired, Nate and Brian went to the cave and got all the medical supplies Nate thought they might need for the operation. He took the smallest suture kits for the blood vessels and larger ones to close the wound later. He also found a magnifier visor and bottles of alcohol. *Oh God, how am I going to do this?* He walked out into the bright morning with his hands full of duffle bags.

Brian closed and locked the cave door. He searched the woods for danger, his father's rifle ready, while they walked back to the bunker.

Caroline was in a lot of pain but kept still and quiet on a small table, waiting for what came next.

Nate read several of Mel's notes on analgesics. He picked up a bottle and held it in a ray of sunlight that streamed in through a loophole. He did the same with two more bottles. "This stuff is all old. And she's lost a lot of blood. Probably too much to use any of this."

"Oh, to hell with it." Caroline ripped at the bandages. "Forget the painkiller. How much can it hurt?"

Brian gaped at her and blinked with his mouth half open.

"You said you can fix me," Caroline said. "Well, stop wasting time. Get to it."

Nate stepped back. "I…"

"Nuts," Caroline said. "The big man has chickened out. Look at him. He's as green as Brian. Martha, you do it. This is a job for a woman's courage anyway."

Martha wiped her face. "Nate is the best friend you will ever have. Why are you torturing him like this? Can't you see...?" She caught herself. "Brian, pump water while I wash my hands and arms." She walked to the pump and picked up a bar of lye soap.

Nate took his filthy jacket off and scrubbed up to his elbows, cleaning swamp mud out from under his nails as best he could. He looked at Martha as a he scrubbed. "There are blood vessels that have to be sutured back together. The smaller ones can be cauterized, but the larger ones are needed, if she is to keep her leg."

Though this was the first Martha heard of Caroline needing such delicate surgery, she nodded as if she were confident she could do the operation.

"I will need your help," Nate said.

"Cindy," Martha said, "light up the gas stove." Nate had just lifted a heavy burden from Martha's shoulders, but the relief scarcely showed on her face.

Gunfire echoed in the distance.

Brian grabbed his father's rifle and looked out a loophole. "Who are they shooting at?"

Nate thought for a moment. "Must be the vigilantes."

"Wow. They're serious, aren't they?" Brian searched through another loophole. "I can't believe they're hunting those lowlifes all the way out here in the woods."

Nate stood erect. "Listen!"

No one said a word.

Deni spoke. "Rotorcraft. More than one."

"Yeah," Nate said. "Coming this way."

The hum turned into a roar and debris flew outside in a whirlwind of leaves.

Brian pointed the rifle out a loophole.

Nate grabbed it. "No." He set it in a corner.

The Huey hovered while four soldiers slid down ropes. They ran and formed a defense perimeter, then got down on one knee, carbines pointing outward.

The ropes were retracted and the helicopter landed. A soldier got out while the blades slowed to a stop. He looked older than the others did.

No one but Brian had ever seen Nate smile so much. "Look at that, Brian. It's Mel!"

"Holy shit!" Brian ran for the door.

Nate pulled him back. "Bolt the door behind me. And no shooting or pointing weapons at them." Nate stepped out and swung the heavy steel door closed. He heard a bolt slide into place as he held his arms up, hands open, and walked toward the soldiers.

When Mel saw Nate, he ran to him and shook his hand. "You son of a gun. You made it! Where are Susan and the kids?"

Nate looked at the other soldiers. He noticed one of them was a colonel. "Susan and Beth got sick and died. Brian is inside with some others."

"Oh hell. I'm sorry." Mel could not possibly be surprised, but it still bothered him. "Jesus Christ, you're a tough son of a bitch, Nate." He looked him up and down. "How in the hell did you keep Brian alive this long?" He glanced at the bunker. "We've been to your farm. It was picked clean by the assholes we're hunting. They didn't burn the house down though."

"Yeah. I know," Nate said. "A lot of my stuff is out on the road, some in disabled trucks."

The colonel spoke. "You the one who booby-trapped those trucks? We lost a man."

"No sir," Nate answered. "It was the ones you're hunting. I did put out a few punji sticks in the woods. Shouldn't be hard to notice. There are dead men there."

"There are dead men everywhere." The colonel eyed Nate closer.

"Some of the stuff in those trucks was stolen from us," Nate said. "We need it to survive until the next harvest. I would like to get back as much as possible."

"We'll see about that later. I hear you were in the Army." The colonel cocked his head.

"Yes sir," Nate said, "in a former life."

The colonel's eyes lit up. "You wouldn't be the one who held that bunch of brigands up at the bridge for so long, would you?"

"Me and my son—and a few friends."

"Colonel," Mel said. "With your permission…I haven't seen his son since I was called in. He's an old friend."

"Go ahead soldier. We will be here a while."

Mel ran to the bunker.

The colonel turned to Nate. "You left a lot of rotting garbage strewn all the way from the bridge to here. I'm sure there's a law against that. But you made my job easier, so I'll let it go this time." He smiled as if it was a private joke only he was in on.

"We were trying to protect our farm so we would not starve. What *is* your job, exactly?" Nate asked. "Is there no Constitution now?"

The colonel gave him a wintry smile. "That's a political question. Ask a politician." He cleared his throat. "You might want to know that Congress is down to thirty-three men and women—both houses—total. The president is still kicking, but his VP died in the plague along with the common folk. There are two left on the Supreme Court last I heard. The plague was especially hard on older people." He made a long sweep with his right arm. "I've got men out there hunting down those you tangled with. We're working in cooperation with your newly-elected county sheriff and several hundred citizens he deputized." His face hardened. "They've had enough of lawlessness and asked us to help exterminate the vermin so they can get on with the business of rebuilding. For the time being, their focus is on extermination, not law. The governor agrees."

"There are two groups," Nate said. "The one that crossed the bridge is the worst, but the others aren't exactly boy scouts. They raided our farm while we were fighting off the first group at the road."

The colonel nodded. "We have most of your boy scouts in custody. They surrendered without a fight. Good thing. There were a few children with them. It could have been bloody. Like this bunch in the woods around here."

"It was bloody," Nate said. "One of your choppers attacked them on the road along with the other group."

Nate stood silent while a radio came to life.

A soldier listened.

When the soldier did not call him over, the colonel turned back to Nate.

Nate spoke first. "Colonel, what hit us? I mean, does the government know where the plague came from?"

"I'm just a colonel. All I know is it spread around the world fast and nearly wiped the human race off the face of the earth."

"Just a colonel, huh?"

"That's right, Mr. Williams. And you're just a civilian."

They stood there and said nothing for ten seconds, both knowing the other was not going to say what he was really thinking.

Synthia was crying for some reason.

The colonel sighed. "As you probably know, there is a shortage of everything because of a lack of manpower. We will be leaving soon. We're low on fuel. And there is no telling how long it will be before you see another sign of government. You will be on your own again, but if I can help you with anything while I'm here, I will."

"We have two women in need of medical care," Nate said. "One is a civilian. The other is Army. She was on leave when it hit the fan. It's not her fault she's AWOL."

The colonel smiled. "Sergeant."

"Yes sir," the soldier answered.

"Get Doc Reynolds here."

"Yes sir." The soldier talked into a radio microphone.

The colonel headed for the bunker. Three soldiers followed with their carbines ready and eyes sweeping the area.

"Mel says he built this place." The colonel rested his hand on a Colt 1911 strapped on his right side.

"Yes," Nate said. "You want to see it?"

"What I really want to see are the people inside."

Brian was introducing everyone to Mel when Nate and the colonel walked in.

Mel spoke up. "Sir, there are people here in need of medical attention."

"Yes, I know," the colonel said. "We have the doc on the way."

Caroline looked the colonel up and down. "You mean the damn Army is actually going to be good for something for a change?"

The colonel looked at her leg and the scars on her face. "I think you'll find the doc useful under the circumstances." His eyes softened. "And it's the Army National Guard, not regular Army."

"Whatever." Caroline grimaced from pain.

Synthia ran and grabbed Nate's leg. She looked frightened. Nate picked her up.

The colonel looked at her and then everyone in the bunker, one at a time.

"What the hell are you looking at?" Caroline asked.

The colonel's eyes darted to Caroline. "People. Extraordinary people. The kind who will rebuild this country, this world."

A helicopter hovered outside.

A young woman soldier rushed in carrying a large pack by the shoulder strap.

"Ladies," the colonel said, "your doctor has arrived." He started out the door.

Caroline took one look at her, lay back on the table, and relaxed. "Good. I need a doctor with the balls to do the job."

The colonel stopped, turned, and looked around the room again. His eyes lingered on Brian and Cindy. "Yes. We will rebuild."

14321818R00135

Made in the USA
Lexington, KY
24 March 2012